HAD A DYING FALL

CARLISLE CRIME CASES #4
A CHRISTOPHER SNOW & ERIN MCCOY MYSTERY

J. M. WEST

MILFORD HOUSE

an imprint of Sunbury Press, Inc.
Mechanicsburg, PA USA

**MILFORD
HOUSE**

an imprint of Sunbury Press, Inc.
Mechanicsburg, PA USA

For information about special discounts for bulk purchases, please contact Sunbury Press Orders Dept. at (855) 338-8359 or orders@sunburypress.com.

To request one of our authors for speaking engagements or book signings, please contact Sunbury Press Publicity Dept. at publicity@sunburypress.com.

ISBN: 978-1-62006-824-3 (Trade Paperback)

Library of Congress Control Number: 2017937158

FIRST MILFORD HOUSE PRESS EDITION: May 2018

Product of the United States of America
0 1 1 2 3 5 8 13 21 34 55

Set in Bookman Old Style
Designed by Lawrence Knorr
Cover by Lawrence Knorr
Edited by Janice Rhayem

Continue the Enlightenment!

Dedicated to my family, friends, and former neighbors—
My staunchest supporters

In memory of Michelle Sheriff Burnette

From *The Twelfth Night*

"If music be the food of love, play on,
Give me excess of it; that, surfeiting,
The appetite may sicken, and so die.
The strain again—it had a dying fall.
O, it came o'er my ear like the sweet sound
That breathes upon a bank of violets,
Stealing, and giving odour. Enough, no more,
Tis not so sweet now as it was before."
                    —*William Shakespeare*

A Complex Sentence

I am a sentence waiting,
You—the grammarian,
Anxious to diagram,
To see what part is missing.
You'll find I'm not so simple,
No subject without complement.
But parse my clauses as you may,
Diagram away; you'll find
The syntax fragmented—hidden
In the subordinate clause.
                    —*JM West*

The Carlisle Crime Case Series

PROLOGUE

May 2009

Waving good-bye to their baby who was driving to PSU for a summer internship, Kelly marveled at Camie's composure and efficiency. She took a deep, shuddering breath and closed the front door against the heat. "You know, now the kids are grown, we should make an appointment with a lawyer about writing a will and—"

Denny stormed across the room, shoved his wife against the front door, held her there, his forearm pressing against her windpipe. "I'll never leave a will so some other man can enjoy what I've worked a lifetime to achieve. Or this." His right hand grabbed her crotch. Understand?" His craggy, chiseled face inched closer to hers, his eyes angry sparks, his mouth a single slash.

She broke eye contact, turned her head aside. "You're hurting me." She tried to gauge his moods, guarding and swallowing her own anger toward her husband of twenty-five years—the man she'd vowed to love until death, the man she no longer knew or liked.

Twenty years older, Dennis Sims had retained the lean frame of his youth, though his silver hair, crow's feet, and slashes framing his mouth revealed his years. He owned the Warehouse, two of the businesses housed there, and rented the four other ground-floor rooms. He and his men were converting the upstairs into urban industrial lofts. Yes, he worked long, hard hours.

"And I don't need your aggravation just now; I've a lot to do, enough to worry about. On top of burying my father and helping my mother with the funeral and their finances, I have deadlines to meet, tenants to cater to,

1

and employees to see." His breath hissed. "Quit nagging. I can't take anymore."

On tiptoes, knowing better than to push back, Kelly held her body rigid, head, back, and palms flat against the front door. He planted his body against hers, pushing. "Understand?"

She nodded. Tried to understand his mood. "Sorry. That's why I thought—"

"Well, don't. I'll take care of business." He released her. "Why don't you concentrate on *your* business: go clean up the mess in the kitchen. You know how clutter gets on my nerves."

Kelly had fixed dinner at noon, packed the leftovers into a Styrofoam cooler for Camie, so she wouldn't have to cook after driving two hours to campus, unloading her gear and groceries. Plus, setting up her room in an apartment she'd share with two others. She sighed, waiting for Denny to release her, saunter to the shed for the riding mower. Finally, she heard the motor spurt, rumbling; the rider lumbered out—a bear out of hibernation.

While scraping and rinsing dishes, Kelly thought. She and her younger sister Shannon planned a lady's day out next week—a New York junket, with lunch at Junior's and tickets to see *The Jersey Boys*.

She could empty the savings account, pack a wheelie, and launch a new identity from there. Cut and color her hair, wear a different style of clothing—consignment, retro—inconspicuous and anonymous threads like the runaways in Thomas Perry's Jane Whitefield novels. No, she quickly rejected that idea.

Four years earlier, their eldest's college preparations drove a wedge between Dennis and Kelly Sims. Since Kelly worked in academia, she helped Drew weave through the maze of college admission procedures, tests, essays, and recommendation letters. In the end, he elected to attend Dickinson because of the tuition remission. Yet he'd chafed under his father's stringent high-school rules, transferring to Drexel his junior year.

Dennis ordered her "to quit coddling the kid," urging Drew to "cut the apron strings from your mother. Time to step up and be a man. Show some initiative: Do something on your own."

When Camie decided on Penn State and insisted on trekking through the admission labyrinth by herself, he'd lauded her. "At least one of our kids shows some backbone. No need to worry about her. She has enough chutzpah for the both of them."

"Why compare them? They have different personalities and strengths. Drew's more cautious; Camie just plows ahead. One day, both will be self-sufficient—," she'd started to explain, when he'd slammed her against a wall the first time.

"Don't contradict or condescend to me," he'd ordered. "You sheltered academics think you have all the answers. What counts is experience in the real world."

* * *

"But why should I leave now?" Kelly argued with herself. "I can't leave my job with its generous benefits after twenty-five years. Besides, I make half of what Denny does. How could I even afford this house? And the utilities? Luckily, my car is paid for.

"Well, a good lawyer will advise you on a divorce," she argued. "You have grounds and photos. Plus, he's refused counseling—'What would people think?' he'd said. And filing a PFA wouldn't work. He'd go ballistic. What damage would he inflict then?

"And where would the kids go for holidays?" Camie had her senior year at State College and Drew's working in Lancaster, having recently become engaged. "No, leaving is not really a viable option. I'll just have to think of something else."

Loading, running the dishwasher, and wiping counters and the island took her as long as Denny's mowing. She heard the downstairs shower running. "I'll fix Denny a sandwich, myself a salad."

While she cut the vegetables, Denny came up behind her, wrapped his arms around her. "Sorry, I didn't mean to hurt you, but you just push my buttons, insinuating I can't take care of the family. Trust me to take care of things. You know I love you; no one else could love you more. Or ever will. Are you okay?"

Kelly nodded but held herself still.

"Heard you mumbling to yourself. When you start answering yourself, time for counseling. Come on; let's go to bed. I'll make it up to you. You know I'll always love you."

She knew better than to say no.

1

Black smoke plumed over orange flames from the backyard. Sparks like fireflies flew. The shed's roof splintered, pieces somersaulting skyward. Flames erupted, feeding on the fuel. The Explorer screeched to a halt in front of a limestone Cape Cod on a corner lot. Requesting fire trucks, the CPD detectives raced around back, waving back curious neighbors. "Stay back! Other explosions may follow!"

Just as the words left Snow's mouth, a second eruption boomed. Wood and metal spewed from the flames, hot and dangerous. Sirens approached, pump and hook and ladder jutting to the curb, with men jumping off and flying to their tasks.

Dressed in full gear, Fire Chief Lane Rusk jumped down from the cab, motioned his men to hook into the nearest hydrant. Lowered his Plexi-glass shield and raced to the carnage. Water spewed forth on the grass and house while white fire-retardant foam arced over that. "Bet the gas grill blew," he muttered. The detectives sprinted to the back door, pounding to raise someone. The house sat mute, dark windows shuttered and curtains drawn against Dawn's fingers of resurrecting light. The light yawned in ribbons, rolling back the grey blanket of night.

"Sorry about Mac and . . . ," Savage said while he and Carlisle Police's lead homicide detective Christopher Snow had sped to the suspicious fire on South Street. "We took up a collection for flowers—had them sent to your house for the family plot."

"Yes, thanks," Snow swallowed hard and nodded. "I can't talk about that right now. It's just too raw." He scrubbed his hands over his face and shook his head. Swallowed over the lump in his throat.

Reese flipped open his cell, called HQ to find out who owned the house. "Court records list that domicile belongs to a Dennis and Kelly Sims." Always the first on the job, Sonja Hamilton, CPD admin extraordinaire, had her pulse on the department and its personnel. She hadn't missed a day of work in five years despite two kids, a husband, and night classes.

"We can't raise anybody here. Their shed just blew to smithereens, but nobody came outside to investigate. Could be on vacation, but we should notify them," Savage said.

"I'll Google them and run a property search. Will you hold?" She hit the keys.

"Will do." Savage answered as he visually canvassed the property. Minutes unspooled as he watched the firefighters.

"Okay. Dennis Sims owns the Party Time and The Sport Hut at the Warehouse. There's a work permit on record for renovating second-floor apartments. Wife Kelly works for Dickinson, coordinator of High School Gifted Programs. Two grown kids, one male, Drew, twenty-five—resides in Lancaster, PA, and one female, Cameron, twenty-one, at Penn State, State College. Let me try Facebook."

The shed continued to burn combustibles. Debris spiraled up the heated waves, then rained upon the lawn; paint cans exploded, spewing syrupy paint like Jackson Pollock. Metal fragments torpedoed. The hulk of riding mower remained, its seat smoldering.

"No mention of a vacation, no photos to suggest that. Oh, look, guess what? Her sister is Officer Shannon Mahoney. You know, a third of the new cycle team."

"Yeah?" Reese turned toward the street, eyes stinging from the smoke. "I've got her number. I'll call her if we can't locate the parents. Do they live in the area?" He rubbed his scruffy chin absently.

"If so, no mention of them. I'll check Mahoney's file, get back to you." Her fingers tapped the keyboard.

"Thanks." He thumbed end, turned his head toward the thunder of cycles. Two of the Musketeers drew to the curb, Chase Rivers first, followed by Gabriel Summers. Threading helmets onto the handlebars, the men bounded upon the lawn to join Savage and Snow. The duo—one short, compact with ferret hair and sharp features, the taller one with finger-tousled blond hair, square jaw, and a cleft chin. Both wore black tees and jeans. Rivers seemed a '60s holdout or an *Easy Rider* fan. Summers looked like his name implied—golden, wavy hair, tanned, and fit.

"What gives?" Rivers asked.

"Nobody's come out to investigate the fire. Do you know the residents?" Snow asked.

"Yeah, Shannon's sister's family. What's the probable cause for entering?" asked Gabe Summers, the leader of the cycle trio. His sandy brows shot up. "Why's Homicide here?" His cobalt eyes roved between the fireworks and the detectives.

"A neighbor called it in. Where's Shannon?" Snow motioned to the house on the right. Spectators had gathered along the street, pointing to and commenting on the fire. Fire trucks continued to pump retardant on the ruined remains of the shed.

"She went to New York City with her sister. I'll see if anybody's home." Rivers jogged up to the front door, rang the bell, the chain on his jeans jingling. No one answered.

"We tried that already. When are they due home?" Savage asked.

"I dunno." Summers pulled out his cell, thumbed his cycle partner. "Hmm. Shannon, your sister's shed just burned to a crisp. Someone called nine-one-one. CFD and CPD are on the scene, dousing the flames, but nobody's answering the door. Call back. We need to inform the homeowners." He ended the call. "Voice mail. Sorry to hear about your wife, boss."

Snow nodded, mesmerized by the fire, the dancing flames reflected in his eyes. Liquid filmed them; he blinked hard, gritted his teeth. Behind him, Savage shook his head in warning. Gabriel nodded in understanding: currently, too raw a wound to rake over.

"I can ride over, see if Sims is working at the Warehouse. "He's trying to get those upstairs apartments ready for the fall semester. Exposed brick walls, pipes and wood beams, clean lines—really sharp looking," Rivers reported. His hands cut angles to suggest a minimalist design.

"Know him?" Snow pulled his attention from the fire to look at Rivers while Summers peered in windows, knocking to raise someone, sliding quickly to the next one and repeating.

"Yeah. Early riser. Six-two, silver hair, sixty-five, a Carlisle businessman. Type-A personality. Puts in ten-twelve hour workdays. Plays poker once a month, softball once a week; the couple entertains occasionally but mostly keep to themselves. Wife works full time, too; she's pretty serious, quiet—opposite of Shannon. Kids are grown. I'm sure you've seen him around town. Ever been to the Sports Hut or Party Time?"

Snow shook his head. "Can't say that I have. Ian keeps me busy now that his mother's—" His throat tightened at the mention of Erin. He cleared it, cupped his hands around his mouth, coughed as the flames and smoke smothered the air. "Summers, come on. If no one's home, we'll notify them by phone.

"Back door's open, sir." Summers pushed; it yawned open.

Snapping on latex and paper booties, the detectives entered the sturdy limestone structure. Through the mudroom past a golden Tuscany print, formal dining room at the right, stairs just beyond, the living room left facing the front. In the great room the clothed body was sprawled across the kitchen island, legs tangled in the barstool, face down, right arm in the sink. Snow hunkered down to study the deceased's face. "Some lividity here. Full rigor. So he lunged for something and . . ." Inspected the fingernails. "But no evidence of a struggle. Left temple bruised badly. Looks like blunt force trauma. Is this Dennis Sims?"

Savage said, "It is: white hair, blue eyes, six-two, about two hundred twenty pounds. Do you see any fatal wounds? Could've had a heart attack. No wait, his left eye is bloodshot." He studied the dead man's limbs, shook his head. "No fatal wounds."

"Strange angle, though. Hefty bruise at his left temple looks like a contusion. Let's wait for Dr. Chen." Snow peered into the sink, where a dirty skillet and spatula soaked, perused the counters and island cabinets for a potential weapon. Peered into orderly cabinets along the wall and under the sink. Nothing sinister jumped out at him.

The petite coroner breezed in wearing a black shift with a kick pleat and blue paper booties over bare feet. Salt and pepper hair styled in a severe bob. Crystal teardrops twinkled from her earlobes. Setting her black bag on the island, she opened it, blew into latex, turning away from the puff of powder, while perusing the body. Then gloved up. All business, Dr. Chen said, "All right, detectives, let's see what we've got here."

Snow watched; Savage's eyes roved over the great room, observing. Tidy but definitely lived in—black leather sofa and merlot recliners, eclectic pieces, some antiques like the hutch with a copper pie sink. Floor to ceiling fireplace, globe lanterns on either end of the mantle, and a towering dried arrangement in the center. Maple cabinets hugged the opposite wall. He eased out the back door, photographed the scratches on the metal door facing. "Lock's been tampered with." His feet left firm patio—a pergola overhead with purple clematis climbing up the posts. Collected a cigarette butt from a shell and a nail file on a window ledge. Dumped water from the patio chair cushions, continuing around until he'd checked all four. A brown barrette fell out of the last one with several blond hairs attached. Dated and labeled, he dropped each into evidence bags.

CSU members arrived, bustled about dusting and lifting prints; their coveralls rustled like dry leaves. Snow joined Savage outside.

Snow gestured toward the neighborhood. "I want names, numbers, witnesses who can catalogue the comings and goings of the Sims family; we need to know customs, habits, conversations, observations, and any unusual vehicles noted in the vicinity. Get timelines of their comings and goings. That also means family car vins, makes, models, mileage."

"Body's in full rigor, so somebody arrived, surprised the occupant. Won't know the details until Chen's postmortem, but track down all you can. The men scattered. He turned to Savage. "When's Shannon returning?"

"They're driving back now. So I'd say around one without stops."

"Interview her. I'll take the widow. Here or HQ."

Dr. Chen checked her schedule on her cell. "Autopsy's tomorrow morning at ten."

"Hey, boss." Zachary Fields joined the group on the patio.

"Search the house, look for anything suspicious—like a possible murder weapon, a blunt, rounded object that can dent a skull. Also take the trash—the entire block; tell Rusk we'd like a report of the shed ruins. List and continue the interviews—employees, friends, enemies, poker players—anyone who can tell us more about Dennis Sims."

"We'll convene at HQ at four p.m. for specific assignments. Hamilton and Huddleston can mine the computer for background."

Fields and Summers helped the driver turn and slide the body, awkward limbs frozen, into a black bag, loaded it on the gurney and into the meat wagon.

The men fanned out to investigate the house and neighborhood while Snow called his office phone, listing reminder messages. "Get Sims's financials, phone records, a list of employee names, relatives, business contacts, computers—home and office." Ended the call. Somebody wanted you dead, buddy. Let's find out who, then why."

Savage's cell pinged. "Savage."

Sonja responded. "Kelly's parents—Gavin and Megan Mahoney—live in South Middletown Township. Two Hundred Front Street in Boiling Springs. That may be on the lake. Phone number—" She rattled off a string of numbers. "Found no listing for another Sims. Anything else?"

"No thanks. I'll give them a call. See if they know where their children are. Thanks. Over, out."

Snow stalked to the Explorer. "Let's go talk to the parents."

No one answered at 200 Front Street, so they trekked around back, where the detectives found the couple on the back porch in lawn chairs eating bacon and egg muffins in front of a ceramic fire pit. The Children's Lake shimmered; golden light cupped ripples in reflecting waves, refracting amethyst, indigo, and deep green beneath wispy fog. A low, calming surrusus accompanied occasional splashes as ducks dipped or paddled amid the loud chirrup of crickets. Trees cast shadows across the water. On the bank across the lake, lights winked on at the bed and breakfast.

Mr. Mahoney stood to shake their hands. The wife nodded, waving them into padded lawn chairs. "I'm Gavin, my wife, Megan." His hair was leached of color, hers a grey and tangled Brillo pad. They wore khaki shorts and oversized Steelers T-shirts.

Snow briefed them on the burning shed. "The bad news: we found Dennis Sims's body in the kitchen. We're sorry for your loss."

"Ohmigod!" Megan exclaimed. Her hand flew to her throat.

"We're trying to locate next of kin. Do you know where Kelly and Shannon are?"

"Boy, that's bad. Did he have a heart attack?" asked Gavin.

"We're waiting for the coroner's report," Savage answered.

"I don't think the girls mentioned taking a day, but, well, I could've missed that conversation," Mr. Mahoney stated. "I went over yesterday morning to borrow Denny's push mower. Mine's in the shop."

"Did you see Dennis Sims when you were there?" Savage asked.

"No, it was early; I didn't want to disturb them. Left a note on the shed."

"Oh Lord, no! Did the house burn, too?" Mrs. Mahoney asked. Wide eyes in her square face registered shock. High cheekbones pinked.

Snow shook his head. "Firefighters have it under control. We really need to locate your daughter."

"Don't you remember Shannon treated her to a day in New York City—for lunch, a play, and shopping? You know, a girl's day out, a diversion. They planned to spend the night, come home early this morning. Would you like coffee?" She indicated the thermos on the table.

Savage shook his head no to Mrs. Mahoney's offer.

Noting their sooty faces and disheveled appearance, Mahoney asked, "How about a cold drink?" He stood, balancing his mug on the window ledge. "Fridge's right inside the back door."

"I'll take a Coke, sir, if it's not too much trouble. Smoke in the lungs." Savage showed his sooty hands, wiped his brow, smudging his forehead. Snow nodded, too, and their host hobbled off to get the sodas.

"We haven't seen Denny lately; he had a half-dozen projects going. Worked constantly. Kelly's busy, too, with the Dickinson camp season just getting under way," Mrs. Mahoney observed.

"What does she do exactly?" Snow asked.

"Her department makes all the arrangements for summer sessions for advanced high school students: robotics, engineering, music, drama, ballet, and the athletic camps. A thousand high school students participate each year. Kelly arranges the schedule, obtains the instructors, and locates scholarships for students who can't afford the cost. Handles orientations. Writes grants, that sort of thing."

"How long has she worked in that capacity?"

"Why, must be goin' on twenty-five years?" She turned to her husband, who shrugged; a smile creased his weathered face as he handed over the Cokes.

"You'd know more than I would about such things," he said. "Yesterday, the girls were kids, you know? Shannon's a cop. And now Kelly's kids are grown. So everything in the shed burned?"

"Yes, sir. Husband and wife get along?" Savage asked.

"About like most couples. Why all these questions?" asked Gavin. He extended his bare legs, crossed his feet, jingling the change in his shorts' pocket. An angry red welt on a swollen knee explained the limp. "I'm sure they have insurance."

"Routine during our investigations," Snow answered.

"You said detectives," Megan returned. She wiped her hands on a damp paper towel and dropped it into the fire. "Do you suspect foul play? My granddaughter left last week for college. My grandson lives in Lancaster. We'll call them."

"We're investigating a suspicious death. What happened to your knee?" asked Savage, pointing the soda can to Mahoney's swollen knee. "Looks mighty sore."

"Reaction to a bee sting." He shrugged. "Swelling will go down in few hours."

"Do you have Dennis Sims's parents' address or phone number?" Reese pulled out his notepad.

"No, sorry. For one, they're twenty years older than we are. Two, we haven't anything in common. And three, they didn't approve of the marriage. His father passed away a few months ago. There's just his mother. I'm sure Kelly can give you Marsha Sims's number," Megan said.

"Well, thanks for your time." Snow stood, glanced at Savage. "If you think of anything else, give us a call. They climbed into the Explorer. "I want to get home to feed Ian and then catch some Zs. I'm whipped. Getting too old for these all-nighters."

"What do you think? Didn't seem too upset," Snow commented.

Savage shrugged. "Maybe it's their age. Like they said, they weren't close. You okay? Need any help?" His espresso eyes ranged over his friend's haggard face, red-rimmed eyes bruised with shadows. Grey and brassy brown bristle peppered his upper lip and chin. "When did you last get any sleep?" Accustomed to insomnia, restlessness, and wariness, the veteran guessed these symptoms were new to his boss.

Snow cast his eyes sideways, then back at Middlesex Road, turning onto Lisburn, and left into Savage's driveway. "Thanks, but we'll manage; it's just a big adjustment. It's tough, but my parents and Erin's dad help. Funny, how much Erin did that I didn't notice until now." Chris changed the topic. "Let me know when you start demoing your kitchen. I can help."

Reese hopped out of the vehicle, stretching. "Not ready for that yet. I'm painting the bedrooms first. But when I get to that point, I'll give you a call. The Musketeers offered to help, too. Maybe one Saturday in the fall we'll attack that job—open up the living area. Have a picnic; make a day of it."

"Double-check with Sonja, see if Shannon took a vacation day. I'd like to touch base with Rusk, too, see how that fire started. We'll interview Sims's mother later."

"Switch it off, Chris. Go home, rock your baby." The lean detective with a military mien tugged his keys out of his Dockers, patrolled the perimeter of his house. Flashing his maglite among the tangle of trees, along the overgrown hedge—he caught iridescent cat eyes. Shoved the key in the back door's lock.

At home, Chris found his mother in the kitchen, warming a bottle. A custard cup held remnants of baby cereal: rice mixed with strained applesauce. "Let me wash up. I'll give him his bottle."

Erica Snow stopped, glanced at her youngest son with concern. He needed a haircut and a shave. Worry lines furrowed his brows. He disappeared into the mudroom to wash up, returned, scooping up his son from his little seat and tossed him gently. The baby gurgled, cheeks dimpling.

"Careful, he just ate, Chris. I fixed you a sandwich for lunch. There's a pasta salad in the fridge, too."

Chris kissed his mother's forehead by way of greeting. Plucked the bottle from the water, tested it, tucked his son in the crook of his arm, and took his wife's accustomed place on the padded rocker in the living room. "Thanks, Mom. I'll eat later. We landed a homicide, so I'll have to get back to work when we locate the wife."

"Oh, I'm so sorry. That happens too often these days. Why can't people settle their differences without resorting to violence? Carlisle used to be such a quaint, friendly, and safe place with church bells pealing the hours . . .

"Oh, the CPD sent flowers—a beautiful spray of baby-pink roses. They're in the fridge. Do you want to take them—"

"Savage told me. Tomorrow, maybe." He hadn't meant to sound curt. "I'm tired, Mother. Thanks for helping. Can you come back in a few hours?" He watched his son inhale milk. "Take it easy, baby. No need to be greedy." Ian's fingers grasped his father's pinky. Despite his exhaustion, Chris smiled at his son's firm grip.

"Of course. And you're welcome. Really, Ian's such a pleasure."

"A treasure," he added, looking at his shiny, auburn waves, vivid-blue eyes, and dark-rust lashes. The infant's eyes drooped; his father gently pulled the nipple out, propped him up to burp him. "How was he last night? Looks like he's losing weight. Is he eating okay?"

"Maybe he's just growing. I'll check with the pediatrician if you like. He's been fussy at mealtimes, but that's to be expected." She omitted the obvious: he misses his mother. "And he's teething." Chris's eyes filmed, then closed. His head leaned wearily against the rocker. Erin's shooting had aged him. His hair lacked its usual healthy sheen; his steps were now labored. Though only thirty-six, he looked forty, weighed down with worry and responsibility.

She sighed at the whims of Fate that tumbled the Snows' lives into uncertainty and turned to tidy the kitchen. Besides tending Ian, she had her own house and garden to look after, though Christopher Senior valiantly attempted to wrest the wretched weeds from the young greens. But if they both didn't hoe the rows every day, Nature would wrestle their gains from them; weeds would choke the tender new shoots and kill the plants. Couldn't let that happen.

2

Checked his watch, nine o'clock: three hours of sleep. Collected Savage, alerted the CSU unit, slid his bubble on the dash, and stomped on the accelerator. Passing I-81 traffic, Snow peeled off the College Street exit, palmed the wheel left on Belvedere, right on South Street. Killed the engine at the curb. Rusk and his assistant Rusty Garrett were raking through evidence at the shed site.

Reese popped a peppermint in his mouth to cover the odor of the beer he'd just drunk and the cig he'd finished. "Get Ian tucked in?"

Snow's eyes slid over Reese. "Give HQ a call, request Fields and the Musketeers. It's a little early for booze. Did you start smoking again?"

"I need to take the edge off. Shrink's trying to give me drugs; I'd wind up a chemical junkie. I'll pick the devils I know." Savage flipped his cell and gave instructions. The garish, yellow-and-black crime-scene tape sealed off the two-story, stone house.

The detectives watched a red Mustang wheel into the drive, the bubble strobing red, blue, and white lights. Shannon Mahoney cut the engine and climbed out of the driver's seat; her sister, Kelly Sims, emerged from the passenger's.

The cop's five-ten topped her sister by several inches. Sims's hair was a burnished maple, her eyes like pond water and pale skin too blotched to judge her complexion, eyes rimmed in red. Grief was etched on both their faces.

"You made good time." Savage checked his watch.

"We were staying in a motel in Jersey when we got the call, sir." Addressing Snow, Mahoney said, "This is my sister, Kelly Sims."

Sims wadded a tissue in her left hand, extended her right to shake, but said nothing, her face closed. She wore black-knit slacks and a leopard-print, cotton sweater. Sniffing, she followed the acrid odor polluting the air. Seeing the ruins of shed, Kelly stifled a shriek, hand over her mouth. "What happened? Is this how it happened? Did Denny die in the shed explosion? He was going to mow later, said he needed gas."

"No," Snow responded. "But when the shed burned, nobody came out of the house to investigate, which seemed strange. We found the back door open, your husband's body in the kitchen."

"What happened? Can the interview possibly wait?" Mahoney said. "As you can see, my sister's distraught."

"I have a few questions for Mrs. Sims now. I'm sorry for your loss, but we need information fast. Savage, if you take Mahoney to her car, I'll talk to Mrs. Sims in mine, as the house, a crime scene, is now sealed until further notice."

"Begging your pardon, sir, but Kelly should have a lawyer," Mahoney said, shifting weight on long legs.

"Here or HQ, your choice. The weather's balmy, and I'm not accusing or arresting anyone yet," he said irritably.

"I know that the spouse is always the main suspect," Kelly said. "But I'll answer your questions. I have nothing to hide." She hefted a roomy leather purse onto her shoulder.

"Does she need a lawyer?" asked Mahoney.

Swiping his hair off his forehead, he answered. "Not for routine questions." He stepped to his vehicle and opened the door. Sims ducked into the passenger's seat as Snow folded himself behind the wheel. Savage steered Mahoney back to her vehicle.

"This sucks big time." Mahoney flipped her cell open. "I'll leave a voice mail at the lawyer's to meet us later. Well, go ahead, Reese, ask your questions."

Leaving his door open, Snow drummed his thumb on his steering wheel but stopped, pulled his recorder from the glove box, identified the case, himself, and Kelly Sims as the vic's widow. "Tell me about your marriage."

Sims took a stuttering breath. "Denny and I have been married twenty-five years, have two grown kids, Drew, twenty-four, and Camie, twenty-one. If you've researched our background, you know what we do. Did you search the house?" The detective nodded. "Then you found the photos."

He decided to play straight with her, since she had Erin's frankness. "You're a victim of domestic violence, yet there are no records of any arrests. Was he a violent man?"

"Not physically, well, not usually. His verbal abuse was a means of control, but he didn't see it that way. Always said he was joking. Sometimes he played the jokester, but I had a hard time telling the difference. Rarely did he threaten me physically, until lately." Olive-green eyes looked solemnly into his. "I can count the times on one hand that he's left marks, but I took selfies and then hid them in case we wound up in divorce court."

"He didn't know or run across them and lose his temper?"

"Oh, well. We both lose our tempers, but he wouldn't invade my privacy that way. We have plenty of photo albums on shelves that he hasn't glanced at in years. Besides, he's not a cop, wouldn't think to look for something taped under a drawer."

"Then in what way?" Snow inquired, turning in his seat.

She sighed, looked through the windshield at her house. She wiped her eyes and blew her nose on the tissue. "Subtle ways. Like telling friends and family I couldn't come to the phone when I was available. He'd say I was in the shower, getting dressed, left for work—that sort of thing." She told the detective about the will comment. "But he's had a tough time lately. His father died in March. He's helping his mother sort out their finances, works ridiculously long hours, which I don't mind. I have plenty to do myself, but I want to downsize; this house is too big for two. He doesn't—didn't—want to move, so we stayed.

"I want to travel; he's a homebody, content with his businesses, buddies, and ESPN." She gave a rueful shrug. "Besides the children, we have little in common. I just hadn't noticed until Drew left for college. When Camie entered Penn State four years ago, everything had to be negotiated: what's for dinner, staying in or dining out, Rustic Tavern or the diner."

"You argued about dinner?" Snow watched her closely. She pulled her long hair away from her face, twisting a scrunchie over and tying it into a loose knot.

"We argued about everything! I'm home nearly every evening to make dinner. If I have stops to make—pick up prescriptions, the dry cleaning, or gas up the car—he'd give me an hour."

"Or what?" Snow asked.

"He'd come looking for me or send Julio."

"Who's Julio?"

"Julio Roberto, his construction manager. Or have his admin Olive run his errands. Or send one of his store managers by to see if my car's in the drive or parked at Dickinson's admin building."

"And if it weren't?" Snow asked.

"He actually came to work a handful of times. He'd stop by with a sandwich, flowers, or just to ask what time I'd be home. But he was checking up on me, as if he didn't trust me."

"Has he always had a suspicious nature?"

Sims shrugged. "Well, he's very possessive and jealous."

"What time did you leave for New York City yesterday?"

"Shannon picked me up about 6:30 a.m. Traffic was heavy. We arrived at 10:30. We parked in a garage, walked to Junior's to eat, and then meandered down the street to the play. Out about five. We window-shopped awhile. Bought this sweater at Macy's. Left the city. Stopped at a diner for dinner and then checked into a motel in Jersey around eleven. Talked some—then turned in. Then my parents called; Shannon broke speed limits getting here." She shredded her tissue.

"When did you last see your husband?"

"When I left. He was eating breakfast, already dressed for work. I was in a hurry."

"Did you have an argument or altercation?" Snow watched her facial expression closely.

"I was preoccupied with getting ready for our trip. Packing water and snacks and fruit in my lunch tote." Sunlight washed over her pale cheeks. She inhaled deeply, let it whoosh out, and wrinkled her nose at the odor of charred debris. Kelly shuddered.

"He let you go on an overnight trip? Sounds out of character given your description of him," Snow commented.

"He trusts Shannon. She's a cop after all. He's taken a few trips himself—gone hunting, fishing, and to softball tournaments. Besides, he loves me; he tried very hard to share. He's twenty years older than I, you know—a bachelor until forty. Some Baby Boomers are more traditional than my generation. He's—was—responsible, frank, possessive, and sarcastic, but a decent man." Her eyes filmed; she blinked and dropped her head into her hands, shaking from shock. The morning temperature hovered around sixty, the heat and humidity rising. "But his mother spoiled him. Growing up, he didn't have to do a lick of work."

"Do you have an address and phone number for Marsha Sims?"

"She lives in North Middleton Township. Two Thousand Circle Drive." She dug in her purse for a pocket calendar, told him the phone number. "She's eighty-five, doesn't own a cell. She'll be devastated. She depended on Denny for so much."

Snow thumbed off the recorder. "That's enough for now. Let's reconvene after lunch. I'll assume you'll stay at your parents'? Are you working tomorrow? Do you have a private office?"

Sims nodded without looking up, unlatched the door. "I'm better off busy. I'll be in the Administration Building on High Street." Rummaged in her bag for a card, handed it over. "First floor, down the hall on the right."

Savage pointed to his watch. Snow held up his index finger. "Then I'll find you, but once we clear the scene, I'd recommend you stay home for a few days. Take bereavement leave. You have a right to have a lawyer present during questioning. Again, I'm sorry we had to intrude, but you need to find other accommodations until your house is cleared."

"I can stay at my parents', but I need my car."

"That's fine—the garage isn't technically part of the crime scene. I assume it's in there?"

She nodded and looked at him—a bit overwhelmed, anxious, and at sea—and climbed out of the vehicle, stumbled over a stone, righted herself, picking her way among dwarf yews that lined the driveway to her sister's red Mustang.

3

Snow and Savage arrived at 2000 Circle Drive, knocked on the door of a brick-and-siding split-level, curtains drawn against the light. Clover, crabgrass, and dandelion choked the grass. Massive oak and maple trees on the lot needed topping. Leggy evergreen bushes lined the front. The storm door was splattered with dried bird droppings. Savage rang the doorbell.

A school bus lumbered by. A retiree trotted out in pajamas to pick up his morning paper. Next door, a dog barked. Birds flitted among the trees; a lone squirrel leaped up; birds scattered. Slowly, the front door swung open to reveal a woman, lean as a lamppost, with white, wavy hair and erect posture. Unaccustomed to the bright sunlight, she blinked her red-rimmed rheumy eyes. "Yes?" Her face, a map of wrinkles, the fume of cigarettes clung to her, a Bic in her hand.

The detectives showed their shields. "Are you Marsha Sims?"

She nodded. "You here about Denny?"

Snow nodded. "So you've already heard? We're sorry about your loss. Who informed you?"

"Kelly called me. It's quite a shock. Your children shouldn't die before you. And we just buried my husband in March. He always handled the finances: bill-paying, the yard chores and such. And Denny's been helping me sort things out."

"May we come in? We need to ask you a few questions." Snow laid his hand against the door.

"Why are the police at my door?" She looked disoriented.

"We're Carlisle Homicide detectives. Your son's death is considered suspicious."

"Oh, I thought it was his heart or a stroke. If you must." She backed away from the door and motioned them to seats in the living room, the walls painted a dove gray with matching wall-to-wall carpet. The men sat on the charcoal sofa, sliding the silver and red throw pillows to the corners so they could lean back.

"What can you tell us about your son?" Snow began, after noting case, date, time, and participants on his recorder.

She settled in a red-flowered armchair next to the arch leading to the knotty-pine kitchen and reached for a mug of coffee on the end table. To the right, stairs led to the next level. Three professional portraits of a teenager, boy, and one girl smiled from the stairwell. The first definitely depicted Dennis Sims's rugged features: sandy hair, a broad, square face, blue eyes, high forehead, prominent nose, and a crooked smile. The second son and daughter had curly, brown hair and eyes, clear complexions but serious expressions. Clearly, the younger two favored their mother had her hair been darker.

Mrs. Sims sipped her coffee and returned it to the coaster. "Coffee?" she offered.

"No, thanks. We just finished ours," Snow said while his former partner frowned but turned his attention to the vic's mother. "What can you tell us about Dennis?"

"He's our livewire—always busy. As a child, he hunted, fished, canoed, swam, and joined Boy Scouts. He biked all over Carlisle. Out the door after breakfast, back home for supper. Lettered in football, basketball, and baseball in high school. Went to college but left his junior year to work construction. He liked working outdoors. Enjoyed people. But he was antsy, constantly moving. Today, the term is hyper."

She waved her hand. "A jokester, too, he often played tricks on his brother and sister. Once he put a tree frog in

Darryl's bunk and marbles in Andrea's bed. Another time he moved their books from one room to another." Her eyes crinkled in memory; she smiled briefly. The blue-veined hands moved nervously. "He was happy-go-lucky until he married. Kelly wasn't right for him, but he adored her."

"Why wasn't she right for him?" Savage queried.

"The age gap, for starters. What did they talk about? She was barely twenty when they married; he was forty, an established businessman. But was she content to stay home, be a homemaker, raise his children, and support him? No, she wanted to work."

"That's hardly unusual today. Most couples have to work to make ends meet," Snow said.

"Can you tell us if Dennis had any enemies?" asked Savage.

"Enemies? I can't imagine. He donated time and money to the community—United Way, the Red Cross, and The Bosler Library. Very charitable, he organized and supported fundraisers for our church and schools. Loved his kids. But he and Kelly had a falling out when Camie was born. She took Drew, left Denny for three months—to take her family to the Mayo Clinic. Apparently, her father suffered from migraines." She shrugged. "Why did they all go? The Mahoneys pulled Shannon out of school, too. That left Denny with everything to do here."

"So he never complained about any problems at work? Owing money or debts he couldn't repay?" Snow asked.

She puffed up. "Of course not, at least not to me. These last few months, he's been helping me with my husband's burial, the obituary, bills, Medicare, and sending out death certificates. Who knew it's so much trouble to die? He comes over once a week to mow, weed, pay my bills, notify all those government offices about whatnot." She flicked her wrist dismissively. "My daughter Andrea comes down some weekends, too, to help with cleaning up and packing boxes. She was closest to her dad. Bless her heart, Andrea cries a lot, misses him.

"But Dennis? Salt of the earth, my eldest was always good to me, never a harsh word between us. Comes to dinner every Sunday." She shook her head sadly, her chin drooping. "What's the world coming to? Did you say murdered?"

"No, ma'am," Savage corrected. "We're treating his demise as a suspicious death, a routine procedure until the coroner determines cause of death."

"What about Darryl? Did he resent his brother being the favorite?" Snow continued.

Marsha Sims looked up in surprise, as if she missed something. "What? No. Darryl lives too far away to be any help. He's single. If you ask me, he and Kelly would've been better suited as a couple. They're closer in age."

"Did they date?" asked Savage, perking up at the possibility of another suspect.

The woman laughed without mirth and shook her head. "No-o! He's been in Norfolk for twenty years. Oh, he comes home for Thanksgiving and Christmas, brings presents, but he's distant, preoccupied. Busy with his own affairs. He flew home for his dad's funeral. Now he'll need to come back for Denny's.

"You wonder if it's worth it—all the work, effort, and energy. Seems a lifetime ago my kids were young, healthy, and happy. Of the three of them, Denny stayed home, came around the most." Her eyes drifted to the recorder. "Now I'm really alone." She sighed, peering into her empty coffee cup. Glanced at the pack of cigarettes on the end table, glanced at the detectives, and then blinked as if startled. "Are you still here?"

The detectives took the cue and pushed to their feet. "Thanks for your help." Snow pocketed the recorder. Savage extended a card to her. "Please call us if you can think of anything else." They left her sitting, staring out the bay window.

Outside, they both heaved sighs. "Guess her boy could do no wrong in her eyes." Savage followed the sidewalk to the vehicle.

"I got the same impression. She may be a bit biased."

"Ya think? My mother had no trouble pointing out my shortcomings on a daily basis." Savage shrugged out of his sport coat and folded himself into the Explorer's passenger seat. "Complained that I was sloppy, careless, and sassy. Nagged morning and night: 'Tuck in your shirt; hang up your clothes; do your homework; brush your teeth.'" Reese's mouth quirked. "Looking back, she was right. My ex, Elena, had the same complaints. But since I joined the Army, at least I'm neater." He shrugged, reached for his cigarettes out of habit, but shoved them back in his pocket when his boss glared at him. Instead, he jiggled his leg up and down.

"You turned out all right," Snow commented, his eyes on the road.

Reese just laughed.

4

She felt anchored, immobile, hollow—tethered to tubes and wires—surrounded by a nebulous sepia sea, steeped in drugs and cocooned in warm cotton. Heard far-away whisperings, interspersed with muffled words like "rest" and "therapy."

Imagined a medbed with robotic spiders crawling over her body, diagnosing her injuries like in that Tom Cruise movie, *Minority Report.* Right hip sore—a dull, persistent ache—a sharp burning when she tried to shift her position. Something squeezing her sore breasts, then, a moaning "ooga—ooga," noise, liquid running. *So, a hospital. What have I done this time?*

A cold, metal disk hit her chest, a stethoscope. She smelled a clean, soapy disinfectant. A different hand feathered along her cheek, tingling as it touched—telescoping warmth and comfort, though the pain consumed her. Even her hair hurt. Couldn't force her eyes to open or her limbs to move, the dull, persistent ache like electric current ran down her right leg. Toes numb.

Trolling, her mind searched for images that might jog her memory as to her current predicament. Nothing recognizable came to the fore, but she knew that second hand—the touch light and gentle, smelling of sandalwood. But the soma beckoned her to dreams where gummy bears lived in a Candy Land world where there was neither pain nor impulse to remember. She slid down on silver ribbons and ran and ran along lanes with birdhouse-sized dwellings. Glancing down at her body, she declared, "I'm a gingerbread man!" She passed an arrow pointing to One Hundred Acre Woods in one direction and paused. The opposite way—Oz. "No, find home," she told her cookie self—peering up and down the lanes, searching for one big enough for people because she had a family somewhere.

She broke off a spearmint leaf and chipped a chunk of almond bark from a tree at the crossroads, plopping onto a handy toadstool to enjoy the sweets. Off in the distance beyond the cotton candy clouds, the West Wind blew a flotilla of bruised clouds her way. "Storm's brewing. Better find shelter."

* * *

At HQ briefing, the Homicide squad met in the room called the Murder Room, formerly Conference One with two white boards, a rectangular table holding a computer, folders, and a landline. Ten steps down the hall on the left, staff members could pop in the break room for coffee, condiments, and store their packed lunches in the fridge. Reheat their sludge in the microwave or brew a fresh pot.

Coroner Dr. Haili Chen summarized her findings: "The deceased had a hairline skull fracture, a broken blood vessel in his left eye, and a brain embolism. The last phalange on right hand was dislocated, which could have occurred when it collided with the quartz countertop, maybe the faucet.

"As per health conditions, he had high blood pressure, as I found traces of Losarten in his bloodstream. He had some carotid blockage, perhaps a former smoker but clear lungs. At some time prior to his death, he'd had a heart attack and a mild stroke. Stomach contents included scrambled eggs and garlic bologna." She paused to flip a page, then sat back.

Chief March said, "Did you call for his medical records?" Dr. Chen nodded. "So did the fracture kill him?"

"Cause precedes effect; I cannot state at this time with any degree of certainty that the fracture alone caused his death."

"The rest of us don't have medical backgrounds, Doc," Savage stated, "so can you just spit it out?" He drained his Sheetz cup impatiently, crushed it, and lobbed it in a corner trashcan.

Casting Reese a withering look, she explained with exaggerated slowness, "More like a chain reaction. A steep spike in blood pressure caused the broken capillaries in his eye, but whether the fracture came first, simultaneously, or followed the ruptured blood vessel, I cannot yet determine. Perhaps when the lab results come back, I can report a definitive COD."

"Then we can't really rule it a homicide?" Snow asked. "Fracture didn't cause brain swelling?"

"No, his temple came in contact with something cold—"

"Cold?" Lieutenant Stuart repeated, as if needing clarification.

"Probably frozen, which would have kept the swelling to a minimum. It contributed to his death, but his preexisting health conditions were also contributing factors."

"Frozen? Like the leg of lamb a woman used to kill her husband, then cooked it and fed it to the detectives? Was that an Agatha Christie mystery or a Hitchcock movie? I can't remember." Stuart smiled. "Then let's just call it suspicious until we can prove homicide."

"Interviews?" asked Chief March. "Obviously, Officer Mahoney cannot assist on this case."

"Mahoney took her sister to NYC day before yesterday where they spent the night; we called them back upon discovering the body," Savage reported. "Mahoney wouldn't comment on her sister's marriage, only to say the husband had a type-A, controlling personality."

"Could the wife have killed her husband *before* they left for the city? What was TOD?" the lieutenant asked Dr. Chen.

"He'd been dead for about twenty hours, but I'd say between eight to ten a.m. Factoring in the cold house, maybe another hour either way. AC was running when I arrived."

"Any other possibilities?" asked March.

"The back door was open, but the lock was scratched and jimmied; we have several sets of finger and foot prints to track down," Snow said. "Glean anything from the neighbors, Fields?"

"Yes, an insomniac, Mrs. Judy Blunt, who lives across the street, claims she saw a dark Mustang pick up Kelly Sims at 6:15 a.m. because she lets the cat out and makes coffee at that time. She referred to Mahoney as 'that blonde biker cop.'"

"How could she see across the road at dawn that clearly?" asked Stuart. He pushed the front office extension button, then speaker, brushed over his sandy crew with his free hand. "Please have Officer Mahoney come to the Murder Room."

"Blunt walked out to get the paper; Mahoney waved at her." Fields continued scanning his notes, as Mahoney entered, helmet in hand, coffee mug in the other, and stood at attention.

"At ease. Have a seat. So your sister's neighbor, Judy Blunt, knows you? Claims she saw you pick up Kelly Sims Thursday around six fifteen."

Mahoney said, "Yes. She just retired, so she has time to spend hours in her yard tending and talking to her flowers, observing the neighbors' business and gossiping. That morning, I remember seeing a pile of tanbark on her driveway."

"Was Dennis Sims alive when you picked your sister up?" asked Stuart.

"I didn't go inside, but Kelly seemed normal, thrilled to go to New York, thanking me immediately for the day out."

"You didn't answer the question. So why did you invite her on that particular day?" asked Snow.

"A belated birthday present. And because she works so hard, rarely takes vacation time, and misses her kids.

And there are no Broadway matinees on Wednesdays." She looked into and then sat her empty mug down. "Over the last seven years, they put both their kids through college. I'm guessing money's tight, but Denny had no objections to our day out."

"You didn't ask how he was?" the chief inquired.

"Why would I? As far as I knew, he was fine. I was focused on our trip—getting to New York, beating the rush-hour traffic, and finding a parking space. Grabbing a pastrami Reuben at Junior's. Then going to see *The Jersey Boys*."

"How was the play?" Snow asked.

"Super! I had no idea the Four Seasons struggled so hard—or had such a troubled past. Or that Frankie Valli nobly paid off his band member's gambling debts. Kelly loved the music. And they had so many hits! The actors sang one after another, narrating their lives between songs. Yes, we had a great day until Savage called."

"Your sister didn't mention her husband or act anxious, guilty, or worried in any way?" asked Fields, doodling on his pad.

"No, other than a passing comment, she said he was worried the apartments wouldn't be done on time. Or wondering what he had for dinner. She thought he was doing too much for a man his age."

"You didn't know about the domestic abuse?" Snow asked gently, making direct eye contact.

"I knew they had their differences, especially lately, but she never told me, no. A few months ago, I noticed bruises on her arms. She shrugged it off, said something about how Denny's dad's sudden death affected him deeply. Helping his mother added more stress and responsibility. His siblings live in State College and Virginia, so it was all on him. Sister Andrea works in the Penn State Alumni Office, and Darryl's a civilian construction foreman at the Naval Base in Norfolk." She stood. "I'm going for more coffee. Anybody else want some?"

March motioned her out as Sonja hurried in. Pagers beeped. "CRMC called 911. A man with a gun attacked a patient in Room 315. Officer injured!"

"That's Mac's room!" Snow jumped up, tearing out of the room, Savage and Fields on his heels.

"Wait. Where's Shadow?" March asked.

Stuart combed fingers through his bottlebrush crew. "Kauffman's keeping her at the K-9 site for training until Mac returns home." He flipped open his cell. "Dispatch, send all available units to Carlisle Regional to hunt for an armed intruder stat!" Snapped it shut, pocketed it. "What the hell happened to Castle? He was assigned to guard her! Sir, I have to go."

March nodded. "Another aborted briefing!" He pushed to his feet to switch on the computer, then Googled ABC News. "Time to requisition more cameras on the streets and in the squad cars. Maybe someone can write a grant for body cams!

"Wish one week could go by without an officer or detective getting injured." He turned up the volume, as a cameraman jounced up the stairs at the hospital, catching scurrying legs, disparate explosions of sound from a creaking cart knocked out of the way to raised voices raining down the hallway.

5

Lethargy lay on her like a lover, pressing her body down and pinning her limbs to the bed. Sounds filtered through her sepia sea like scuttling crabs, muffled shouts, the groan of bedsprings, something metal hitting the floor, skittering across the slick linoleum. *A gun!* Sensing danger, Mac tried to climb into consciousness; her mind willed her eyes to open, but her leaden body refused to obey. Then the hubbub faded, so she drifted back into dreams.

* * *

Snow shouldered into the room to find a blonde wearing hospital gloves leaning against the vacant bed, extending the handle of a snub-nosed revolver toward him. Chris strode over, snapped back the privacy curtain where his wife lay sleeping while beeping machines monitored her vitals.

Her doctor appeared in the doorway, almost composed. "Erin's fine. The intruder didn't reach her, thanks to her friend." He indicated Mac's CI, Jean du Bourbon in drag, formerly the Revolutionary War reenactor Marquis de Lafayette.

"Where's Greg Castle?" Snow stopped, bent over, hands on knees, huffing after charging up three flights of stairs and running the length of the hallway past the nurses' station, beating Savage, who took the elevator. Glanced at his slumbering, undisturbed wife, her auburn curls framing her pale face against the pillow. He sent Fields to cover the rear. "Can you identify the assailant, Doctor?" Snow asked.

"No, he wore a stocking over his head, barreled in waving a gun in one hand, a knife in another. He was quick. Your man didn't even have time to unsnap his holster. The guy was average height, five-eight, sandy hair poking through; my guess—military or cop."

"Yeah?" Savage asked. "Why?"

"The fatigues, the build, and the way he moved," Dr. Cook said.

"How's Greg Castle?" Snow asked.

"He's in surgery with a knife wound to the abdomen. From behind, I shot a hypo of Lydocane into the assailant's gun hand; then your friend here slammed the door on his wrist. He managed to disentangle himself, knock me down, stumble over me, and escape in the confusion." He proffered the hypo in a sealed glassine.

"Thanks. Think we can get DNA off of this?" Savage asked.

The doctor shrugged and then nodded. "Possibly."

Savage strode down the hall, shield displayed, approaching the nurses; Fields cordoned off the area, both shaking their heads—no sign of the assailant. Savage canvassed the floor, leaving the nurses to Fields. Snow ordered, "Call HQ, have them check local hospitals, doctor's offices, and urgent-care centers for a man with a strained or broken wrist."

"One more thing." A shaking hand extended a clear plastic bag. "I have the bullet we extracted from your wife's hip last week."

"This came from a sniper rifle." Snow studied the smashed, spent bullet, and then shook du Bourbon's hand. "Thanks, man, for protecting Erin. Why are you here?"

"Watching Mac. She's vulnerable until you find her Battle of Monmouth shooter. And she's my out-of-jail ticket. I found out the Revolutionary War sharpshooters climbed into trees, many of whom the Sixth Regiment doesn't know or remember because they were extras hired for the rehearsal." He leaned against the bed, tugged off the blonde wig. Aristocratic, long, thin fingers feathered through his sandy shag.

Snow approached Mac's bed, enveloped her hand in his, then stroked her cheek gently while he made sure she was sound—well, had no new injuries. "Did you get a good look at him?"

"No, he was disguised. Doc's right, though. I got the same impression. I'd say current military—Army. Yes, he could've bought them at an army surplus, but they fit too well—almost molded to his form, and he wore sergeant's stripes. You see Matt Damian in the Bourne movies?" Snow nodded absently, his attention still on his wife. "Similar height, build, and boyish look. The man's dangerous; no wasted movements. Had he breeched the room, he would've . . ."

"God, I know! Wake up, Erin. I need you!" His fist clutched her hair. He dropped to his knees, level with her face. "Please, babe."

"Careful, man, don't bump her IV!" du Bourbon warned. "The doc said to let her rest. See her eyes? She's dreaming. When she wakes, she'll have all this . . . ," he waved his arm over her right side, "to contend with. I imagine the physical therapy for a hip replacement is intensive, a big adjustment at her age and with a baby, too. Sorry, man. I feel responsible." He tossed the wig on the empty bed, rounded it, and sat down, letting the high heels slip to the floor.

"No, I'm responsible," Snow argued. "I kept reminding her that the regiment needed a Molly Pitcher, kept pushing her to the limit. Hey, her color's improving." He stopped, kneeled beside her bed. Brushed her cheek with his fingers. "Are you staying with her?"

"You're touching her; she knows it. Damn straight; the bastard might come back." Du Bourbon flashed a smile and his knife and then furtively sheathed it behind his back with a glance toward the door.

In the hall, Snow approached the doctor. "Let's move her to another room under an assumed name, say Erica Slaughter. Better yet, to Health South or another physical therapy site. Keep it off the records. And what's Castle's current status?"

"All right. He's still in surgery, but he'll pull through. We've done all we can do at this point. If you insist, I'll discharge Mrs. Snow, but she goes in an ambulance."

The detective nodded agreement. "I'll ride with her. Call me when she's ready.

"Savage, when you're done here, check the gun and bullet into Evidence and have Ballistics trace the revolver's make and model. Fields, after finishing your interviews, get the security cam disks. We've got a description; let's see if we got lucky enough to snare an image." Pausing in the third-floor lounge, he called HQ and informed his chief of his ten-twenty, the men's assignments, and requested CSU to dust CRMC Room 315 for prints.

"Yes, sir. After I get Mac settled, Savage, Fields and I are headed to Party Time and the Sport Hut to interview employees."

In route, Chris rode shotgun, leaving EMT Hemmer to monitor Mac. Then called home to check on Ian. The driver backed into the rear entrance—ambulance beeping —of the physical therapy building, unloaded their patient, and transferred her to a bed. The records on the table read "Erica Slaughter." Attendants hooked her up to new monitors. Snow paced until du Bourbon entered the room, dressed casually in a golf shirt and jeans with sandals.

"Note the name change," Snow confided quietly. "Thanks for keeping an eye on *Erica.*"

6

Party Time and the Sport Hut were open for business.
Heavy, metal mesh smothered the Warehouse windows.
Snow and Savage pushed through the glass door. Inside,
worn hardwood floors underfoot and warm exposed
beams overhead. Bins and counters boasted balloons,
party favors, and giftwrap for all occasions. A helium tank
stood beside the counter. The detectives strode through
the front to the arch of the sports store and stopped.
"Well, I'll be damned," Snow remarked.

"Hey, top cop, what's up?" Tyrone Bender swung out
from behind the glass display cases to shake the
detectives' hands. At six-five, two-thirty, he looked every
inch the basketball star who had assisted Carlisle High to
its '86 championship. The basketball team members
smiled from a 24" x 28" framed wall poster.

Was it only last year he'd been accused of murdering
his wife? His brother was behind bars for the crime.
"How's it going? How's Tamara?" Snow asked. Mac had
taken to the toddler, who'd been locked in her mother's
car at the crime scene, and sent the little girl gifts on her
birthday, Christmas, and Easter.

"Good, man, good. We're all good. Well, except my
boss. I'm really sorry to hear about his death. He was a
real dynamo, always moving. Gotta hand it to him—a real
go-getter."

"So you're the manager?" Savage asked, peering at the
sports memorabilia: local school posters adorned the
walls. A basketball backboard with a net and rim was
mounted at one end of the room. Display cases ran the
length of the store, a soccer goal at the opposite end.
Basketballs hung in mesh laundry bags on hooks along

the walls. In the middle, racks of sports clothes gave off that fishy, chemically new scent. Midday, only a couple customers trolled the floor. A twenty-something held up a Penn State jersey. An older woman selected a boy's Steelers windbreaker. They made their purchases and scurried out the rear door.

"Got a few minutes? We need to ask a few questions about your boss," Snow said.

"Olive? Could you cover the registers?" He spoke to a woman wearing a black pantsuit strolling through the store.

She smiled tightly, nodded at the detectives. "Sure."

"Thanks. Come back to my office." Bender laughed as he led them to a corner desk with two chairs and a computer, papers piled in a metal organizer on the corner, receipts impaled on a nail. "How about a soda?" Bender pulled some bills out of his pocket, fed them into the corner vending machine. Out popped three Cokes.

"Sure, thanks. I'll get right to the point," Snow laid his recorder down and asked the same questions he'd put to the widow, then moved onto the business. "Just to inform you, CPD has requested all records associated with the stores and the apartments." He motioned upstairs with his thumb; they could hear the pneumatic zip of an air hammer and drone of a drill. Feet shuffled around.

"Do you need sales slips?" Tyrone frowned, trying to make the connection. He scratched his head and looked at the new cash registers.

"Not just yet. Does Sims have an accountant?" Savage asked while watching two new customers enter.

Bender turned to Reese. "Not that I know of. I hand the receipts over every month after I total sales. Business is slow at the moment but peaks during the different sports seasons. You know, fall—football, field hockey, and soccer; winter—basketball and swimming; spring—baseball and softball." His hand swept the room. "We get a boost during playoffs."

"And Party Time?" Savage inquired with a lift of one brow.

"You'd have to ask Olive. She manages it, plus handles correspondence and office calls for the boss."

"We will." Snow made a note. "Any problems with the business? Any unhappy or irate customers threaten Sims? I noticed the heavy-duty mesh." Canted his head toward the windows.

"Yeah, we had a couple of break-ins last fall. Last time had to replace the cash registers and add security." He indicated the cameras in the corners pointed to the counters and doors.

"How often do you change the disks?" asked Savage.

"Rerecord every twenty-four hours." Two more female customers entered, conversing quietly with each other.

Before Snow could frame his next question about the other tenants, a rat-a-tat concussion riddled the front, shattering the door, sending glass projectiles flying in every direction. The security alarm screamed. Women squealed, twirling in confusion; others ducked. Bender motioned for the customers to get behind the counters.

"Get down and away from the windows!" yelled Snow.

"Sounds like an assault pistol," Savage muttered. Both men scrunched down, unsnapped and unholstered their weapons, and rushed the front door. Poking their heads carefully through the doorframe, neither could see the shooter. Besides their unmarked sedan, four other cars dotted the parking lot. A brick with a note attached rolled to within five feet of the door as a rusted Olds blew past, never stopping.

"Cover me." Savage duckwalked outdoors, retrieved the brick, and scrambled back through the vacant doorframe. By that time, Bender had silenced the alarm. Thumbed Carlisle Glass on his cell to replace the front door panels with Plexiglas, and ended the call. The detectives walked the perimeter while the store manager checked on Olive and the new customers still huddled behind the party goods counter.

Pale with shock, Olive shook her head, rubbing her forehead that struck the counter while hunkering down. "No, I'm okay, really. I'll just get some coffee." Bender indicated her forehead was bleeding, matting her dark hair. "I'll ice it and put a BAND-AID on it. I'm sure the detectives want to talk to me."

"Ladies, are you a'right?" Bender asked, helping each to her feet. The blonde nodded, brushed offer her jeans. The brunette looked furtively out the door, her dark eyes glazed.

"What the hell was that?" Bender asked the detectives while unearthing a broom and dustpan to sweep up the glass.

"No, leave it. You'll have to close." Savage flipped the OPEN sign over. "This is now a crime scene. Ladies, I'll need a statement," he addressed the silent women huddled in the corner. "Are you all right?" The customers nodded mutely.

"All right." Bender and the detectives returned to his desk where the manager waited until Snow had called the CSU and ordered B&Ws on the scene. "Comb the outside, front, and back." Ended the call. "Well, that injected some adrenaline into the system." He breathed deeply and chugged his Coke. "Now, what can you tell me about the other tenants? We'll want to speak to them, too."

"The first room houses Good Dog Rising, a dog obedience school. Second one's empty at the moment, but a barber's moving in soon. The third's a hair and nail salon. What did the note say?" Bender asked. He chugged his soda in one long gulp.

Savage donned latex and unwrapped the plain, white paper and turned it around for the others to see. "PAY UP OR ELSE!!!" Dropped it and the twine into a glassine. Dated and labeled it. Bagged the brick. "Have any idea what that means?"

Bender's chocolate eyes widened in surprise. "No clue, man, but it sounds like somebody owes a loan shark money."

"Any idea if Sims owed money or had any enemies?" Snow asked, raking blunt fingers through his hair.

"I would've said no. Now, I'm not so sure," Bender replied, eyebrows furrowed.

After a few more questions, Snow and Savage concluded the interview, handed Bender their cards, and moved on to question Olive Dayton. After getting statements, he motioned for the others to leave. Then the detectives trooped out, around the corner to the other tenants. Finally, they climbed the stairs to question the construction crew.

"Can't stop now, gentleman," claimed Julio Roberto, standing amid the materials and debris of four lofts roughed out, the galley kitchens and bathrooms piped in, but the suites lacked walls, insulation, and trim. His right hand clasped a claw hammer; his left indicated the rolls of pink insulation stacked around the perimeter.

"We're on a deadline." He pulled off his ball cap that left a sweaty rim around his inky curls, his tee was wet under the arms; a tool belt circled his tan cargo pants. Wiping his forehead and glancing at the two other men, he motioned for them to continue working.

"We're investigating a suspicious death. We can go to CPD Headquarters if you'd rather, or obtain a subpoena," Snow said, his jaw set but voice level—eyes on the hammer.

Savage made a gesture toward his pistol. "Put the hammer down slowly please."

Roberto gave each man a measured glare but did as he was told, then untied the toolbelt, set it aside, and pointed out to the fire escape. He lit a cigarette once they'd stepped outside.

Snow put similar questions to him that he'd asked Bender and Dayton, and though his answers were brusque, they coincided with the others' answers. He asked about the remodeling particulars.

"For one, the apartments are already rented. We got thirty days to complete them. Appliances are ordered, and plumbers are coming next week. Drywall goes up. Then we set the tile and lay carpet. We caulk and paint week after that."

"When was the last time you saw Sims?"

"He stopped by last Tuesday to check on progress. Left tile and carpet samples, told me to pick them up at Lowe's." The man inhaled, held, and then let the smoke filter through his nose. Savage shifted uncomfortably, trying to avoid the cancer sticks, then whipped around to inhale the second-hand smoke.

Snow continued. "Please call us if you think of anything else, especially if you find out Dennis Sims did anything out of the ordinary to attract unwanted attention. We're trying to track his movements last week, interview his contacts." Snow extended his card.

"Do you know if he had financial obligations?" Savage asked.

Roberto shrugged, pocketed the card. "Don't we all? One thing different." He held up his index finger and then pointed to the front wall of the Warehouse. "That shooting ten minutes ago." His lips tipped into a lopsided smile as he crushed the butt into a small bucket of sand with nicotine-stained fingers. He opened the steel door for the detectives, nodding for them to precede him into the building. "Did you talk to his banker or the wife?"

"Not yet, but we will. Thanks for the tip." Snow motioned for Savage to lead the way downstairs, and they exited the Warehouse.

7

Kelly slipped through the doors of Mary Grace Alwine's
front office along a strip of offices: an ENT, a Physical
Therapy Center, dentist, and others off of Alexander
Spring Garden Street. Pushing through the second door,
she entered a quiet reception area painted taupe and
decorated with soothing watercolor abstracts, swirls of
sea green and blue against a luminescent opal canvas.
Instrumental music played softly in the background; a
closed door led to her friend's office and consulting room.

Swinging the inner door open, Alwine appeared,
wearing a cream-colored blouse over lavender slacks. She
smiled, hugged the friend she'd known since high school.
"I'm so sorry about Dennis. You must feel overwhelmed. If
I can do anything . . . ," the sentence trailed, as she
lowered herself to an armchair rather than sit behind her
desk and gestured Sims to the other chair.

"As a matter of fact, I need to talk to you." Kelly's chin
trembled as she fought for control, fisting her hands in
her lap.

"I think I know what you're going to say—that you're
the prime suspect in your husband's death, assuming it
wasn't accidental."

Kelly Sims nodded affirmatively. "The detectives found
the selfies."

Mary Grace leveled her calm, brown eyes at her friend.
"That was quick. How did you explain them?"

"I told the truth." Kelly crossed her legs, leaned back
in her chair, smoothing her hands over the armrests.
Finger combed the hair off her forehead. Cracked her
knuckles.

"Roll your shoulders a few times. Would you like some tea?"

Kelly shook her head and glanced at her watch, too jangled. "No thanks. I'm going to Messiah to interview a prof who's going to teach Chinese—the language and cuisine—at summer camp, but I don't know what to do next." She loosened her shoulders.

"I'd recommend tai chi thirty minutes a day for starters." Mary Grace smiled slowly, signaling that she knew Sims wanted practical advice. "Have you retained a lawyer?"

Kelly shook her head again, pulled a spiral notebook from her purse, showing her friend. "I made a list: make funeral arrangements; write obit; call caterer and Dennis's lawyer, retain my own lawyer. The kids are coming home today. On top of work."

"Don't you have bereavement leave?" she asked. Kelly nodded. "At least take your personal days."

"I know. I will. But that's not it. I'll miss my husband, but I'm relieved, because I thought . . . Never mind. The cops, detectives, sense that I'm not grief-stricken. It's like perpetual storm clouds have dissipated; the sun's shining. I'm free to come and go without restrictions, without twenty questions, without his hovering over me or feeling guilty when I've done nothing wrong."

"You've been under constant, considerable strain lately since your decision to divorce. Do the authorities know about it?"

"No, I can't tell them! Don't you see, the more I tell them, the guiltier I seem. And we fought Thursday before Shan and I left for New York." She yanked a tissue from the box on the table between them, rocking the ivy beside the box. Steadied the plant.

"Physically?" Mary Grace asked.

Kelly nodded. "He lunged for my throat but I smacked him—first time since Camie was born—right up side the head. No, well, there was one other time. Then Shannon rang the doorbell."

"What did Dennis do then?" Her therapist leaned forward.

"Nothing. Just glared through me and motioned toward the door. So I grabbed my wheelie and scatted before he changed his mind."

Mary Grace watched her friend shred a tissue. Carefully she leaned over, took Kelly's damp hand. "It doesn't look good, I grant you, but go about your business with your head up. It sounds cliché, but live one day at a time, in the moment. You'll grieve in your own time and your own way. And If Camie and Drew need to talk, I'm here.

"And I'll see you once a week, let's say Wednesdays over the lunch hour. No charge. You can vent. Take at least three days off of work to concentrate on your list. I can help if you like—at the funeral home and at your house. Act as buffer if you need one." She smiled, thumbing dark-brown bangs off her forehead.

"What if they arrest me? And I lose my job? I'll lose the house! And I have no idea what shape Denny's businesses are in; they were his bailiwick. Plus, Camie has another year of college left. Thank God Drew's graduated and working, so I needn't fret about him.

"And Denny's siblings consider me a gold-digger anyway. They don't know the hell I've been through." Kelly stopped, shaking. "We don't ever talk about it."

"Take several cleansing breaths. Focus on one day at a time. Can you identify the song playing?"

Kelly listened to background instrumental. "It's from *The Lion King*—'The Circle of Life.' I get it. I'll try." Tears rimmed her eyes; she blinked them back, dabbed them with a clean tissue. Plucked out a couple more for later.

"You're not alone, although it may feel that way now. People will offer condolences, bring food, and send flowers and cards. Beyond that—most are uncomfortable with death and usually evade the issue, so in time you'll need coping strategies about dealing with single life. And you know about the stages of grief. You don't seem angry."

"I know. Oh, I'm depressed—" She waved her hand over the list. "—but my emotions are out of kilter! Hot, cold, but that may be menopause." Her hand gestured, erasing. "It's the police I'm worried about. They've already questioned Shannon and my parents and interrogated me last night and promised to see me again." Impatiently, she combed her unruly chestnut waves, rummaged in her purse for a barrette, and then clipped them back.

"Take off work so you can attend to your family. Follow your to-do list. Comfort the kids. Call me. I'm serious about the tai chi, a half hour morning and afternoon if you can manage. Or take a brisk, half-hour walk. In the meantime, . . ." Mary Grace stood, eased over to the credenza housing the CD player, opened the end cabinet, extracted a DVD, and handed it to Kelly.

"Thanks." Kelly looked at the cover, the model's pose, linked hands reaching for the blue sky. Behind him lay a tranquil tropical bay. "I know. One day at a time. I hope I can; I'll try. Thank you." Sims patted her friend's hand absently, consulted her watch, and stood up. "Okay, Wednesdays at noon. Next time, I'll bring lunch for us both," she promised, brushing the lint from her skirt. "And thanks for listening. I'm not calm, but at least the panic has receded somewhat."

"You can always see your doctor about something to calm your nerves, but I find ten milligrams of melatonin work pretty well. Take another if you wake up in the middle of the night." She stood, escorted Kelly to the door, and hugged her again. "Call me if I can help. I mean it."

Sims nodded and left the office, then the building. "Fifteen minutes to Messiah College." She coached herself. "You can do this; finalize the camps. Then I'll take off. One day, no, one hour at a time, waiting for the next ax to fall."

Suddenly, a red truck veered into the intersection in front of her; she jerked her steering wheel right onto the shoulder of the road, standing on her brakes—squealing in complaint—to avoid a collision, honking the horn. "I had the green light, you freakin' moron!"

But the truck driver sped on, oblivious or unfazed by the near miss. The car behind her honked his horn, drove past. He glared impatiently while Kelly's limbs quaked, her heart thrumming in her throat, temples throbbing. Her hands clutched the wheel, frozen in place. Glancing in her rearview mirror, she waited until traffic cleared and the light turned green again to proceed slowly through the intersection and onto I-81 to head to the college.

8

Erin awoke, eyes gritty and heavy, drowsy from drugs, her body still anchored to a bed. She blinked, staring at grayish-blue walls. Her body tensed, awakening the pain in her hip and abdomen, spreading down her right leg. Numb toes tingled, so she rotated her left foot, then the right. Something had happened, then the memory of the shooting stung her. Her hand roved over her hip, which felt strange, something alien planted beneath the skin. Tears slipped down her cheeks. Biting her lip against the pain, sharp as a taser, she closed her eyes and tried to contain it.

Swiveling her head, Erin saw the body slouched in a padded lounge chair, head back with eyes closed, the lines across his forehead relaxed. His full lips were slightly parted, but his arms crossed his body—as if he begrudged the nap he obviously needed.

On his knees, *The Patriot*'s banner headline yelled: "FATHER PETITIONS COURT FOR CUSTODY." Slug below read: "Emma Hawthorne Going Home?" And a composite article: "DEFENSE ATTORNEY FILES FOR A DISMISSAL OF CHARGES!"

Oh yeah. My stint as Molly Pitcher ended with an injury. Ian? Where's the baby? She patted the bed. How long have I been here? This isn't CRMC. She forced her limbs and shoulders to relax, knowing that her in-laws and Dad were helping Chris care for Ian. She felt her breasts, realizing someone had pumped milk for the baby. *That's why they're sore.* "But damn it, some asshole shot me at the Battle of Monmouth reenactment. I'm going to catch that bastard!"

Chris startled at her words, scrubbed his hands over his face and scooted to her bedside. Took her hand, kissed her palm. "You're awake. God, Erin, you scared us all. I'm so sorry this happened to you." He stared at her chapped lips. "The nurses bring you ice chips every day; they melt. Here, drink some water." He poured a glass, adjusted the straw, and held it to her lips until she swallowed. "How do you feel?"

"Like I was dragged to hell and back—still on fire. My hip burns, my back aches, and my neck . . . What happened? I remember being shot. Where are we? How's Ian? And Shadow? Why am I so sore?" she whispered.

"Ian's fine but fussy; he misses you. Corey's keeping Shadow at the K-9 site but brings her home on weekends. You've had a hip replacement. We're in Health South, where you have to undergo physical therapy."

"Why?" She couldn't comprehend his words.

"The bullet shattered the joint." He made a fist. "This is your ball at the end of your femur." He cupped his other hand over it. "This is the socket attached to your pelvis. The bullet separated them."

Stunned, she stared at her husband, letting his words sink in.

"Does it hurt much?" he asked. His hand slid up and down her arm. "I'd hug you but don't want to jar you! But the worst part is you lost the baby. I wanted to tell you first, so you wouldn't be upset when the doctor—"

Her tears flowed unimpeded as recognition slowly dawned; blood pulsed through her, an ocean in her ears. Something dropped within—emptiness invaded her soul. "So I *was* pregnant." Feelings cascaded through her: the rush of anger, sadness, grief, remorse, and depression plummeting her mood. "It's my fault! I said, 'Oh no,' like I dismissed the notion. Didn't have time, didn't pay attention." Tears welled; she flicked them away. "Too focused on work."

"You knew? Why didn't you tell me? I'd have talked you out of playing Molly Pitcher if—"

Erin laid a hand on his arm. "I didn't know for sure. I felt one tiny blip at Margie Hawthorne's wake, but I thought . . ." Her eyes connected with her husband's. "It was morning sickness—"

"Not a flu bug when I made you spar! I'm so sorry, babe, for pushing you. For being too rough with you. For expecting you to shoulder so much—a job, an infant, and me when you push yourself hard enough." He gathered her in his arms and held her while they cried. "We put a marker in our family plot with the date. The squad sent roses, which Mom and Dad took up yesterday.

"But how is that even possible? Didn't think you could get pregnant while nursing," he wondered aloud.

"Obviously, it's possible!" Erin lay back against her pillows.

"Take all the time you need to rehabilitate and grieve." He resumed his seat, kept her hand in his, rubbing the web between her thumb and forefinger with his thumb.

Erin shuddered. "I don't know what to say. Just feel sad, empty, and sore. Jarred to the bone. Wasn't I at Carlisle Regional? I dreamt of a ruckus in my room. What happened?"

"It wasn't a dream, babe. Don't know if I should tell you now, but your shooter tried to attack you in the hospital then escaped."

Then he told her the details. "We moved you here under the name Erica Slaughter."

"So I'm your mom and my grandmother? So my assailant's still at large? What happened to Greg Castle? He was guarding me."

"Had surgery for a knife wound. He's recuperating, too."

"Knife? I thought I heard a gun sliding across the floor."

"You did, Erin." Chris glanced at the waning light, draining away, dusk surrendering to darkness.

A steely resolve rolled up her spine. "In the hospital—the same man who shot me at the battle? We're going to catch him!"

"Damn right! We recovered the pistol." He told her about the gun, a partial print on the bullet in the chamber, the doctor's description, and the CPD's work to track him down. "But it's tough slogging through all the regiment's data. Nobody at the hospital recognized him, because he wore a stocking over his head."

"Did he leave any DNA?" Mac asked.

"Perhaps on the hypo when the doc shot Lydocane in his hand. We sent what we had to the lab, but not all the reports are back. Chris described du Bourbon's role. "He saved your life by slamming the door on the perp's wrist. We're tracking hospital and doctor offices for a male patient with a sprained or broken wrist. Your informant has info for you. He dresses in drag as a CI, but wears male civies under his current alias, John Bowie."

"You recover the bullet from my hip?" Mac asked.

"Yes. The battlefield slug came from a sniper's rifle. Guy was hiding in the trees—reenactors and your shooter, too, apparently. According to Bowie, the extras who swell the numbers during battle aren't actually in the regiment or even known to its members. Just hired for the battlefield reenactments. Your assailant came and went, undetected."

Mac closed her eyes, leaned back against the pillows, her face strained and gaunt. Auburn curls spiraling into dreads.

"Okay. That's enough. You're exhausted. Your dinner should be coming along soon. Let me run home, check on the baby. I'll come back after supper. Rest until then." He stood, kissed her chafed lips, and massaged her shoulders. "You've got knots in here. Try to relax," he whispered.

"Please bring Ian when you come back; he needs to nurse."

"Then we'll have to stay the night." Chris looked skeptical.

"He can sleep in his pack 'n' playpen. Perhaps they can find a rollaway bed for you. Will you also bring me my laptop?" She held his hand until he nodded, released it grudgingly, watched him back out the door.

Minutes later, a tray bearing dinner arrived: a creamed soup and Jell-O. While she tested a spoonful, in saunters a man with a sandy shag wearing jeans and a tee. "John Bon Jovi?" Erin asked.

The man clasped a hand over his heart. "You've slain me! Don't you recognize me? Well, you're half right. Formerly Jean du Bourbon of the Revolutionary War's Sixth Regiment Reenactors, I'm John Bowie now. CPD calls me Tootsie when I'm in drag. It's quite a lark." He smiled his crooked smile, waiting until she was ready to ask.

Mac let a minute slide. *He looked different—plastic surgery?* Though her hip was throbbing, she tried to smile. "I owe you. Thanks for saving my life. Surprising, since you tried to kill me last month. Still, I thank you, kind sir, for your valiant efforts on my behalf. What's your cover?"

"Flattery will get you everywhere!" He flicked his wrist at her. "I teach French as an adjunct at three area colleges. Moved to Lancaster. You know I wouldn't have shot you! Empty revolver, remember? So, when I'm not minding your bedside, I hang around the ordinaries following the regiment to pick up information on your shooter."

"I doubt anyone would recognize you. Have you had surgery?"

"Oh yes. Now we have something in common."

"Mine was necessary," Mac commented drily.

"As was mine!" du Bourbon insisted, lowering himself to the lounge chair Chris had vacated. He'd had his eyelids lifted, his jaw firmed, added a few pounds, looking toned and tanned. "Your shooter is young, a stranger, the tavern owner tells me, and likely military."

"What tavern? Did someone recognize him?"

"The Brandywine Inn, a reenactors' watering hole. Alcohol loosens tongues. This kid said he was on leave, wanted to sign onto the Civil War reenactors. Either had the wrong war or the incorrect place. Anywho, the bartender said he sounded Southern, Army, based on his fatigues. Still, that's a wide swath to cover."

"How'd the barkeep know? Did you get a name?" Mac leaned forward, winced as her hip tendons pulled, eased back onto her raised pillows. "Did he pay with a credit card?

Bowie shook his head. "A no-brainer. Only man in the bar with a buzz cut. The barkeep remembers the conversation. The kid was looking for a female cop playing Molly Pitcher."

"Now you've got my attention."

"Payback," Bowie guessed.

"Great! Thanks. That's not enough info to track him down, but someone with a grudge is looking for me. So it has to be an old case—someone I arrested."

"How many we talkin' about?" Du Bourbon brushed his bangs off his forehead. "My CI lingo sound legit?"

Mac smiled. "Well, a little too erudite and polished for an informant, but keep working on it. I imagine hanging out in bars will do it, but I haven't seen your Tootsie getup yet."

"With makeup, I look pretty!" He posed, one hand on his hip and modeled. "Did the doc recover the bullet?" du Bourbon asked.

"Yes. Chris sent it to the lab today."

"Grooved?" he probed.

"Yes, but not from a Pennsylvania or Kentucky long rifle. Too new, Chris said the bullet came from a sniper rifle."

Bowie nodded. "Anyway, I'll let you rest. I'll be outside until hubby returns." He winked. From behind his back, he brandished a CD case, handing it to her. "Check it out."

"You're getting really good at this, du Bour—er, Bowie. Glad we could work something out—to keep you out of jail."

"The pleasure is all mine, I assure you. You can call me John." He bowed, brought her hand to his mouth, grazed his lips across her knuckles, and tucked the case in her hand with the exaggerated aplomb of Lafayette—his former role, then faded from view as the door wafted shut. Erin's eyelids drooped. Muffled sounds beyond the closed door shut out the world, induced sleep.

Dreams spun on the sound of water swirling into a wooden bucket; she held on as it filled, overflowed. Her grandmother, Ora Slaughter, gesturing madly, motioned for her to duck down. Hearing a sudden pop, her body dropped into the river. Letting go of the heavy load, she floated until wet Colonial garb dragged her beneath roiling water, turning her as it purled in eddies, poured over rocks, the churning white foam choking her. Knowing if she woke, she'd drown, her body floated on. Blood oozed from the wound, staining the water rusty, carrying her into "darkness visible," Lucifer's abyss in *Paradise Lost*, darker than a month of midnights.

9

Wednesday Snow called HQ. "I'm returning to the Warehouse. Did Ballistics come back on the weapon? When's the briefing on the Sims death? Thanks. Over, out." He studied the bullet holes. "Nine millimeter automatic? What would be the point for a drive-by when cops were inside?"

"Probably didn't know we were there. Had an unmarked sedan—remember? Like the note said. A warning. 'Pay up,'—all in caps. Sims must have a skeleton somewhere." Savage examined the ground for any evidence CSU may have missed. "All the casings were collected, apparently."

"I get that, Reese. Pay up what? Salaries? Debt? Blackmail? So we need to look beyond the wife, as long as she and Mahoney stand by their NYC story. Somebody else had a beef with Sims."

"Neighbor verified their story. Mahoney dropped off play tickets, restaurant and parking receipts—time stamped. Seems like a solid alibi to me." His knuckles brushed across his scruffy beard.

"Let's see if the wife will give up the financials," Snow ventured.

"Got the impression it's not the wife's permission you need but that foxy admin's." Savage ragged his eyebrows, a Groucho Marx imitation, index and middle fingers holding an imaginary cigar.

"Then let's go see this foxy Olive Dayton." Snow shoved through the Party Time door a second time. Again, Dayton was traipsing down the stairs wearing a toast-colored top with a scoop neckline, revealing cleavage, paired with tight, black Capris. Her black hair nested atop her head. She stepped over to greet them, hand extended. "Detectives. How can I help you?"

"Perhaps you can shed some light on what happened to your employer." They followed her back to her office in a cramped nook under the stairs. Tucked in the left corner, a file cabinet held newspapers and flyers announcing sales. A coffee station stood to the right. Opposite them sat a computer on a metal desk, a stack of mail beside it. Shelves along the back bore party samples and catalogues. She stirred powdered creamer into her coffee. "Coffee? I just made a fresh pot. How do you take it?"

"Go ahead, have a seat. I'll pour a couple," Savage offered, already upending two take-away cups, adding creamer, one packet of sweetener to Snow's, leaving his own black, and snapped on the lids. Lowered himself to the chair by the door so he could canvass the store, keep an eye on the entrance.

"We have a few questions." Snow set the recorder on the desk.

"Sure, as long as no customers need me. Tyrone's not here yet."

After identifying participants for the recorder, Snow asked, "Are you aware of anyone, maybe a dissatisfied customer, who bore Dennis Sims a grudge? Or disgruntled business partners? Evicted tenants?"

She shook her head. "He has no business partners that I know of. Just employees. He pays us bimonthly like clockwork. He's a stickler for promptness. We have two store managers, two clerks per shift each—a.m. and p.m. —and the construction crew upstairs. The Going Postal store doesn't belong to Dennis. The four tenants provide income, but they deal directly with the boss. Now, I'm not sure what changes may occur."

"How do you account for the drive-by shooting yesterday? The note with the brick said 'PAY UP.' Can you explain that? You're not nervous about returning to work today?" Savage asked.

She smiled tightly at him. "It's a mystery to me. Well, I'm a little anxious, but we're open for business as usual. I'm not being paid to sit at home. Why are you assuming the note was meant for Den—Mr. Sims?"

Snow observed her set features for a minute: her etched brows like boomerangs and lids dusted with lavender eye shadow. "Unless you tell us otherwise, it's his business. Do any of his employees have gambling habits?"

Her hand went to her throat. "What? How am I to know that?"

"How long have you worked here, Ms. Dayton?" Savage asked.

"Twelve years. I started on the cash register." Her nose lifted a notch. She sipped her coffee and then rested the mug on a coaster. "Worked my way up." Then leaned back, crossed her arms.

"Then I imagine you know a lot about the business. Income, inventory, expenses, personnel—that sort of thing," Snow said, noting her defensive gesture. "Who handles the finances?"

"Tyrone and I manage the inventory, sales, ordering, and displays, but Mr. Sims handles the accounts. Or used to," she amended.

"Does Mrs. Sims have any input in the businesses?" Savage asked.

"She doesn't know the first thing about it. Dennis managed the businesses, his wife their house. A traditional man, he was the breadwinner. She came in twice a year for birthday supplies for her kids' parties. And maybe a couple more times for sports clothes. That's all."

"Can you provide us with the financial records for the past year?" Snow asked.

"Why?" Her back came up. "Do you have a subpoena?"

"We're investigating a homicide, ma'am. We can get one. Excuse me." Savage stepped out to use his cell.

Snow explained, "It's routine to examine everything about the victim's life in order to catch the killer. Evidently, he owed someone money. That's a powerful motive for murder. We need to track that person down. Find out why he'd shoot at the building and throw bricks with a note containing threats."

She nodded without commenting; her eyes flashed on Savage.

"Well, I can give you this year's monthly statements for Party Time, both income and expenses. I assume Tyrone already has?" Snow nodded. She tapped keys on her computer; the printer hummed, spewing out pages of spreadsheets.

"We're looking for anomalies. Do you have salary data for employees?" Snow continued.

"Subpoena's on its way," Savage reported.

Dayton's lips thinned primly as she manned the keyboard. Surrendered the requested data reluctantly as if it were her own personal property she was handing over.

"And how well did you know your boss? Did you have a personal relationship with him?" Savage added as they stood.

Her face pinked. "I resent what you're implying. He was my employer, period. Demanding—a bit obsessive— but decent. He was married—perhaps not happily, but that's not my concern."

Savage's obsidian eyes bored into hers. "Care to explain that last sentence?"

Dayton opened her mouth, glanced at the recorder, and then shook her head. "No."

Snow thumbed off the recorder. "Thanks for your time. If you remember anything relevant, please give me a call." Laid a card on her desk. As they strolled out into the sunshine, they met Detective Fields with two uniformed officers.

"Here's your subpoena for all records, sir. Computers and phone logs, too. When we're done, I'm stopping at the deli for sandwiches. Want anything?" Zachary turned to go inside.

"Yeah, an Italian sub with everything but hot peppers," Snow said.

"Same thing for me plus the hot peppers." Savage dug some folded bills and a handful of change from his pocket, pulled out a ten and five. "Fountain Cokes, too."

"First, go get the computers and have Huddleston access and print all bank statements. Find out if Sims held accounts at other banks. Savage, we're going upstairs for another round with Julio; he never mentioned how long he's been in Sims's employment or what other work he's done in the past. Or other clients he's had. Let's see if he admits watching and reporting on Kelly Sims.

"I'd also like to know why Ms. Dayton trips down the steps every morning around nine thirty. Oh, and, Fields, just stick the subs in the fridge at HQ. We'll head back there after we're done. Thanks."

10

"Sonja, did you receive a ballistics report on the slug that the doc dug out of my hip?" Mac asked via her iPhone.

"Whoa, woman, working your own case when you're on medical leave? How you feeling? You sound lucid. They got you up and about yet?" the CPD admin responded.

"Yeah, the PT had me on a treadmill for a few minutes. Slow going. Seems I have to learn how to walk all over again. Then we did water aerobics; then she gave me a massage. That was nice. Just wish I had her energy. Anything on the bullet?"

"Yes, ma'am. Short bullet came from an M24 Remington sniper rifle made for the US military and cops since the 1980s. Do you need all the info on bore, twists and radial lands and grooves?"

"No, that's good. Any prints?" Mac inquired.

"From the bullet? Nothing noted in the report other than a partial with too few points to ID. The results aren't back yet from the pistol confiscated in your hospital room. How long will you be in rehab?" Sonja asked.

"Haven't asked that question yet, but I have my laptop. If anything on my case comes in, you can e-mail me."

"Roger, dodger. Get it?"

"Not very well, and yes I get your pun." But Erin smiled. "That's it. Thanks. Say hello to the squad for me. Hope to see you in a few weeks. Bye."

Mac eased the CI's disk into the slot on her laptop to watch the surveillance at the bar. Her assailant had his back to the camera, partially turned to order another beer. Definitely military, but she didn't recognize him, and his body blocked whomever he was talking to. His left leg jiggled constantly. Some faces she recognized: reenactors Winters, Shultz, and Ferris in a lively conversation at a round table to the left of the bar. Backed it up, watched it again. And again. Closed the laptop, laid it aside. She'd check the news and her e-mail later. Lay back against the pillows and dozed.

* * *

Kelly broke the news to her kids when they returned home as she requested, explaining the bare essentials about the police presence and their inquiries.

"Why is Dad's death suspicious? Are they sure it wasn't another heart attack? He had one in 2000." Drew paced and frowned, rubbing his neck and shoulders, easing the strain from driving from Lancaster. "I'll have to take a week off and tell Jenna, which means I'll lose time at Christmas. Well, it is what it is."

"Dad's dead? NO! What happened? Mom, you're not involved, are you?" Camie's face scrunched in concern as tears slid down her wan cheeks. "I know you guys haven't been getting along." She brushed her tears away but more filmed and fell.

"Don't be dramatic, Camie. Of course Mom didn't do it. She's a saint to have put up with Dad." Drew's brows knitted in concern. "Don't go around saying shit like that out loud. You could get Mom in a heap of trouble, arrested even. The house may be bugged. THINK!" Turning to his mom he added, "You were with Aunt Shannon in New York, right?"

"Yes. Let's sit on the patio. I made lemon-orangeade. Let's not argue; I'm frazzled as it is. Can we just focus on the things we need to do? I wrote the obituary, and I'd like you two to make sure I didn't omit anything or anyone. We have a meeting in an hour with the funeral director to decide—"

"Daddy's gone. I didn't get to say good-bye!" Camie flounced onto a patio chair, buried her head in her crossed arms, and cried. "He was mean to you sometimes, but he was always good to me." Long, honey and caramel strands of hair cascaded across the girl's crossed arms, jagged sobs shaking her body.

Kelly put her arms around her daughter's shoulders. "I know. No one had a chance to say good-bye." She motioned for Drew to sit down. He poured drinks, grabbed a cookie from the plate, and bit down.

"Nana made these. Her chocolate chip cookies are always soft and chewy. Look, Camie, Dad wouldn't want us carrying on like this. We're grown. We have to do what he'd want us to do: soldier on. Take care of Mom and the businesses. Want some hot tea?"

"No. Easy for you to say." She continued crying, variegated blond locks hiding her face.

"Go ahead and cry. It's part of the grieving process," Kelly soothed. Drew picked up the typed paper on the patio table, read through it once. Twice, frowning. "Not just Uncle Darryl. You forgot Aunt Andrea—though we haven't seen her for years." He pinched the bridge of his nose, blinked and looked toward the ruined shed. "Someone needs to clean that up. It's an eyesore. I'll do that when we're done at the funeral home if the firefighters are done with their investigation."

"You're right. How could I forget his sister! Your dad's family was so distant. Let's see, Darryl must be fifty-five. But the elderly lady who sat with the family at his dad's funeral; she's related but not a sibling," Kelly said.

"A cousin," Camie mumbled into the table. "Married and moved to Scotland. Jane Fitz-something. We can get the guest register from Grandma for her last name."

"See, that's helpful. Thanks. Now sit up," Drew said. "Did Dad leave a will?"

"He said he wouldn't . . ." Kelly let the sentence die. "No, I don't know for certain. I should call Abrams and Koontz for sure."

Sitting and scanning the obit, Camie added, "You have to say the *late* Marshall Sims for Grandpa." She inserted the word.

"What about in lieu of flowers, send donations to the Heart Fund—or did Dad have a favorite charity?" Drew asked.

"No, we want flowers. Flowers make it bearable. I want to pick out the spray for the casket. Not white lilies but red roses or carnations," Camie volunteered. "All crinkly with cares."

"What about the Warehouse? Did he leave you the businesses?" asked her eldest, his dark brows knotted in concern, his mind running ahead of his sister's.

"Drew, I just said I don't know. Why would he? I don't know anything about—," Kelly answered.

"Because you're his wife, Mother. Okay, call the lawyers. We need an appointment ASAP. At least he has burial plots, right?"

"Yes." Kelly sighed, remembering how morbid she'd thought buying the plots was years ago. She searched for the file and phone number. Paged through it.

Suddenly Drew started coughing. Covering his mouth, he thumped his chest, continued hacking. He reached for the lemon-orange drink, tipped it over. Camie jumped up, sprinted into the kitchen for water and paper towels. She pushed the glass into Drew's hands, mopping up the spill. He accepted it, nodded his thanks and sipped. His mother rubbed his back between his shoulder blades. Eyebrows furrowed, she listened but detected no wheezing.

"Want some hot tea with honey to coat your throat?" his sister offered.

Drew shook his head. "No thanks. I'm good."

"When did this coughing start?" Kelly asked.

"Just now." Drew shrugged away. "Thanks. I'm okay." He hesitated. "I just wanted to tell you—" Eyes canted to Camie.

The doorbell pealed. Threading through the house, Kelly padded toward the front. Two CPD detectives flashed their shields. She sighed resignedly, stepped back, ushered them in.

"We're here to interview Drew and Cameron Sims, if they can spare about twenty minutes. I'm Detective Fields and this is—"

"Detective Savage," Reese finished, striding in. "How are you doing, ma'am? Holding up? We also need the family's prints or saliva swabs to eliminate you all as suspects."

"We're trying, Detective. They're on the patio." She gestured through the kitchen to the back. "Camie's a little fragile at the moment, so go easy, please. I have to make a phone call."

A cycle rumbled up to the curb. Kelly opened the front door again. Shannon balanced a casserole in a foil pan and held a paper bag between her teeth. She paused while Kelly took the bag. "Mom sends lasagna and garlic bread, so you needn't cook tonight."

"Then I hope you are all coming over to help eat it."

"Sure. Thanks. I never turn down a home-cooked meal." Mahoney strode through the living and formal dining room, eyed the pile of unopened mail. "Kel, you might have bills to pay in that stack. Do you need help?"

"No, I think they're all sympathy cards, but I'll get to them later. We're working on the obit, final arrangements, and finding out if Denny left a will. And your detectives are grilling my kids, probably about Denny's and my relationship."

"They had to know about the abuse." Mahoney made room in the fridge for the lasagna, moving the half watermelon up a shelf. "Why you never reported him, I can't guess. He was an unpredictable, temperamental bully, thus dangerous. You were always a hair's breadth away from a hospital visit or worse."

"Not always. He's been curt and sarcastic as long as I've known him but never mean and violent until the kids left home. He loved us. Really!" Her voice quivered. She dropped the loaf of bread on the table as the front bell pealed again. "Oh, damnation."

"Had a funny way of showing it," Shannon remarked.

"I'll never make this phone call," her sister complained.

"Go ahead. I'll get the door. Oh, hello. Thank you, Mrs. Blunt, how kind. Yes, the viewing is tonight. You can ride on the back of my cycle!" Shannon offered. "Of course not, I'm kidding. See you tonight then." Swinging back through, she popped the tray of deviled eggs into the fridge; her sister was conversing earnestly with someone on her cell, so she wrote a note, *Gotta get back to work. See you tonight. S.*

The detectives got the family's prints and mouth swabs, questioned their movements from Thursday to Friday, then ushered themselves out. Kelly Sims returned to the patio. "We have an appointment with the lawyers tomorrow after the funeral. Most of the guests should be gone by then. If not, Mom and Dad can play hosts."

The only unplanned incident at the viewing and funeral was the detectives observing people parading past the casket with final farewells, family members lined up on either side, shaking hands, sometimes hugging a friend or neighbor. Mahoney was wearing a lapel camera to catch any disgruntled, angry, or suspicious faces in the crowd.

The Party Time manager, Ms. Dayton, walked the line stiffly, her manners perfunctory. Tyrone Bender, in an impressive, perfectly tailored black suit, black shirt, and tie, paid his respects. The construction manager, Roberto, seemed uncomfortably restricted in a tight sport coat. Neighbors Mr. and Mrs. Blunt, the Rogers and Stewards, and a steady stream of strangers filed by. One short guy with hair gelled back swaggered in and mingled but didn't pass by the casket or greet the families.

Mahoney paused by Savage, eyes scanning the crowd. "Viewings are sordid rituals; I'm not having one at my funeral."

Reese shrugged indifferently. "Life is for the living, but some find comfort and closure in these rituals. The viewing is like visiting the deceased's last-known address. The dead don't care. Did you get a shot of everyone?"

She nodded. "Last-known address? That's weird. Anyway, closure is a myth for loved ones. We always miss them and keep them in memories in our hearts and minds."

He let her comment slide. "Good work. Get the photos processed by tomorrow's 9:00 a.m. briefing." Distracted by a call, he excused himself, strolled outside the stuffy, stifled quietude into clean, crisp air—a slight breeze ruffling the leaves—a river in the trees. Outdoors, he could relax, take a breath. "Yes, sir. We've got it covered. If the perp attended, he's one cool customer. She did. Fields is filming outside from the car. Give my regards to Mac and Ian."

The next morning Snow and Summers attended the funeral while Fields again filmed attendants discreetly from the Explorer. Overhead, lavender clouds with grey bellies threatened rain; one like a hammerhead hovered ominously above them.

The graveside service was blessedly brief. Kelly Sims's daughter broke down, but her maternal grandparents stepped in to pull Camie aside, sit down, and comfort her. All in black, the wife and son held up throughout the ordeal, shaking hands with mourners, nodding and thanking those who came. At one point, Drew leaned over, whispered in his mother's ears; she blanched, reached for his arm for support, and nodded solemnly.

One individual slipped away during the Psalm reading, so Savage followed unobtrusively to get his plate numbers. Others beat a path to their vehicles ahead of the rain, leaving the family alone as the casket was lowered to its final destination.

11

Returning from walking in the wave pool, Mac eased onto her bed, her alien right hip refusing to coordinate with her left. "I feel like Ahab in *Moby Dick*. *'Call me Ishmael.'*" She sighed, feeling akin to both. Turning to the packet of photos Chris had left in her bedside table drawer, she scattered them out on her bed, poured over them with her magnifying glass, studying facial expressions. Mahoney's and Sims's families—parents and kids—displayed genuine grief.

Using her cell to record comments, she said, "Widow seems stoic, no tears." Another woman with wispy, bluish-white hair looked disapproving, or maybe bitter years turned her mouth upside down. Another woman looked hostile; Mac turned the photo over, reading Mahoney's scrawl, *Ms. Olive Dayton, Party Time manager.* "Did she have something going on with the deceased?" She sat aside the questionable ones. "Another, a Hispanic male, Julio Roberto, seems ill at ease." She stopped, recognizing the candid of former mayor. Paged through a few more. Finally, a man with slicked-back hair looked smug. She sat his photo aside, too, because he looked like someone out of *Good Fellas*.

When lunch came, she ate absently while listening to Snow's interviews. "Sounds like you like the wife for this." She pulled the thick file, pored over the reports. "But Kelly Sims has an ironclad alibi."

She booted up her laptop and checked their databases for Salvatore Carrelli, the name on the back of the last photo. Currently on parole, the man did time for noncompliance for child support: three wives and five children! "Why did you attend Dennis Sims's funeral?

Does he owe you money? A smoking gun—and a pretty damn good motive for murder!"

Scanning the bank statements, she found a copy of a $5,000 check to First Loan, Carrelli's financial institution. He also owned an Italian eatery on Simpson-Ferry and several Mechanicsburg apartments. Peering through the glass, she tried to read the notation at the bottom of the check; the scribble was illegible.

Picked up the phone, e-mailed Chris a message about the Carrelli connection, and described the CD her CI had left her, describing the rear-view and partial profile of the suspect in her shooting.

* * *

At the CPD Homicide squad briefing, Snow listened to Chen's update on the lab reports. "Tox screen came back with traces of nicotine, an elevated level of adrenaline, and the blood pressure medication in his blood. Scar tissue indicated a prior heart attack, as I mentioned earlier. Early signs of atherosclerosis and the burst blood vessel in the left eye. I'm prepared to declare Dennis Sims's death a homicide with the health issues a mitigating factor."

"Could the bump on the head have caused the uptick in adrenaline?" Snow asked.

Chen nodded. "In addition to the fact that type-A personalities have higher levels of cortisol and epinephrine in their systems.

"COD?" Savage asked.

"Blunt-force trauma, high blood pressure, and excessive adrenaline induced a massive embolic stroke."

"Say again?" Fields scratched his head.

"A stroke, Detective. Read my report." Dr. Chen tapped the file.

"All right. It's official," Chief March said. Stuart stood by the white boards to list COD, suspects, and case facts as each detective reported.

"The drive-by shooting points to someone other than the wife," Snow reported. "Shooter used a nine millimeter automatic, tossed out a brick and a warning note with "PAY UP OR ELSE!" No prints. Bank records indicate a connection to one Salvatore Carrelli via $20,000 bank loans in 1995, 2000, and 2007."

"Carrelli attended the viewing and the funeral—the first to leave both," Fields added. He smoothed his palm over his crew cut, nodded at the camcorder. "A spiffy dresser, by the way. Looks like he's wearing a silk suit, Versace or Armani."

Savage added, "Sims's employees seem satisfied with him as a boss. No gripes there. The Warehouse tenants paid their rent regularly. No smoking guns there."

"CSU found multiple prints, mostly the Sims and Mahoney family members throughout the house, as expected, including Shannon and her parents'. Four unidentified prints with no match in AFIS." March scanned the report.

"Rusk reported that a rupture in a faulty propane tank or leak in the gas grill caused the wood shed to burn down. Suppose the timing was a coincidence," Stuart commented.

"No incendiary devices?" asked Savage.

"Apart from the combustibles in the shed?" Stuart shook his head. Laid down the marker, rolled up his sleeves.

"So we have a *natural* conflagration and a homicide occurring simultaneously?" Savage's eyebrows quirked in disbelief.

"We don't know that. Once in a while, accidents happen," acknowledged March. "Interviews turn up any suspects or shake the wife's alibi? Apparently, marital fires simmered, too."

Snow said, "Yes, Kelly Sims has evidence of spousal abuse but never reported her husband, which gives her a powerful motive. The Party Time manager's holding back, but that may be loyalty to the boss. And Huddleston's going over computer records and correspondence; Mac's combing through Mahoney's photos. But now we have to track down this Carrelli." He tapped his finger on the man's photo.

"How is Mac recuperating, by the way?" asked March.

"Slowly, but improving now that Ian and I are spending nights with her. Her recovery will take awhile. I gave her Mahoney's photos from the funeral and Sims's bank records to keep her mind occupied." He stopped short of mentioning her nightmares and brooding over the baby she lost. "She's in rehab under an assumed name."

"We should send her flowers," Dr. Chen noted.

"Good idea, tell Sonja to send them to the domicile." March turned the pages of the lab reports. "Oh, send Castle's family a Giant gift certificate from the Sunshine account. He may be laid up awhile; with three kids, his wife may need help with groceries. Anything else? Oh, hell yes. Where are we on Mac's shooter?"

Dr. Haili Chen stood and nodded. "Yes, sir. If I may go?" He waved her out, so she gathered her files and slipped out quietly.

"We've got a CI tailing the reenactors, but we should call the FBI to search for current Army enlistees. A bartender said he sounded Southern, according to Mac. If he's not from Pennsylvania, then he's crossed state lines."

"On what grounds?" The chief frowned, jotted a note in the margins of Mac's file.

"Her CI has a photo of his back and profile taken from a surveillance tape; he's wearing desert camo. Asking questions about a cop who played Molly Pitcher," Snow responded.

"How do you know he didn't buy it at an Army Surplus store?" Savage put in, one eyebrow jutting up. He tipped his chair back.

Snow said, "I don't for sure, but it fits him too well, and he was the only one at the regiment's favorite watering hole with a buzz cut. We don't have the resources to investigate her case thoroughly; the FBI does. She's convinced it's someone connected to a perp she arrested. I trust her judgment, but counting her years in uniform, that's ten years of records to search."

"Okay. See if Sonja or the intern has time to cull the files for a convict with a military background who's been recently paroled, discharged, or who's AWOL. That'll mean computer and paper files. Get a still of that surveil photo, see what Huddleston can do with that. And send it to Agent Howard; see if it's good enough to run through facial recognition software."

"Do we need someone to keep an eye on the widow Sims?" Fields sank his teeth into a raspberry-filled croissant, his second pastry. Flakes dropped to his shirt; he dusted them off. "Hmm."

"Are you offering? The Musketeers are doing occasional drive-bys. The family seems preoccupied with funeral arrangements. Visitors drop off food. Besides, Kelly Sims has a solid alibi. Let's follow these other leads, see what falls out," March said.

"I have time to tail Mrs. Sims." Zach smiled, his eyebrows wiggling up and down suggestively.

Jay Huddleston, CPD IT consultant, knocked on the door.

"Enter!" The chief motioned him in. "Find something of interest in the Sims' computers?"

He pushed his Lennon glasses up the bridge of his nose, took Mac's empty chair. "Yes, sir. Some irregularities. First, he owed Salvatore Carrelli over $20,000, which is in arrears. But that's not all. Sims has bank accounts in five different banks and credit unions and does a lot of transferring of funds. He borrowed money using the business as collateral multiple times to start more projects, like the Warehouse apartments.

"Finally, the tenants—seems Sims has at least twelve —made regular payments, because the Party Time manager keyed the data on the spreadsheets she provided, but they don't correspond with any deposits anywhere, unless he put them in personal accounts, which we don't have. Nothing in his domicile unless data's stored on his home computer, which I don't have either." Huddleston looked up, his eyes canting to Snow and Savage, indicating an oversight on their part.

The chief responded, "Then get a subpoena to seize the home computer and anything else you need. Talk to the wife again, too. I must admit, Huddleston, I can't even follow what you just said. Did the guy break any laws? Would that cause someone to kill him? Why kill him at home if it's business related?"

"I can't answer your questions, sir; I'm not an accountant or a detective, but Dennis Sims was being very creative with his financing, skating a thin line legally. I'm surprised he didn't flag an IRS audit." Huddleston frowned as he scratched his head, disturbing thinning, blond hair, which he pushed absently off his forehead.

"That's the point," Savage quipped. "Somebody got tired of waiting for him to pay up, got payback instead."

"Could be a motive for murder, but why send the warning after he's deceased?" Stuart spoke from the white board, writing "*Illegal fund transfers?*" under Sims's name.

"A message for the wife? Sounds like the hired hands were a day late or light on grey matter. Let's track down Carrelli, rattle his cage. If he clams up or refuses, then we'll have a man with a motive. We already know he has means and opportunity, plus he's on parole. Let's find out who's on his payroll." Snow pushed away from the table to stretch his legs, pocketing his notebook.

"Dismissed, people. Let's get cracking. Somewhere along the way, someone slipped up, and we're going to catch it. Snow and Savage, take Carrelli, and go see what the widow knows about the family finances. Fields, confer with Mac; report your findings. Then monitor the widow's movements, track her cell. If time permits, trace Mac's shooter; the Musketeers can help. Huddleston, keep digging. So far, the press is still doting on the Hawthorne case, so maybe we can ease under their radar on this one."

"That's because it's more titillating—teen kills her kidnapper and maybe her mother. Surprised she hasn't sold the movie rights." Savage snagged a donut and dashed for the door before the rest could comment about a second trial.

Hand fisted on his hip, Stuart asked his boss, "Doesn't anyone believe innocent until proven guilty anymore?"

March shrugged, scraping his files together. "People are voyeurs; they're relieved someone screwed up worse than they did, so they'll devour the salacious details, gossip about the girl, and consider their assumptions fact. Must be fifty different angles the media can recycle. It's salacious and sells newspapers. I'll be in my office."

12

"**First Loan's** located in that strip mall in
Mechanicsburg on Simpson-Ferry. We'll check there first.
Are there other possibilities?" Snow asked Savage as they
sped along. Passing the PNC Bank, they finally reached
Windsor Park Shopping Center where Snow whipped into
the first available parking space.

Pushing through the glass door, on which modest,
blue stenciling read First Loan Financial, the detectives
encountered a receptionist with a mass of tangled, black
hair wearing rectangular glasses perched low on her
sharp nose. Looking up from her computer, she blinked
and smiled dutifully. "May I help you?"

The men showed their shields. "Here to see Mr. Sal
Carrelli."

She frowned, nonplussed. "Do you have an
appointment?"

"We do. It's called a homicide investigation. Just buzz
us through if he's in," Snow ordered.

Instead, she picked up the landline, tapped a button.
"Carlisle Homicide detectives are here to see you."

A long minute passed before Carrelli appeared,
gestured them back a short hall with offices on either
side, mirroring one another. Restrooms on the left, the
rear exit at the end of the hall. Turning right, he ushered
them into the last office simply furnished in gunmetal
gray with his credentials mounted on the wall behind the
desk. A closed, sleek, silver laptop was centered in front
of a swivel office chair, a stack of files beside it. Two
straight-back, wood chairs faced his desk with a view of
parking lot. "How about coffee or soda?"

The detectives nodded. "Thanks. Cream and one sweetener for me, black for my partner." Snow sat down, adjusted his Dockers, pulled out his recorder. "You don't seem surprised to see us."

The man lifted the receiver, repeated the requests. Leaned back. His tanned, lined face denoted many years, many miles, yet he appeared dapper in his pressed, dark-navy suit and spotless red tie. His manicured nails showed meticulous attention to detail. "I'm not. You're probably here to ask about Dennis Sims's financials. First, I hope you have a subpoena." Savage slapped it on the desk. Carrelli glanced at it briefly without picking it up. "Second, I have a better chance of clients honoring their debts if they're alive. What would you like to know?"

The receptionist entered with two steaming cups, handing one to each. Savage switched cups, taking the black one. "Thanks."

"Christopher Snow with Detective Reese Savage interviewing Salvatore Carrelli," noting the case number, date, and time. "Can you explain why he owed you in excess of $20,000, which seems to be in arrears?" He tested the coffee's temp, sipped.

Carrelli shrugged indifferently. "That's not a lot of money. He borrowed funds to renovate his kitchen and refurbish the Warehouse in the late '90s, then again to pay his kids' college tuition, and currently, to build the four apartments above his businesses. He was good for it but sometimes fell behind when apartment tenants either failed to pay their rent or trashed their place when evicted. Or when he needed to repair or replace windows, appliances, or whatever. I wasn't worried; he would've paid eventually. Besides, he offered his businesses as collateral. One alone is worth at least twice that."

"So you didn't send any collectors to rough him up or remind him he had an outstanding debt?" Savage asked.

"Please, gentleman. Such tactics went out with Capone. There are collection agencies for that these days." Carrelli's fingers hovered protectively over his laptop. Then he sat back again.

"Had you notified a collection agency that his account was in arrears?" Snow probed as Savage took notes.

"I saw no need. He's been a client for over twenty years."

"Why would he obtain loans from you instead of his regular banks in the first place?" Savage asked.

"I imagine he's done both; he kept various accounts in different banks and other financial institutions. Maybe to keep the businesses separate from his personal finances? Perhaps Mrs. Sims can enlighten you. Or even Ms. Dayton or Mr. Bender, his store managers." He opened his hands and shrugged.

"He regularly transferred funds back and forth among different accounts and various institutions. Do you know why? Did any of his checks to you ever bounce?" asked Savage.

"I'd have to check the records, but off-hand I can't remember any returning with insufficient funds. As a self-employed entrepreneur, he had a knack for knowing what would sell in this tight market. As a landlord, he bent over backwards to accommodate his tenants, but sometimes unexpected expenses catch you up short." Again, the indifferent shrug as he examined his manicure. "He was good for it."

"How long has the debt been outstanding?" asked the lead detective, his pocket notebook in hand.

"However long ago the apartment renovation began."

"You know, we can go downtown, put you in the box. You're on parole. So your life's squeaky clean, or what will we find when we toss this place?" Savage's carbon eyes bored into Carrelli's muddy, bloodshot ones.

"Let me check." He opened, refreshed his laptop, and brought up a file. "Seven months. That's nothing. I've had other loans in arrears for a year or more."

"Then what do you do?" Savage seemed interested.

"First, write them a letter. Then notify the collection agency."

"Okay, go ahead and print the Sims file." Snow tapped the subpoena as a reminder.

"I can't imagine what good it will do." But Carrelli complied.

The printer hummed to life, raking the pages through.

"We find our best suspects tracking the victim's finances." Snow looked out the window. A shadow outside cast the window in shade; then Julio Roberto, wearing painter's overalls, passed by. Savage nudged his partner.

"Is Julio Roberto one of your *collectors*?" Snow asked.

Carrelli turned to look, but the man was gone. "Collectors? No, but I hire him for construction projects. He's a good worker, an independent contractor, solid citizen, legal, and a family man. I assure you, Detectives, everything's copasetic here.

"And I report to my PO weekly; he also drops by unannounced. I've got two ex-wives, a current one, and five kids to support." He started fidgeting with the Cross pen on his desk, dropped it, and pushed away. He shuffled the papers together and thrust them across the desk. "Here are Sims's records. Anything else? I have an appointment in ten minutes." Standing, he checked his watch.

"Fine. We'll just peruse your office while you're gone." Snow stopped the recorder. "We'll take the computer, too."

"You can't do that. How can I access my records and accounts?"

The man bristled, straightened to his full height, all of five-seven.

"Don't twist your boxers. We'll leave the secretary's here," Savage offered. "And don't leave town in case we need to talk again."

"This is outrageous!" He huffed out the door mumbling something about a police state trampling individual rights.

Detective Fields and Officer Summers passed Carrelli on their way in, striding down the hall to assist in the search. The former with his brush cut and Boy Scout looks contrasted sharply with the shaggy-blond, jean-and-leather-clad biker.

"Remember. Take only what refers to Dennis Sims and his family. Oh, and keep your eyes peeled for any records pertaining to Julio Roberto; he's connected to both Carrelli and Sims. And the computer—" Snow directed.

"Yes, sir," Fields jumped in. "Goes to Huddleston."

Snow's cell played the refrain from "Stand by Me." "This is Mac; I'm going to pick her up." Then he called HQ to inform Chief March.

"I'll stick around and help with the search," Savage said. "Maybe get a home improvement loan." His facetious smirk coaxed a smile from Snow despite his preoccupation with Erin.

He folded himself into the Explorer and zipped off, wending his way through heavy traffic to Health South.

13

Tying her wayward curls out of the way, Mac struggled to dress. Underwear, slacks, and a short-sleeve cotton sweater took fifteen minutes. Socks, ten more. Forget the shoes, since she had to go out in a wheelchair anyway. The therapist left a walker to aid her trip in going to the bathroom—a condition of her release.

"Don't forget to walk twenty minutes morning and evening until you can maintain a regular gait. You need to break up the scar tissue around the wound and joint. Otherwise, it will be more painful in the long run. Walk straight, heel to toe. I notice you've been swinging your right leg out, then stepping off. Mrs. Snow, I wish you'd stay a few more days," Tracy sighed.

"Chart says Slaughter, but it's McCoy, but technically, you're right," Mac responded, inching the walker along. "This is ridiculous. I'm not even thirty." She stopped, perspiration prickling her scalp, trickling down her spine. Breathing through the shocking pain. "No, a week's long enough. I have an infant at home I have to take care of. No need to hover!"

Her physical therapist stayed close to her right elbow to offer a helping hand. "I saw your photo in *The Sentinel* when your baby was born, so I know your name. What a story to tell him! Careful. Slide rather than lift the walker; it has wheels. You're dragging your right foot." She stepped around Mac to guide her leg. "At least come back to use the wave pool."

"I'm tempted to hit you with this," grumbled the patient. "Why is the bathroom so far from the bed?"

"Handicapped accessibility. Look, I know you're frustrated. Though the walker provides better stability, would you rather try the cane? We have ordinary ones, but I'd recommend the one with three feet that swivels. Works better on uneven surfaces and in ice and snow."

"It's May, Tracy. I won't be using anything in ice and snow. Are you related to Clark Winters?"

"I don't think so. Who's he?" Winters moved behind Erin, gently eased her closer to her walker. "It's easier if the walker surrounds you rather than you trailing along behind." She laid her hand against Erin's back. "Straighten your back. There's no hurry; take your time."

"Easy for you to say. Winters is a reenactor who portrays General George Washington during the Revolutionary War. We met during our last case. Chris is coming to pick me up, so I have to pack up my things. Gather up his files."

"Oh yeah, I read about that. A teen acquitted for killing her kidnapper. Now the daughter may go on trial for killing her mother, right? Two trials within three months, and she's what—sixteen?

"After you go to the bathroom, I'll pack up your stuff and call for a wheelchair. Do you have a preference for a cane handle?"

Erin threw her a malevolent look but inched along, caught a walker leg in the gap between the door and the frame. "Shit." Stopped, jerked it back—pain radiating from her hip. Lifted it over the threshold despite the therapist's advice and lowered herself, stopped. "Why the hell didn't I do this before I got dressed?" Unbuttoned, unzipped, eased down on the throne, grimacing when pain stung again. Tracy stood in the doorway. "Privacy, please?"

The PT shook her head. "I need to verify that you—"

"I'll call you, Mommy, show you before I flush. Want to wipe me, too?" Erin felt her blood pressure climb, flush her face. She took a deep breath, puffed it out. Tracy stepped back and eased the door to the frame, leaving it unlatched. She turned to pack her patient's belongings and request wheels for transport.

The Explorer rocked to a stop at the front curb, idling. Snow hopped out to help his wife into the passenger's seat, then took her suitcase, folded the walker, and took the cane from an attendant. When he noticed her scowl, he stowed them in the cargo bay.

He handed her a Massey's chocolate milkshake when she'd settled in. Her stormy face transformed into a sunny one. "Oh, thanks. Aren't you wonderful, thoughtful, and kind?"

"And you can chase it with a fountain Coke. I got you both."

Her eyes swept over his brassy, light-brown hair, his deep, amber eyes, and the laugh lines feathering their edges, shadows beneath from lack of sleep. His solid jaw and cop's build. "I really love you." She drew on the straw. "Omigod, that's heavenly!" Then turned; the car seat was empty. "Where's Ian?"

"Napping. Don't worry; he'll wake up soon. Let's just get you home first. I've missed you, babe." He caressed her face, and then trailed his finger along her jaw. "I'm really thankful you're alive." Coughed, cleared his throat, then focused on driving. "Let's stop for Chinese takeout. How do you feel?"

"Like I have an alien part embedded in my hip. It feels strange."

"Does it hurt much?" he asked gently.

She finished her shake, set the cup down, and picked up the soda. "Only when I move, but, yes, it's painful. But I have meds! How's Shadow?"

"She comes home weekends, patrols the grounds, then searches every room for you. Corey's been working with her, but I haven't had a chance to talk to him about what. The dog's restless, jumpy. She'll be glad to see you. We'll have to be careful she doesn't knock you down in her eagerness, especially when you're holding Ian.

Erin nodded without commenting. *How on earth am I ever going to go back to work or function at home, let alone work in the field? It took twenty minutes to go to the bathroom.* Tears filmed her eyes, and then spilled onto her cheeks. Angrily, she swiped them away.

Chris reached over, closed his hand over hers. "Don't worry, babe, everything will turn out okay. You just need time. And you can work your shooting and the Sims's case from home, just as you've been doing. You're the one who found the Carrelli connection; we confiscated his computer. I'll bring the records home when you're ready. But let's just have supper and enjoy being together tonight." He wheeled into Chen's restaurant. "I already called it in. Be back in a jiff." True to his word, he climbed back into the Explorer within minutes, handed the paper bag to her, and they motored home.

They passed the limestone farmhouse on the left, the burgundy barn farther down on the right. As they approached the limestone bungalow at the end of the tree-lined drive, an orange ball glowed on the horizon. Prolific red and yellow roses bloomed at each corner of their bungalow; mountain laurel bracketed the front door. A birdhouse occupied the right corner of the gable that guarded the vermillion door.

"I can't take off right now because of the Sims' case, but your dad and my parents can help for a few weeks until you feel you can maneuver alone. We'll all have to adjust to a slower pace. Chief March said take the month off. Well, three weeks left, actually. Desk duty for awhile."

The garage door rolled up, swallowed the Explorer and its occupants.

14

Kelly Sims parked in front of Mary Grace's office but remained seated for a few minutes to collect her wits and catch her breath. Facilitating the funeral, consoling the kids, and reading of the will—he had left one after all—disposing of the shed ruins, selling Denny's Beamer, and meeting with Ms. Dayton, Mr. Bender, and the construction crew had sapped her energy.

She hadn't given the tenants a thought. "Make an appointment with a realtor to sell the rental units. Return to work. Act normal. Hell, no wonder the man was tense, preoccupied, and angry. Way too much on his plate." She took several deep breaths, grabbed her purse, the deli bag, and climbed out of her white Altima, smoothing her sleeveless, black tunic over white walking shorts.

Mary Grace greeted her with a quick hug. At five-four, she had a compact, sturdy body tending toward stockiness, but self-discipline and a healthful diet balanced with yoga kept her trim. Two glasses of iced tea sweated on the glass table between the chairs. "I see you're running yourself ragged. Is there anything I can do to help?" she asked, watching Kelly withdraw subs from a tote.

"Two Italian hoagies! Listening is a great help. I'm overwhelmed, but we'll get everything done eventually. The kids are a blessing! But I really miss Denny's efficiency and organization, even though I chafed under his regimen. I'm not so organized. Now that Camie has returned to college and Drew to his job, every room, every call, every ring of the doorbell tenses me up."

"I see. You feel the interruptions are distractions? You need to focus to get X, Y, and Z accomplished?"

"Exactly." Kelly pulled her bushy hair back off her neck and secured it with the scrunchie she wore on her wrist. "But it's more than that; I've wasted so much energy arguing or bottling up my emotions, tip-toeing on eggshells in fear of Denny's hair-trigger temper. Over time, the stress debilitates me."

"All the time? That must have been exhausting."

"Not early on. When Drew and Camie were little, we concentrated on them and their activities. Well you know, like you do with Alyssa. Life flowed along smoothly—for the most part. Yes, we had skirmishes along the way, too. Too many to mention. Now it all seems so pointless, so much wasted energy when life is so short."

Her friend nodded, waited, her hands resting in her lap. "You said after the kids went to college, the dynamics changed."

"We lost that connection, became strangers. Stupid little things started stacking up, bothering me: Denny had never changed a diaper, opened a can, helped with meals, or picked up a tool other than a hammer and duct tape to fix anything around the house. He left doors open, never offered to help with the kids' baths.

"He contradicted everything I said, trying to control every conversation, every decision on every trip we took, every item we bought. I had to consult him for whatever I bought the kids. Had some smart remark for everything. My anger simmered as I stewed, resented the situation. Sorry, I'm whining. And truly, I'm grateful for the house, kids, my family, and friends. And I love my job."

"And you are above all such marital games?" Mary Grace cocked her head to one side, studying Kelly's reaction, waiting.

Kelly scrunched her nose and shook her head. "Not at all; I can be moody and bitchy—stubborn, even argumentative if I know I'm right, but I never once *instigated* an argument. Never pissed him off on purpose."

"Why did you stay with him?" Mary Grace wondered.

"God help me, I loved him, truly. The fiery chemistry we had! He was a Galahad in bed!" She pinked at the admission. "And I didn't have the resources to start over. Besides, Drew and Camie adored their daddy. He read them bedtime stories, played with them, talked to them sensibly—yelling at them only when he thought they were in danger. He attended school activities and parent-teacher conferences. I don't think he missed a single ball game or swim meet. And was always home for dinner promptly at six."

"So his good traits balanced the deficiencies."

"I think so, but it's hard to explain the constant strain, the bickering over every little thing." Kelly stopped a moment to wipe the condensation from her glass with the napkin and take a bite of her sandwich. "Is your marriage like that?"

Mary Grace smiled, her face serene. "No. Ted and I share responsibilities equally. On days that I come home late, he makes supper. He'll go to the grocery if the fridge is empty. He does laundry, but then I also mow, weed, trim, and help plant flowers and shrubs. Rake leaves in the fall—whoever's available does the job. And it takes all three of us. Alyssa has her chores, too." Mary Grace asked, "How did his behavior make you feel?"

"How do you think?" Kelly shrugged. "Marginalized. Powerless. Angry. Frustrated. Tense. Our culture still valorizes males, objectifies women: we have unequal salaries, greater expectations, and more constraints."

"Only you can change how you feel. Did you tell Dennis how you felt—that you needed his help at home or some space for yourself?"

"Sometimes, but he had so much business to attend to that I felt guilty asking for help. He was so sociable and affable outside the home; we entertained regularly early on. But inside . . . ," she paused, "he became another person entirely."

"A Jekyll and Hyde?"

Kelly smiled at the analogy and shook her head. "Not quite, just minus the nice-guy façade."

"But you work full time as well," Mary Grace pointed out.

Kelly shrugged. "Like many, he never considered academia work." She flicked her wrist. "Some ivory-tower fluff. Called it an excuse to socialize with young studs."

"That's a telling comment: jealously covering his insecurity. But he never objected to your working outside the home?"

"As long as it didn't interfere with home and family. If I had a late interview, meeting, or function, I'd ask Shannon or my parents to fill in until Denny got home. Shannon's been babysitting for us since she was thirteen. My mother-in-law watched them a few times, but she's much older, so I didn't want to impose."

"So he wasn't physically violent until lately?" asked her friend.

"Yes. Well, sarcasm's his favorite tool. He's famous for the last word, the cut, repartee, and the putdown. I asked him once why he pushed me until I lost my temper. He said, 'Because you rise to the bait so easily.'"

"But why would he bait you?" Mary Grace frowned, sat her empty glass down and took another bite of her tasty sandwich. "These are excellent—really fresh ingredients."

"They're from the South Street Deli. Exactly. I think it amused him. Kept him in a one-up position."

"Marriage isn't a competition, Kelly."

"Ours was—or at least a contest. I found it easier to let the comments slide just to keep the peace until I lost my temper. And Vesuvius erupted and then his mood matched and then exceeded mine. Fireworks usually followed!" She flicked her hands out.

"And when that didn't work?" Mary Grace asked quietly.

"I'd leave, take the kids home to visit my parents, to a movie, or go shopping. Growing up, the kids always needed something: a pair of sneakers, school clothes, and haircuts. Or I needed to taxi them to school activities, doctor and dentist appointments."

"He wouldn't retaliate?" Mary Grace wondered.

"Not usually. Work, a call from a tenant with a broken pipe, or a neighbor wanting to borrow trimmers distracted him. If his store managers called about a break-in, or even with a question or concern, he'd go handle it personally." She crunched the ice in the bottom of her glass. "In time, I learned that silence was the best tool to avoid a discussion that escalated into an argument."

"Would you like more tea?" Mary Grace offered.

"Oh, no thanks. I've taken up enough of your time. I have an appointment with Denny's lawyers and a realtor. I have questions about the businesses and plan to see the Warehouse apartments. Again, thanks for listening. It really helps." She lugged herself to her feet and hugged her best friend.

"Why don't we meet for lunch at the Back Door Café at eleven next week? My treat," Mary Grace suggested.

"That'd be great! Be good to get out. See some different scenery. And maybe visit The Bookery. I could use a good mystery for distraction. Then I'll fix lunch the week after." Kelly smiled, shouldering her purse, feeling a bit less tense as she slid on sunglasses and emerged from the building. "Would they have the latest Louise Penny novel?" she mused aloud. Then she noticed the homicide detectives approaching. *Now what?* And frowned, her key fob poised to unlock her car.

15

"**Weɗ like** to ask a few questions about your husband," Detective Savage said, showing his shield.

"Why? I have an appointment with a lawyer in half an hour. I need to grab something to eat for dinner while I'm out."

"All right. We'll go along with you. We're close to Panera Bread and Applebee's. Choose one for lunch." Detective Snow took her elbow and escorted her to his Explorer.

"Here," Savage held out his hand for her keys. "I'll follow in your ride." He smiled, confident his Mediterranean good looks would ensure her cooperation. She unlocked the vehicle and tossed the key ring to him.

"No thanks. I've already had lunch." Then she shrugged. "Sure. Panera Bread. I like their salads." She ducked into the Explorer's passenger seat, smelling baby powder, a spicy scent like General Tso's chicken and a whiff of sandalwood. Latching the seat belt, then folding her hands in her lap, she waited for the detective to speak.

"How have you been holding up?" Snow asked. His eyes took in her casual attire, rusty hair corralled at the nape of her neck and then returned to her moss-green eyes.

She darted a glance at him, surprised at his concern. Shrugged. "One day at a time. The funeral was difficult. Now I have to address a host of things I wasn't prepared to do. It's overwhelming."

"Like the businesses? Sounds like a heavy load to carry."

"That's one of the reasons I'm meeting with his lawyer. To simplify my life, but there are complications," she admitted—using a hand to brace herself when he cornered.

"Aren't there always? Sorry to burden you further, but we need to know more about the family dynamics." He palmed the SUV into a parking space. Savage pulled into one in the next row, climbed out, locked her vehicle, and returned her keys.

"Thank you," Kelly said. "Nothing for me. I'll order a strawberry chicken salad to go when you're done."

While Savage ordered, Snow ushered her to a vacant corner booth at the front, set up the digital recorder, and then excused himself to help with the trays. The men returned with their combos, took seats opposite her. Savage sat a cup of iced water in front of Sims.

Once settled, Kelly waited for the questions. "Thanks."

"We've just talked to Sal Carrelli," Snow began, summarizing their conversation with him. "Were you aware that your husband owed him money and switched funds among at least five different bank accounts?"

"Why? No," she shook her head. "He never discussed business with me. He kept the household accounts separate."

"Yes, well, that's logical, but we can't fathom the rationale for moving money around. Also, why would he have a running account with a loan shark when the banks loaned him money?"

"Who's Sal Carrelli? We have checking and saving with Commerce Bank for household expenses. All of my salary goes there, and Denny contributes about half the rental income to that."

"Carrelli runs a *financial* institution called First Loan near his pizza joint in Mechanicsburg," Savage commented. "Your husband has a $20,000 account there, in arrears."

Kelly Sims's eyes rounded, her mouth rounded into an O. She gulped some water, coughed, sputtered. Waved her hand in front of her mouth. "Wrong pipe. Excuse me. I didn't know that."

"Okay. Are you saying you had access only to the housing accounts?" Snow clarified, surprised.

"Correct. You won't find my name on any business checks. Those were strictly Denny's. And he rarely discussed business at home, unless he received a call. I could hear his end of the conversation, but he usually took it into his home office.

"It's the main reason I'm meeting with his lawyers later. I want to sell the businesses, but he left my son, Drew, The Sports Hut and our daughter, Camie, Party Time, but neither want them or can be here to manage them."

"Wow!" Savage remarked. "Rejecting established businesses—why? Are they independently wealthy? Do you resent that?"

"Of course not. Camie's still in college, and Drew works and lives in Lancaster. He's getting married in the fall. Neither has the time or inclination for the businesses; their lives are elsewhere. Camie may return after graduation for a while, but I expect she'd like to spread her wings, too. And I enjoy my job at Dickinson. Besides, I could hardly begrudge my kids' inheritance."

"As his wife, you're entitled to half unless there'd been a prenup. All right. Let's back up." Snow switched tactics. "What time did you leave your house last week to go to New York?"

"I told you: about six thirty, maybe a bit earlier."

"You're not sure?" asked Savage.

"No. I was busy gathering my overnighter, purse, jacket, and umbrella. Fixing coffee, scrambling eggs for Denny. Not watching the clock."

"Did you invite Shannon in?" Snow asked.

"No, I just hurried to the door, so as not to keep her waiting."

"Why not?" asked Savage.

"We were in a hurry to beat rush-hour traffic. Listen," she consulted her watch, "I have an appointment downtown in fifteen minutes. We've been over all this before; it's all on tape. So if you'll excuse me, I'll be on my way." She folded her napkin, dropped it on the table, and scooted along the bench. "I need to order my salad."

Snow and Savage stood, both finished. "We'll accompany you. Perhaps the lawyers can answer our questions." They emptied and stacked their trays on top of the bin on the way out.

"You can't listen to privileged information," objected Sims, collecting her strawberry salad, shouldering her purse, and slipping out the door. She strode to her vehicle, popped the trunk, and slipped the salad into an insulated cooler.

Snow handed her the subpoena. "If it pertains to Dennis Sims, we can." They followed her to Pit and Pomfret, veered to the curb. The door to the Abrams & Koontz's office was cracked open. Savage leaped out, Snow behind him, palmed his pistol. Kelly Sims mounted the steps behind the detectives.

"What the hell—" No receptionist to greet them. They cleared each office—finding an unconscious man sprawled on the floor behind his desk, hands restrained behind his back. Checking the man's pulse, Snow blew out a breath. "He's alive."

Savage hit 911 on his cell.

"Nine-one-one. What's your emergency?"

"Man breathing but unconscious. Looks like a hit to the back of the head. Send an ambulance to the corner of Pitt and Pomfret, Abrams and Koontz Law Offices." Then speed-dialed HQ to report a B&E. "Yes, sir, we'll need CSU to dust, cordon off the area."

"Can you identify this man?" Snow raked his fingers through his hair, pulled gloves out of his pocket. Puffed gently, tugged them on. Lifted the man slightly to loosen his tie. Cut the plastic restraints; the wrists flopped to the floor. A swollen, bruised knot bloomed at the base of his skull, the purpling easily detected through his salt-and-pepper crew.

"That's Dennis's lawyer, Paul Abrams." Kelly frowned, dropped to the nearest seat, hands clasped between her knees. "What are you looking for?"

Snow patted the man's pockets, lifted his wallet, checked the ID. Savage gloved up, paged through files in the cabinet labeled Q—T.

"Dennis's files are missing?" Kelly guessed.

"How did you know? What time was your appointment?" asked Savage. He threw her a suspicious glance, as though her presence presaged the violence.

"One o'clock. Why else would Mr. Abrams be knocked out, the receptionist out to lunch, and the office ransacked? I'd really like to know what's so damned important about my family. Why are strangers targeting us? What did we do?" Palms up, her face scrunched in consternation, as she sidled out of the way.

"Evidently, someone wants a secret to remain hidden." Snow checked the office door and windows for forced entry. "Office must have been open."

"Omigod! What happened? What are you doing to my boss?" A short, stocky woman with silver threads in her sandy pageboy picked up the phone. The detectives showed their shields; she placed the receiver back in its base. Then she approached Mrs. Sims, concerned. "Are you okay?"

Kelly nodded. "I'm Kelly Sims. Shocked, that someone would break in during daylight to steal my husband's files right before my appointment. Now I have no clue what to do. And poor Mr. Abrams, knocked out on my account! I feel responsible—like I've done something to disturb the order here. Oh, sorry. This is Detective Snow, CPD Homicide." She pointed to Reese. "And Detective Savage."

"Bonnie Reed, the office manager." She hunkered down to examine her boss, her hand reaching toward his forehead.

"Don't touch," warned Snow, though he had. "This is an active crime scene. An ambulance is on its way."

"Do you have paper files backed up on the computer?" asked Savage, following her to the front as an ambulance crew lifted and rolled a gurney through the front door, down the hall.

Carrying crime scene kits, a CSU team, two men and a woman, white overalls rasping, donned paper slippers and padded past them, nodding as they passed.

"Not the older ones, but we've scanned in the advanced directives, wills, and forms from the last nine years. Inputting all this data is an arduous process." She seated herself behind her front desk, tapped a key, refreshing the monitor. Keyed in a password. "I'll print what we have on Dennis Sims, but he's been a client for twenty years, so files preceding 2000 won't be here. Sorry." The printer whirred to life.

"Let's get him to CRMC." The crew hustled out after stabilizing the patient. Savage closed the door after them, checking the locks and windows for damage. None. "Well, not much point in staying, boss, with the CSU here. We won't find out anything today."

"How about you drive to the Med Center, interview Abrams when he wakes up. If he can ID his assailant, we'll get an arrest warrant. I'll tag along with Mrs. Sims to her house—see what pops up on their home computer. You can pick me up when you're through with the lawyer." He pinched the bridge of his nose, blinked his eyes rapidly several times as he straightened. "I'm going to see if I need glasses one of these days." He tossed Reese the Explorer keys.

"Nah, you're probably just tired. See you later." Reese slipped quietly out the door. He nodded at Kelly. "Mrs. Sims, thanks for cooperating."

Ms. Reed collated the papers, stapled them, and handed them to Snow. "I can't understand why someone would steal those records. They're typical forms. I'm sorry, Mrs. Sims, about your loss. Your husband was a nice, polite, well-respected businessman. Always took the time to say hello, chat, and joke with the boss." Color crept up her neck, remembering the off-color jokes. "If there's anything else?"

Kelly Sims shook herself, realizing Reed was talking to her. "Sorry, wool-gathering. Thank you. I'll call to reschedule once Mr. Abrams recovers and returns to the office; I apologize if I caused this." She stepped outside.

"It's not your fault," Reed offered, but gazed askance at the disheveled office. She returned to the safety of her desk but remained standing. "You don't think the intruder will return?"

"No, ma'am, not with the police presence here." Savage indicated the CSU team photographing the man's office, lifting prints, and collecting evidence. One was cutting up a square of carpet stained with blood. Another bagged the plastic zip ties.

"How long will they be here?" Reed whispered.

"As long as it takes, a couple of hours or until they've gathered all the evidence. Thanks for your cooperation," Snow said to Reed, following Sims, handing her a card. "Call me if you hear any news."

16

At 769 South Street, Kelly poured two glasses of lemonade, offered the detective one.

"Sure, thanks." They carried them to the living room.

He paged through the Sims' legal forms while waiting for the widow to settle, noting the will's specifics. He set the recorder on the coffee table between them. First, he Mirandized her. "It's routine that you be informed of your rights. Reed's right, nothing unusual here—other than the kids' bequest, at least nothing pointing to secret financial transactions. Why did your husband leave the businesses to the kids?"

"I guess he wanted Drew and Camie to have them. I have the house and half the income from the tenants. That's why I had an appointment with Mr. Abrams. I wanted to liquidate the businesses; I'll give the proceeds to Drew and Camie. When I sell the apartments, I'll put that in savings or pay off the house and bills."

"Life insurance?" Snow looked into the woman's eyes, her black lashes a sharp contrast to her pale complexion and the copper highlights in her hair, which accentuated her freckles. "If you don't mind my saying, you and Shannon don't look like sisters."

"No. She favors my mother's people, I look like my dad's." She sipped her drink, the ice cubes clinking as she sat the glass down. "Scandinavian," she said in response to Snow's raised eyebrows. "Yes. Dennis had a $100,000 policy on him and me."

"Why did your husband owe a man named Salvatore Carrelli $20,000?"

Her eyes widened; her fingers splayed against her chest. "You mentioned that before. Whatever for?"

"It's not clear, but apparently he habitually borrowed to finance his next project. I assume these funds went to remodeling the Warehouse apartments. A Mr. Julio Roberto claims the apartments are already rented. They look sharp and pricey; one wall with exposed brick and high-end appliances ordered. Are you aware of any of this?"

"Yes, I knew about them, just not the details. As I said before, Denny managed the businesses, while I supervise the house, kids, and manage a full-time job. That's enough! I think I mentioned his traditional values." She crossed her legs and arms protectively across her chest.

"That didn't suit you?" asked Snow.

"It's not that. Dennis just didn't consult me about his business. In fact, he managed our checkbook and gave me fifty dollars a week for expenses." She frowned, her mouth an angry slash. "Which didn't even cover the kids' needs."

"An allowance?" Snow's eyebrows shot up. "What were you to do in an emergency—illness, accident, or disability?"

"I don't think he planned on having any. Except for vacillating blood pressure and a heart attack nine years ago, he seemed very healthy for his age. He hated going to the doctor but had annual checkups.

"Anyway, I used plastic for most of my purchases and the fifty for my personal expenses," she explained.

"How did you meet?" asked Snow, trying a different tact.

She smiled slightly. "His truck rear-ended my car on my first day of work twenty-six years ago. He insisted I go to the ER and then escorted me there, notified my employer, and called a tow-truck. I wore a neck brace for weeks, had some physical therapy."

"Was your vehicle totaled?"

She nodded, sinking back against the sofa cushion, lifted her hair off her neck, removed and absently retied the scrunchie around it. "My insurance sent me a check for the car's value. He paid the balance for a new car. Bought me flowers. Took me to nice restaurants, movies, and concerts. We visited the Jersey Shore, Niagara Falls, and New York City. Within three months we were married. In another three, we were expecting Drew."

"Swept you off your feet? So when did all this change?" Snow tapped his pen against his notebook. Thus far, he'd written down nothing, let the recorder run.

"We were fine for years. We hit a rough patch when Camie was born, but once we mastered the routine of two kids, we got back on an even keel. Busy with the kids, our jobs, the house, and yard. We took vacations every summer: Ocean City, Outer Banks, and Disney World. You know how it is. You're married with children."

He nodded, indicated for her to go on.

"I don't really know. We drifted apart. He spent more time at the job, and so did I, once I was appointed coordinator of the Summer Program. We socialized less, until one day I realized that we didn't socialize at all. Not that it mattered." She shrugged.

"When and why did he become abusive?" he asked.

"Because he could. He didn't consider his behavior abusive. Claimed he was teasing, that I had no sense of humor. He was always outgoing, affable with neighbors, glad-handed strangers, telling jokes and stories. Talked for hours on the phone—business, with friends, and some networking and fundraising.

"He was very different at home. The harder I tried to please him, the more sarcastic he became, so I just quit trying. Took a self-defense course at Dickinson. He thought my fighting back was sexy. Whenever he started manhandling me, I took the selfies for proof whenever I filed for divorce."

"When did you file?" His attention sharpened, put pen to paper.

"I didn't. I was going to as soon as Camie was settled." She shrugged. "In another year."

"Talk about a motive for killing someone," he pointed out.

"Oh, please. I'm five-eight, one-forty. He's—was—six-two, two-twenty. Who would win any fight?"

"Depends on what kind of weapon you'd have. You never retaliated?" Snow wondered.

"Yes, I slapped him once and threw coffee on him another time. Tell me you've never bullied your wife? Ah, you're blushing! If you're going to arrest me, do it. If not, I have a ton of work to do. So if you'll excuse me." Kelly stood abruptly, arms akimbo.

"Sorry if I offended you. Please plan no trips. Matter of fact, I'd like you to surrender your passport now." He dropped his card on the coffee table. "We'll talk again after we interview Mr. Abrams."

The widow barked a bitter laugh. "Did you find one when you searched the house? Weren't you listening? I don't have a current passport. Except for day trips or an occasional meal out, we haven't travelled anywhere together in the last seven years."

"You don't have a safety-deposit box?" Sims shook her head. Snow stopped recording, rose to his feet. "Thanks for your time. I'll see myself out. Call me if you have anything to report, anything to share, or if you unearth any useful information. Someone's going to a lot of trouble to hide something, which may be the motive. I hope you're leveling with me. Withholding information or evidence is obstructing justice. If you're innocent, then I trust you'll help us find his killer. If not, you and your family may be in danger.

"Oh, yes, I'll be sending our computer guru, Jay Huddleston, for your computer." Snow pulled the subpoena from his pocket, laid it on the coffee table beside his business card.

She nodded, ignored the card, and walked him to the door.

Snow called Savage. Then they swung around HQ to complete his paperwork on the Abrams crime, then called it a day.

17

At home, Chris trudged wearily into the bungalow where Ethan McCoy was wiping cereal from his grandson's face, hefted him out of his baby seat, and lowered him into Erin's arms. She propped her legs up on the oversized ottoman.

Chris winced at his wife's pale, pinched features, the walker parked beside the rocker. "How's everyone?" Chris unknotted his tie, slid it off. Rolled up his shirtsleeves and washed the scum of the day off in the mudroom. Returning to the living room, he kissed Mac and rubbed the baby's auburn waves. Ian's eyes locked onto his mother's when he nursed. Returning to the kitchen to help his father-in-law, Chris said, "Thanks for helping." He pitched his voice lower. "How'd Erin's first day at home go?"

Ethan nodded. "Fair to middlin'. The lass tries, but she's frustrated 'cause progress is slow." The timer beeped. Ethan slid on oven mitts, pulled a turkey noodle casserole from the oven, and sprinkled shredded cheddar over. Chris found a salad in the fridge, poured iced tea, and set the table. "How's the homicide business?"

"Frustrating, like running into walls. Went to see the vic's lawyer, but someone beat us to him, knocked him out, and stole the files. So we had to report and process that crime scene."

"Sounds like someone is taking drastic or desperate measures." Ethan tossed the mitts aside, leaned against the counter. "Putting bits and pieces of a case together must be difficult."

"Yes, and time consuming, but it relates to our homicide, so we have to follow up." Chris moseyed back to the living room to hoist Ian to his shoulders to burp, pat his back, giving Erin a brief respite. "How's my big boy? Look at you: wide-eyed and bushy-tailed. Hey, you scratch yourself, buddy?" He looked at his son's nails.

"Yeah, we had to cut them. Little lad has a temper. Erin, supper's on. Oh, an officer delivered Mac's arrest files." Stacked in a corner of the living room, four file boxes waited.

Chris nodded, and then pivoted, jouncing Ian with one hand and offering Erin the other.

"She can do it, Chris," Ethan stood in the doorway. "Come on, Hop Along Cassidy! Up and at 'em!" Her husband stepped back.

Mac pushed the ottoman aside, reached for the walker, pulled it in front of her. With studied patience, she took a breath, grabbed the handles, and pushed herself up, shuffling toward the kitchen.

"Walk, Erin," her father ordered.

"Easy for you to say." The joint pain jolted her hip and radiated out. Gritting her teeth and perspiring with the effort, she balanced on her left leg, but swung the right out. She stopped, concentrated. Raised her right foot, stepped forward, and winced, the pain tightening the lines along her eyes and mouth.

Chris sat Ian in his playpen where toys leaned crazily against every mesh corner. The baby crawled for the stuffed hedgehog. Pulling the chair out, Ethan steadied it as Erin eased down sideways, pushed the walker aside, and turned to the table.

"Why is the walker wearing tennis balls on its back legs?" Chris asked.

"Dad did that." Mac smiled tightly. "Easier to scoot the damn thing across carpet and floors." She grimaced in distaste.

"It's only temporary," Ethan commented. "You'll be walking alone in no time." The trio ate in silence until the doorbell pealed.

Chris hopped up. "Got it." Corey Kauffman let Shadow off the leash as they entered. She bounded into the kitchen, rounded the table, her tail madly thumping the wall, wagging her entire body. She rushed at Erin, sniffing her hands and licking her face.

"Hey, girl. You've been good for Corey?" Erin wrapped an arm around the excited, wiggling dog. "I missed you!"

Ethan got up for another plate, scooped up a hefty portion, and set the fork beside the plate. "Take the load off. Eat."

Erin checked the clock: nearly seven. "You've fed Shadow?"

"At five thirty. Thanks." Corey accepted the plate, sat down at the end, and took a bite, shook his head at the salad. "I never say no to a home-cooked meal. This is damn good." He forked in more. The stocky veteran operated the K-9 Instruction site for training police dogs. "Shadow's up to snuff. Smart and swift, she found everything I hid—and more. Turned some rabbits out of hiding, but she moped around evenings, missing Mac."

"Thanks for training her. I appreciate it."

He smiled at the only female K-9 handler he knew. "How's the hip, Bionic Woman?"

Mac shrugged, smirked. "Brand new, improved parts, I'm told." She picked at her salad, spearing an olive. "Rehab will take time." She frowned, sighing in resignation, trying to ignore the pain poking her hip. "I'll live."

"Shadow will help you get in shape," Kauffman pledged.

"I'll have to rely on voice commands for awhile since I won't be able to keep up with her," Mac admitted. "Dad, this casserole is really tasty. What's in the sauce?"

He beamed at the compliment. "Thanks, babe, my own creation. It's the roux I make for Thanksgiving: chopped onions and celery in butter, added flour and chicken broth. Poured over cooked noodles. Grilled the chicken tenders, laid them across the top. Added cheddar jack and chopped parsley for color. I could've added broccoli, though, now that I think about it."

Snow's cell piped up. He excused himself, ducked into the mudroom. A few minutes later, he returned. "That was Savage. I've got to go to Carlisle Regional. Sims's lawyer woke up. We need to interview him before he talks to the widow."

"What happened?" asked Mac. She laid her fork down. Shadow lay down at her handler's feet, her eyes following Ian's movements. Grunting with the effort, the baby tried vainly to reach the dog.

"Abrams was assaulted today in his office. I'll be back as soon as I can—an hour or so. Thanks again, Ethan, for all your help, and Corey for training and keeping Shadow. I brought the legal forms for you to peruse, Mac, if you feel up to it.

"Why or what did Dennis Sims do to bring a murderer to his doorstep? We seem to be one step behind the killer." Snow grabbed his keys and weaved around Ian's playpen and the dog, his hand on the mudroom door, which led to the garage.

"So the widow's in the clear?" Mac asked, keeping an eye on Ian's grasping fingers. With her paws under the pack 'n' play, the shepherd's nose sniffed the baby, but Shadow kept her distance.

"Well, she seems clueless about the business end of things but knows more than she's telling. Back soon." The door clicked as he left.

Ethan stacked and carried dishes to the sink. Corey, in his worn, ragged Redskins shirt and tan cargo shorts, added his to the pile. "Thanks for the delicious dinner. I haven't had a meal that tasty in ages. I've got to get back. I'll come work with Shadow, if you need me to, until you get your legs back under you." His weathered face cracked into wrinkles. "Don't get up. I can find my way out."

Mac smiled. "Thanks for the offer, but Shadow won't let me sit still for long. And thanks for keeping her on par with the other K-9 units. I'd hate for her to fall behind on my account." She extended her hand; he clasped it, and then strode through the front door.

After they left, she lowered her head onto her crossed arms. "How am I going to manage Shadow, I don't know yet; she can out walk me! It's overwhelming. Don't know what I'd do without you and Erica, Dad."

"You'll figure it out. I'll bathe the lad and get him ready for bed. Come on, little man. Let's clean you up!" He hoisted him up. "Just a blip on life's radar. I'm thankful you're mending; it could have been much worse. Keep working; you'll improve gradually. Eventually, you'll be almost like new. Chin up, lass, the worst is behind you!" He smiled encouragingly.

Shadow dropped down beside Mac, nudging her hand, her cue for a treat. "Okay, girl, but I didn't give you a command." The shepherd cocked her head quizzically. Mac patted her, swung her legs around, grabbed the walker, and pushed up. "Let's find something for you to chew on. But then I have to work on these files."

18

Letting the past sit, Mac turned to the forms from Sims's lawyer. Scanning them, she found nothing dramatic—a living will with a DNR order, last will and testament, list of properties and designating his son power of attorney in case of the father's incapacity. "Now, that's unusual. Why not the wife?" Sims left his wife the house and half the rental income, modest stipends for his employees, his kids—the stores, and Shannon Mahoney and her parents he left the other half of the rental income. "What? Why was Sims so generous with his in-laws? Hmm." Her spine and scalp tingled, piquing her curiosity. "Note to self: interview Mahoney. Wait, didn't Savage do that?" She pawed through the box Chris brought home, found the tape labeled S.M. and slotted it into a recorder.

"Being noncommittal, are we? Savage is not usually so easy-going on interviewees. We need more info." She dialed HQ, requesting Mahoney's cell, left a voice mail message for her to stop by the bungalow tomorrow at ten.

Ethan appeared with Ian decked out in knit PJs. "Ready for a fill-up." He offered Erin an arm.

She set aside work, and taking halting steps, feeling the right hip pull, pain hitchhiking a ride, eased into the rocker. Took her son. "Thanks, Dad. Without you, I'd be in a world of hurt." She smiled at the bear of a man's retreating form.

"Ah, lass, that's what dads are for." He whistled for Shadow, who shot after him; they disappeared through the mudroom door.

Ten minutes elapsed. Mac burped Ian, switched sides, slipping a pillow under him. She hummed and wiggled his toes gently, running her thumb gently up his instep. Ian's eyes grew heavy; he lifted his brows to try to stay awake. By the time her dad returned, he was sleeping on her shoulder. Her right leg tingled from being extended so long on the ottoman.

Gently, Ethan lifted the baby and eased into the couple's bedroom to settle the baby in his crib. Shadow glanced up at Ethan but settled beside Erin, her face so earnest, her brown eyes locked on her handler, checking Mac's face. Mac dug another treat from her pocket and rewarded the dog. "I'm okay. Good girl." Scratched the back of the dog's neck.

Sighing, she picked up the Sims folder again. "What other anomalies are you hiding?" she asked the deceased.

Ethan reappeared, hefted the first file box, set it beside the sofa, sat down, and opened the lid. Slid his glasses from his shirt pocket and onto his face. Extracted the first file. Opened it, crossed his legs, and began reading.

"Dad, what are you doing?" Erin asked.

"You're working Chris's files, I'll work yours."

"What are you looking for?" she asked.

He smiled. "Anomalies. Your shooter may be in here. Because he'll come at you again, I can't rest until he's behind bars. I'll start with the most recent and move backwards. Looking for an ex-con or former military with sharp-shooting skills," he asserted.

"Sure. Sounds reasonable." Mac dropped another interview into her recorder, pushed play. "But you don't have to pour over my incident reports. I imagine they can be pretty boring."

Ethan looked up over his bifocals. "Nothing about you is boring, lass." His eyes skimmed pages. Hearing something, Shadow's head reared up. She scrambled to the door, barked—ready to pounce. The purr of a cycle signaled an arrival.

"Sit, Shadow." Erin reached for her walker, but her dad waved her back, beat her to the door, greeted the guest, and stepped back.

Shadow's throat rumbled. "Shadow, come," Erin commanded. The dog trotted back to her, dropped by the rocker. "Lie down. Stay." Upon compliance, she rewarded her with a dog biscuit.

Officer Shannon Mahoney approached, stood at attention, her honey and caramel hair pulled back in a low ponytail, the wind-blasted tendrils twisting around her face. "Sir, I have a conflict tomorrow. I'm on my way home. If it's convenient, can we do this now, or do I need my union rep to make an appointment?"

"What?" Mac said. "The interview's not about you, well, tangentially perhaps. I have additional questions to ask about your sister Kelly and her husband." She checked her iPhone: 8:00 p.m. "Sure, have a seat; we can knock this out in an hour. "Uh, this is my dad, Ethan McCoy. Dad, one of the CPD cycle patrol officers, Shannon Mahoney."

"Pleased, I'm sure, to meet a comely Irish lass who can handle a Harley. If you don't mind my saying, you don't look Irish—or like a cop. The blonde hair and biker outfit." He reached for her hand; she shook his and smiled.

"Sir, my mother's ancestors were Scandinavian."

"That explains it. I'll move to the bonus room." He heaved the open box into his arms. "Coffee, tea, or soda? My daughter's . . ." He let the sentence string out, glancing at Erin, who had managed to stand, girded by the metal walker.

"Water would be fine. I'm just coming off a shift."

"Nothing harder?" Ethan asked.

"No, sir, thank you." Shannon shifted. "I'm riding the bike."

"Have a seat, Mahoney. We'll get right to it." Mac eased back down, ejected the interview she'd been listening to, slotted a blank cartridge in her old recorder.

Ethan handed her a bottle. "If you change your mind, I turned on the Keurig."

"Thank you. She snapped the lid off and drank. "This is fine."

Then she dragged a ladder-back chair over, sitting opposite Mac.

"On the morning you left for New York, you told Savage you didn't enter the house because you were in a hurry. Could there've been another reason? You knew about the domestic abuse?"

Mahoney hesitated a second, then huffed. "I didn't *know* until Kelly told me, but I suspected. I know the DV signs, did a paper on it at the Academy. Denny displayed a number of them, especially his verbal put-downs, dominant and aggressive behavior, though I imagine he toned that down when our family was around. On balance, he was mostly polite and jovial when we were around. But always had to have the last word. But I never heard him threaten her."

"Did you notice a falling off of family visits or get-togethers?"

"Definitely, but we wrote it off to both Kelly and Dennis being busy, overworked, and stressed out. Hell, I'm too busy to go home often, and I'm younger and single, but the job . . . Well, you know its demands."

"Yes, I do. Was Dennis Sims controlling?" Mac asked.

"Extremely. In my opinion, he was jealous and insecure, knowing that Kelly's smarter and better educated; she dated others before they married, so why pick him?"

"Why did she?"

Mahoney shrugged. "I don't know. He was rugged, masculine, and athletic. And debonair. Looked chipped from rock. He exuded an aura of authority. Had powerful forearms, thigh, and calf muscles—like a runner or weightlifter. People noticed him.

"He was also a seasoned raconteur—very friendly and entertaining. Early on, she admired his maturity, frankness, and reliability. At first, he adored and doted on her. Called her 'fresh and fetching.'" She paused for a breath and another sip.

Mahoney reminded Mac of that mannequin outside the Glass shop on Pomfret: a perfectly sculpted, tanned, blond, unblemished, and long-limbed clothes hanger.

"Was their age difference ever a factor?" Mac inquired.

"I'm not sure what you mean. In what sense?" Shannon asked, her cop demeanor slipping for the first time.

Mac shrugged. "In their relationship."

"Not to Kelly. He was established, owned a house, and bought her a new car when he totaled hers. Slowly, he reined her in, demanding to know where she was, decided what she wore—no sundresses or anything revealing. Accused her of flirting with other men when she was just conversing. Chipped away at her self-esteem. Thank God I stayed single." She rolled her eyes.

"Did he ever threaten her, the kids, you, or your parents?"

"Me? Hell no." Emphatically stated. "Kelly?" Her hand tipped sideways, like riding the wind. "They jousted verbally. He could be emotionally abusive and possessive. Maybe it was the age factor: he always expected her to acquiesce to his experience."

"Did you encourage her to report the verbal or emotional abuse?"

"No. I didn't consider it my business unless she asked me. She didn't. Kelly loved Dennis; she wasn't afraid of him."

"Really?" Mac sounded dubious, shifting her weight and dropping her feet to the floor. Pushed the ottoman aside.

"Kelly had RAD training. Rape Aggression Defense System—part of the college's public safety program—to give women self-defense training in case of assault. Are you familiar with it?" Mac nodded. "Approximately twenty percent of college students experience rape, so Dickinson provides positive steps for coeds to protect themselves.

And the course is open to employees. My sister could defend herself and probably did on occasion."

"Did you know she planned to divorce Sims? Maybe he found out. That morning, they fought. Did she club him with a leg of lamb and then leave for New York?" Mac suggested to ease the tension.

"Do you have any proof? Begging your pardon, sir, that sounds like a plot for a murder mystery. Sounds like a lot of work." Mahoney smiled tightly. "Kelly came to the door within seconds after I rang the bell.

"You said she didn't act upset, strange, guilty, or anxious that day?" Mac asked.

"She may have felt guilty for taking the day off, but Dennis took hunting, fishing, and boating trips now and then. Played cards and softball. Hobnobbed with friends. He could hardly complain if Kelly took a day off. Besides, she was with me." She crossed an ankle over the opposite knee, leaned back.

"Did you see anyone lurking around the house that morning? Any strange vehicles drive by or parked on the street?"

Mahoney shook her head. "No, but I wasn't in cop mode. I was treating my big sister to a day out as a birthday present. She likes Broadway plays but hadn't seen one in years."

"Why not?" Mac shifted in her chair.

Mahoney shrugged. "Priorities like putting the kids through college and her job, I imagine. Both take time and money."

"Why did your brother-in-law leave you one fourth of the rental proceeds, your parents an equal amount, and his wife only half?"

For the first time, the CPD officer blinked, eyes widened slightly, then she coughed and drank, recapped the bottle, lobbing it from one hand to the other. "Perhaps because we've always helped with the kids: babysitting, taking them on trips, entertaining them when Kelly and

Dennis were busy or sick. I assume it's his way of compensating or acknowledging our commitment to family."

"Were you aware that he was $20,000 in debt, used the house as collateral to renovate his businesses and the Warehouse apartments? In effect, creating a lien on the property?"

Shannon looked at her, eyebrows popped up, nonplussed, shaking her head. "I had no idea."

"If your sister can't repay the arrears, she may have to sell their properties. She claims no knowledge of her husband's business dealings. And today, his lawyer was knocked unconscious, his files stolen. Who would do that? And why? That's a motive for murder, and your alibi is the only thing saving your sister from being arrested, since she was the last person to see her husband alive. What can you tell us?"

"I'm sure they have insurance." Mahoney shrugged, but her eyes strayed to Shadow, who was growing restless, paws inching forward. Mac released her; she whined and shifted to the door, her eyes beseeching. "I can let her out," the cyclist offered as she eyed the walker.

Ethan must have overheard or sensed the dog's need; he clambered down from the bonus room. "Thanks, but I'll take her for her evening constitutional. *Ahem.*" He coughed, latched the leash onto Shadow's halter ring, and they trotted outdoors.

Mac kept hammering Mahoney with hard questions, looking for hesitations, evasiveness, lack of eye contact, or too much information—all clues that she was lying. But Mahoney batted answers back for an hour, until Mac finally shut off the recorder. "Thanks for coming tonight. What's the scheduling conflict tomorrow?"

"We're briefing the FBI tomorrow on your shooting. Rivers and Summers are going undercover. I'm partnering with Isola Perez and a dozen other FBI agents, searching military bases for your perp. Bartender said he had a

Southern accent, so we'll start at Quantico, work our way down to Georgia, then Florida. Huddleston and Agent Howard are covering facial recognition software. Too bad we don't have prints to run through CODIS or AFIS."

"Or the military databases. Yes, sounds like searching for a needle in a straw tick," Mac observed. "Did the lab report any DNA from the hypo at CRMC that the doctor injected into the assailant?"

"No, DNA results take longer than the other evidence. Just following orders." She stood up, smiled crookedly, pointing to Mac, and then herself. "Chief loaned us out for Jubilee Day in two weeks. Mom's working the NCADV booth handing out domestic violence pamphlets. Our whole family usually participates, but Camie's at State College this year. And I'm riding a horse!" Dusting off her pants, she returned her empty bottle to the island. "Thanks for the water."

"How's your sister coping?" Mac knew Mahoney wasn't assigned to the Sims homicide—conflict of interest, but they could talk.

"Shaky ground. Too much to do, but at least her family's always had her back. We finished, sir? Good luck with your hip." Knocking hammered the door. "I'll get it."

Defense Counselor Denise Wilhelm stood on the other side, nodded to Mahoney, marched in.

"You've been served." She slapped a subpoena into Erin's hand. "Wednesday, 10:00 a.m. Grand jury convened re my appeal."

Mac nodded, biting back her last question, as Mahoney exited, Wilhelm right behind her. An engine started, purred, revved up, and the cycle sped away. Followed by a quieter vehicle crunching along gravel.

Ethan returned with Shadow, whistling *O Danny Boy*. He refilled her water dish, pushed through the gate, and laid five files on the island. "I pulled that DV case, Keller's wife, the Valentine Day's snowstorm, and the Flowers sisters arrests. I'm bushed. Calling it a night. Chris called; he's on his way." He leaned over, kissed his daughter's temple. "Take your meds. Get some rest. The case can wait until sunrise." He chuckled and waved as he shuffled out, then returned. "Oh, found this outside by the chimney." He laid the piece of roofing tile down.

"Thanks for making dinner and watching Ian. Drive carefully!" Mac leaned back, totally exhausted, wishing for the strength she'd left on the battlefield. *Ping!* Outside, a sound like an engine ticking down or her wind chime tinkling arrested her attention. She listened with all her senses. Waited for Shadow to react.

A tapping at her chamber door? Nothing but darkness. *What if I open the door?* "Quoth the raven, nevermore." She laughed shakily at her macabre mood. "From Poe to Shakespeare: 'Once more, into the breach!' Will the homicide case against Emma Hawthorne never end?" Then she brightened, tossing the subpoena aside. "I'll call ADA Lawson; maybe we can get a continuance." *Or maybe not.*

Resigned, she grabbed the walker handles, hoved herself up, rolling toward their bedroom to check on Ian, and then bathe. Stopped, wondering: *How do I get into the shower? I need to lift this leg into the tub.*

She stood over the baby, propped on his side, a rolled blanket at his back, golden auburn waves muted by moonlight, eyes roving beneath delicate, blue-veined lids. In sleep, his mouth sucked gently. One tiny fist tucked under his chin, his small chest lifting and falling, his leg twitching occasionally. He'd just started sleeping through the night—a big help but still woke early.

Mac unbuttoned her shirt. Hands reached around as a voice whispered, "Let me do that," his hands brushing against her breasts as he undid buttons. Chris slipped it, then her bra off her shoulders. Unsnapped and unzipped her jeans, easing them down her legs, trailing his fingers along the back of her thighs and calves, raising gooseflesh where he touched. Lifted her left foot, tugged the slacks away, then her right foot, gingerly. Slipped off her panties slowly, stood. Lifted her gently away from the walker, into his arms for a lingering kiss. "How about a shower?"

* * *

When he heard the tires crunching, noting the husband's arrival, the black-clad, masked intruder dropped soundlessly from the roof. Freeing the grappling hook caused pain to knife through his sprained wrist. The falling cord set the wind chimes tinkling like coins, but the grinding garage door masked the noise.

Stealthily slithering among the trees into deep shadow, he scrunched down, padded quietly out, jogged down rows of corn—rustling restlessly—until he reached the road. His vehicle hulked in the shadow of massive fir trees.

Peeling off his gloves, coiling the rope around the hook, he stuffed all into his rucksack. Tossing his equipment into the back, he slipped into the driver's seat. Rolled down the window, waiting, listening to night sounds until he was sure no one had followed. Keying the ignition, the vehicle slipped away, its plates covered in dusty, red clay. More miles ticked off the odometer as he motored to the remote cabin.

19

Dawn brought cloudless skies, the sun's rays drying the dew that smoked off the grass and cars in the parking lot. A police detective sat in the chair in a private room at Carlisle Regional, gazing out the window, then whipped around abruptly at the sound of the bed cranking up.

"Need some ice for that bump?" Savage asked.

Paul Abrams touched the raised goose egg at the base of his skull and groaned. A headache bloomed. Abrams nodded, pushing the button pinned to his hospital bed. A nurse materialized carrying an ice pack and a pitcher of water.

"Here you go." She placed the pack behind his head, poured a glass of water, whipped a straw from the bed table, snapped off the paper, and bent it—handing the plastic glass to her patient. "I'm Melinda Wagner, your day nurse." She took his temperature and blood pressure. "You've had a concussion." She continued her ministrations, noted his temp and BP on his chart. "Your breakfast will be along directly." Her clogs squeaked as she exited and Snow strode in.

"What happened?" Abrams asked Savage. "Do I know you?"

Savage smiled and showed his shield. "Detectives Reese Savage and Christopher Snow, Carlisle Homicide. Hoping you could tell me. Did you see your assailant?"

The middle-aged estate lawyer shook his head, winced. "No, he attacked me from behind." Brought his hand back to his lap.

"Do you remember anything at all about yesterday's attack?" Savage eased his notebook out, extricated the mini pen from the spirals. Flipped it open. "Sounds, scents, anything at all?"

"Yesterday? Have I been out all this time?" He rubbed his temples gently.

"You woke up last night but were hardly lucid," Snow said, leaning against the doorjamb.

"Well, to answer your question . . ." The man's face scrunched inquisitively, grey eyes on the water pitcher. "Yes, a scent—not aftershave, not soap, but faint—like suntan lotion—lime and coconut. I heard nothing at all, or I would've turned . . . tried to defend myself." He stopped, drew his knees up. Dropped his hands.

"Any idea why you were assaulted?" Savage rolled one shoulder, then the other, tired of sitting.

"No, I can't think . . ." He paused. "I had an appointment with Mrs. Kelly Sims, to go over her husband's papers." His knuckles rubbed the stubble along his jaw and his chin.

"Yes, the Sims file was stolen from your office, so Ms. Reed ran some duplicates off the computer. But we found nothing unusual. Why would someone steal Dennis Sims's legal papers?"

"I have no idea why anyone but the family would be interested, let alone knock me unconscious in broad daylight for them."

"Someone keeping secrets? Did Sims have skeletons to hide?" Savage inquired, lifting one brow. He unfolded his six feet from the chair, carried it to the man's bedside, sat it down, and eased himself onto the seat.

"I'm not at liberty to discuss my clients' privileged information, but I assure you, his—"

Savage slapped the subpoena on the bed, jarring the patient.

"The man's dead; CPD's conducting a homicide investigation. I suggest you cooperate. We searched your office yesterday—" Abrams's eyes enlarged—"It's a crime scene. We confiscated your computer. Out IT guy is combing through files as we speak.

"I'd say that the butt of a handgun dented your skull. If the assailant didn't find what he wanted, he'll return. Next time, he may not stop with a pistol whipping. You'll need police protection. Did Sims have any secrets, to your knowledge, that got him killed? Twenty years a client, he must have confided in you." Reese explained the shooting at the Warehouse.

"Why the scare tactics?" Snow joined the conversation.

"The only thing out of the ordinary I remember is Mrs. Sims leaving for several months in the eighties. She drove her family to the Mayo Clinic to find out the cause of her father's migraines."

"Why did the whole family go?" Snow prodded.

"You'd have to ask them, but I think her father had medical issues. I recall that Drew Sims was little; Kelly was expecting."

"What was Dennis Sims's reaction? He didn't go along?"

"Oh no. He had businesses to supervise, apartments to maintain—that sort of thing. I can't remember his saying anything other than he missed his family." Abrams rubbed his finger along the side of his nose. "He rarely left Carlisle. Just took the occasional family vacation or attended a sporting event. He was a busy man—always hustling. He was on the City Council for years, an usher at his church, and doted on his kids. I can't think why anyone would want him dead." He massaged his neck gingerly.

A kitchen aide shoved the door aside, delivering the patient a hearty breakfast, plunked it down with the utensils wrapped in a napkin, then exited. The bump on Abrams's head had not affected his appetite; he tucked into the food eagerly. Stopped to add milk to his coffee, then returned to scooping up the eggs, cutting the turkey sausage with his plastic knife and fork.

"Who stands to gain the most from his death?" asked Snow.

Abrams put down his fork, munched on a piece of toast. "That's just it. With the debt he left, I'm not sure anyone will benefit. The Mrs. will have to liquefy most of her husband's assets to repay the outstanding loans. He had life insurance to cover funeral costs. My guess is it'll take a year to straighten his affairs." The man wiped his hands on his napkin and swallowed his coffee.

"Were there any surprises in the will?" Savage wanted to know, turning from the window.

"Yes. Dennis's bequest to Shannon Mahoney was overly generous in my view. He knew about his debts, so his wife should have received the lion's share." He scratched his head. "Why would he do that? If I were her lawyer, I'd advise her to contest the will. Under Pennsylvania law, Mrs. Sims is entitled to half."

"Good question, Abrams, good question," Snow commented. "Thanks for your help. You have our number if anything else pops up. We'll return your computer when we've pulled Sims's files. I'll have officers drive by your office and home on their rounds for a few days." He dropped a card on the man's empty breakfast tray. He motioned for Savage to follow as both their pagers beeped. "Shit, we can't catch a break," he observed.

Reese glanced at his pager. "Dispatch. What the hell? Another homicide?"

They double-timed out of CRMC, bolted through the glass doors, and jogged to the Explorer. Snow tapped his pager for the address.

"Dispatch. Nine-one-one from 769 South Street; your circus, Detective. Report to the scene. An ambulance is also in route."

Bubble up, Snow switched on sirens and lights. The SUV tore along Alexander Spring Road, code three, parting traffic and running red lights. Walnut Bottom Road whizzed by. Cornered on Belvedere, blowing through stop signs. Then right onto South Street, braking at the curb.

20

The front door yawned. Donning blue booties and latex, the detectives strode past crime scene techs, reached the kitchen where an EMT hovered over Mrs. Mahoney. The stocky blonde attendant slipped an oxygen mask over the unconscious woman while talking into her shoulder radio —reading stats quickly as she wrapped the BP cuff around the patient's bare arm, which crinkled like crepe paper while Hemmer stabilized her neck. "One eighty-eight over ninety. Starting IV. Set up for an EKG stat. Transporting patient to Carlisle Regional. One, two, three."

"See you at CRMC," remarked Hemmer. He and the woman hoisted Mrs. Mahoney onto the gurney and rolled her out the front door. Lights whirring and sirens screaming, the ambulance tore down the street, splitting the neighborhood serenity.

A mop and bucket sat beside the island—the barstools moved aside. Open boxes were stacked next to the door leading to the home office. Other flat cardboard leaned against the dining room table to be made into boxes.

The detectives roved around the living area, checking doors and windows for broken locks or forced entry— some evidence of a crime.

"Let's walk out. Looks like an accident," Savage observed. He called it in to HQ.

"Did someone kill Mrs. Mahoney, too?" Mrs. Blunt hovered just across the street, wringing her hands. "This used to be a quiet, safe neighborhood when the hospital was on Belvedere." Her uneven, white hair was pinned in place, the flowered housedress stopped at her shins; she wore scuffed, canvas tennis shoes.

"No, ma'am. Looks like an accident. The EMTs took her to the hospital. Did you see anyone else here? Where is Kelly Sims?" asked Savage.

"You're such a handsome, young man; you look familiar." Mrs. Blunt smiled up at him. "Oh yes. Mr. Mahoney took yard waste to the recycling center. Left maybe half hour ago. He'll be back, I'm sure. They're helping Kelly pack up her husband's stuff. Sending stacks of books off to The Bookery, I guess."

"Where's Kelly Sims now?" Snow repeated the question.

"At work, of course." She turned her head to study the other detective. His light-brown, brassy hair combed back, kicked out at the neck. "You look like that Irish singer, but you could stand a shave and a haircut." With that, she turned, padded up her driveway to her modest dwelling, shaking her head.

A black Chevy truck rolled down the road, signaled, and pulled into the drive. "What's up, gov'ner?" Mr. Mahoney stepped down, shook hands with the two detectives.

"Sorry to have to tell you, but an ambulance just took your wife to the hospital," Snow said. The man's stricken expression made him explain. "Looks like she slipped and fell."

The crime scene techs packed up and filed past the trio in the driveway. At the rear of the van, they climbed out of their white overalls.

Savage asked, "Do you need water? A soda?"

Mahoney shook his head. "I need something stiffer. I know, not while I'm driving. I have to head to the hospital. No, let me lock up first." He trudged up to the door, closed it, inserted and turned the key, then pocketed it.

"Mind if we go along, ask you a few questions? It'll be awhile before the ER doctor will discharge your wife." Snow tossed Savage his keys and climbed into the passenger's side of the old truck.

"Nice job on the shrubbery. Mrs. Blunt said I need a trim and shave, too." He chuckled. "Are you okay to drive, sir?"

Mahoney nodded absently, intent on the road. Gripped the wheel in both hands to hide the trembling. "What happened to Megan?"

"We just arrived, but the EMT said it looked like she fell while mopping." While in route, Snow questioned the man about the family's trip to Minnesota. Asked for records or memorabilia from the trip.

"I had migraines so bad I blacked out. Light made 'em unbearable. I'd got nauseous, vomited—everything hurt down to my teeth and hair. Doctors around here couldn't account for them, so my family doctor finally referred me to the Mayo Clinic."

"Did you serve in the military?" asked Snow.

"Yes. Did a tour in 'Nam. Incurred a head injury from a mortar shell. Concussion, embedded metal shard—which docs removed. But that was a long time ago, son. Migraines didn't start until the kids came along. Kept getting worse. So my physician referred me to the experts."

"So what happened at the clinic?" Snow braced his hand on the dash while Mahoney made a fast turn into the med center's parking lot and whipped into an empty space. Braking suddenly.

"All kinds of tests. You name it. I had it." He shrugged. "EKG, EEG, brain scan, MRI." He shook his head. "Tried meditation, massage, and yoga, too. I like the massages." He smiled slightly.

"What'd they find?"

"TBI. They gave me trial meds—anti-cytokine therapy —that had only previously been tested on mice. That and Alka-Seltzer Plus did the trick. Also weaned me off caffeine, MSG, sugar, and processed foods."

"You were there three months?" Snow jotted notes as they talked.

"Two, but counting travel time, yes. Kelly drove mostly. We stopped along the way: the Larry Byrd museum/restaurant in Terre Haute, Sea World in Sandusky, Ohio. Let's see, uhm—and Falling Water. Who would want a house hanging out over a waterfall that way? A clever design, but low ceilings made me feel claustrophobic—and damp.

"In Ohio, I remember Shannon chowing down on Big Boys—three-decker cheeseburgers with all the fixings. She'd just turned sixteen, so we spent a few evenings letting her drive around mall parking lots. The women shopped a bit."

"Kelly was pregnant? Seemed a trip like that would be hard on her." Snow watched the man's expression. For a second, Mahoney looked baffled as though his mind blanked.

"Oh yes, Camie arrived early." He nodded, turning off the ignition. "Mind my asking why you're asking so many questions about our past?" Mahoney opened the driver's door, stepped out. "What does our Mayo Clinic trip have to do with anything?"

"The past informs the present. Most homicides are committed by someone the victim knows. Trying to find out who killed Dennis Sims and why means examining *everything*, past and present. The case is still open; the leads are drying up. Who's your family doctor?" Snow shoved the passenger's door open, climbed out. Stared at Mahoney over the cab's hood. "I'd like records, receipts, photos—anything you have from that trip."

Savage drew alongside in Snow's vehicle, idling.

"Dr. Masland. Still don't see how it helps with your case." Mahoney shrugged. "I'll tell my wife. She may have a photo album. But I don't know if we kept the medical records from twenty-odd years ago. Maybe the doctors did. Have a good day, Detective. I need to see how Megan's doin'." He ambled across the parking lot, aiming for the ER doors.

"I'll wait out here until you've had a chance to talk to your wife. We need to return to the Sims's house. I'd like to talk to your daughter further."

"She won't be home 'til five," answered her dad. "So I'll be here until Megan's discharged." Mahoney turned toward the ER doors.

"Okay. In that case, we'll see you later. Have a good day, sir."

Mahoney hiked up his pants, sighed, and disappeared through the entry doors.

Snow flipped his cell, called HQ, requesting a subpoena for Gavin Mahoney's medical records in Carlisle and at the Mayo Clinic, dating back to 1987. Climbed into the Explorer.

21

Kelly Sims arrived home at five thirty to find blood on the granite counter, an abandoned mop and bucket. Connected the dots immediately. Letting her purse drop to the stool, her eyes noted the blinking light: voice mail. Her cell tweeted. "Oh, God, Mother!" She punched "talk." "Hello?"

"Mom's okay," Shannon assured her sister. "They stitched her forehead and sent her home about an hour ago."

"What happened?" Kelly kicked off her heels, massaging her instep. "Looks like she fell against the counter. There's blood on the island. Did anyone break in, scare her?"

"No, you're right. Slipped and fell, called 911 herself. Dad had taken your yard waste to recycling, so he wasn't there when it happened. Ambulance crew, Homicide detectives, and CSU all arrived on the scene at once. I bought Chinese. Mom and Dad ate some. She's sleeping now. No need to rush over. Matter of fact, we've got leftovers. What about I bring them by?"

"Sure." Kelly opened a bottle of white wine. Took out another stemmed glass. Shannon rarely brought dinner over. "Is there something else we need to talk about? Why were the Homicide cops here?"

"Their former crime scene. Yes, Snow accompanied Dad to the hospital. He wanted to know all about the Mayo Clinic trip, what we did those three months we were gone. Pour me a glass. See you in fifteen."

Nuking the veggie lo mein, dim sum, and shrimp fried rice, Kelly watched Shannon quizzically. Her sister peeked into lampshades, ducts, and outlets. She mouthed, "Bugs?"

"How are you holding up?" Shannon nodded, rolling her forefinger—asking Kelly to follow her lead, converse.

She poured wine. "Good days, bad days." Kelly wobbled her hand. "I wake up, thinking I'm dreaming, and the day's work dawns on me. I can handle work; it's home that's overwhelming. When I get home, I can sit for hours staring out the window without seeing what's there. Sometimes, the days get ahead of me. Then I play catch-up, scurrying all around, accomplishing nothing.

"Or I try to read." She gestured to the paperback, *Winter Sea*, on the end table. "Usually Kearsey's stories carry me away; her prose just flows, but I can't remember the last paragraph I read."

"You know you're a suspect, right?" Shannon asked. "Here, let me plate that for you. Let's take it out on the patio. Lovely day—temperate, low humidity: 'What is so rare as a day in May?'" she misquoted a poem she remembered from high school, picked up the plates while Kelly carried the wine glasses.

"Not a perfect day, but at least the sun's shining. What, now you're the weather forecaster?" Kelly looked at Shannon, her eyebrows quirked as she dusted off the patio table.

After they settled at the patio table, tucked in a few bites of lo mein, Kelly said, "Okay, why are you acting like you're on TV? Is the house bugged?" she whispered.

Shannon forked in more rice. "I love this stuff. Phones, for sure. I didn't find any bugs in the great room or kitchen. "Has Homicide asked you for birth certificates yet?" She sipped wine and nodded.

"No, why would they want them?" Kelly asked.

"Motive for murder," her sister answered. Stopped chewing. Finger-combed her hair back, clipped it in place. Leaned back, stretched out, crossed her legs at the ankles. Huffed out a sigh.

"Oh, really? Yes, I have the originals. I can make the detective copies, but they won't arrest me because of birth certificates."

"They're following the money, asking invasive questions. And McCoy called me in for another interview, wanted to know why Denny left me such a generous bequest," Shannon said. "I'm uncomfortable about it, too. It raises questions."

Kelly speared a shrimp. "Oh! Well, he owes you for a lifetime of babysitting, for one. You're my kids' second mother, and we're grateful for your support. I couldn't have worked without your help." She dipped the dim sum in soy sauce, took a bite.

"Kel, he should have left you everything. Aren't you the least bit mad about the will?"

"Am I frothing at the mouth? Your mean 'angry.' No, I'm not. You, Mom, and Dad deserve financial compensation. If Denny's mismanaged our finances, I'll deal with it. Sell the businesses and the Warehouse. Drew and Camie can't run them from Lancaster and State College."

"What if you lose the house? Let me give you the other half of the rental money. I feel guilty taking what's rightfully yours."

"You're joking, I hope. Think of the irony. If I lose the house, I'll move into a smaller one, which I've wanted to do for years. Let's wait until I've talked to the lawyer, see how the finances shake out. Don't worry. Why don't you buy your own house? Are you still rooming with Gabriel and Chase?"

"We're renting a yellow three-bedroom rancher outside of Boiling Springs. I have the master and en suite. They share the Jack and Jill bath, but they also get the study. There's a three-car garage for our bikes and cars. Screened-in patio. Nice spacious yard in back; we put up a volleyball net." She shrugged, tipped back the rest of her wine. Poured another. "Don't feel the need to be saddled by a mortgage. What if we transfer again?"

"Why would you do that? You just started with the Carlisle force three months ago. It's ideal, really. Close to your family, a smaller community. Not as much crime as York," Kelly argued.

"This case has added a lot of heat. CPD considers me a suspect, too. McCoy interrogated me for an hour the other night. Kelly, do not underestimate these detectives. They'll hound us until the last dog has died. We'll all wind up serving time." She shifted her weight to reach for the wine bottle and read the label: *Red Tail Chardonnay*. "Hmm. Tasty."

"Glad you like it. Wouldn't they have already arrested me if they were going to?" Kelly looked drawn and tired, with new worry lines etched in her forehead. She, too, leaned back, crossed her legs. Sighed.

"No incriminating evidence: first, though, you had an excellent motive, but you also have a solid alibi. Evidently, they lack the murder weapon. Kelly, Kelly. Why didn't you just divorce Dennis when your marriage hit the skids?"

"You know why. He wouldn't allow it. And get a PFA order? Like a piece of paper would keep him away from me? I would've been in real danger then. He would've stalked me to my grave or had Julio or somebody push me off a cliff, drain my brake fluid, punch the radiator, or any number of other things. Those are just the ways he told me about." She shuddered. "Let's go in. It's getting chilly, now the sun's setting." Pale opal topped with salmon rimmed the horizon.

Kelly continued. "As it turns out, I don't have to flinch, wince, dodge, or whisper. Or tiptoe around the house, swallow my anger, or bite my tongue on a retort. Or listen to an unending stream of commands. I'm telling you, in the last five years, he'd grown worse.

"He climbed into the middle class with hard work, but his blue-collar mouth and manners . . . every other sentence the F bomb. It's such an ugly, violent, degrading word." She stopped. Patted the napkin against her mouth, held it there to stem the words. "Sorry, I don't mean to dump on you. No longer a subordinate, now I can enjoy the solitude. Seconds sparkle, minutes unspool, and jewels of thought beckon like a lover. I've shocked you!"

Shannon stared at her sister as though seeing an alien. "I had no idea you were so introspective. Sorry that I couldn't help you more. I should have reported him. Domestic violence is epidemic, and it usually escalates. Four out of five women experience some form of physical, emotional, psychological, or sexual violence. Twenty percent—and that's just the reported cases! You're right: When the wife leaves, that's the most dangerous time for her. And it sounds like Denny's violence was escalating. But you never asked for help." She reached out, rubbed her sister's arm. Stood, gathered the plates, and returned indoors.

Kelly followed; shut the patio door. "No, I never asked because . . . well, because I made my bed. We had the children. Denny was a good father and provider. Early on, we had fun and the chemistry sparked. In bed, he was gentle and generous, working to satisfy me as well." She blushed. "As he aged, he changed, and so did I after Camie . . ."

Her sister put two fingers to her trembling lips. "I'm so sorry. I was so absorbed in my own misery." Shannon hugged Kelly, rubbing her back, as tears blurred her vision. She shook her head to snap out of the doldrums. "Let's have coffee. Got any dessert?"

"You were a teenager; you had a right to be self-absorbed. Nothing homemade: I have raspberry gelato and mud pie in the freezer."

"Massey's custard?" Shannon's eyes brightened. "Hot fudge?"

"Of course." Kelly pulled the mud pie from the freezer, the fudge from the fridge, popped off the lid, and stuck the jar in the microwave while Shannon rummaged through a utility drawer for a dipper. "Next drawer over. Grab two spoons. And . . ." She whisked a canister of whipped cream from the fridge as well.

"This stuff's like a brick. You could knock someone out with it! Why do you keep your freezer so damn cold? Can't you dial it back a notch or two?" Shannon asked, wrestling to scoop it out.

"It's called frozen for a reason, Shannon. Let it set out for five minutes or nuke it for thirty seconds. I'll make coffee." Taking two mugs from the cabinet, Kelly handed her sister a packet of sweetener and creamer from the fridge.

Shannon muscled the custard into cut-glass dessert dishes, dribbled each with warmed fudge, and squirted a dollop of cream on top; the sisters spooned the sundaes down.

"Yummo. Don't know how this will mix with the wine." Shannon paused, spoon in midair, studying the mound of coffee, fudge, and crushed cookie bits.

"Then don't drink any more. You're driving anyway," Kelly pointed out reasonably, licking the luscious off her spoon. She eyed the stove clock. "It's getting late. Do you want to spend the night? Then you can tell me more about your interview with McCoy. And I'll crack open another bottle of wine. Shiraz this time. Let it breathe."

"Why the hell not? May I borrow some PJs or a tee?"

22

Erin's eyes popped open. Wilhelm's subpoena stared at her from the end table. Looked at her clock. *Testifying today. Get up; shower before Ian wakes. Move. The mind is willing; is the body able?* She'd attended water aerobics at PT for two weeks and walked twenty minutes twice daily. As the weather warmed, she felt like a slug dragging her right leg along, the pain dogging her every motion. Showered, started the coffee, hobbled to the mudroom, let Shadow out.

"Shadow, come!" Erin put the dog's breakfast in her dish.

Chris shaved, bolted into the shower for a quick once over, toweled, dressed. Peeked at his sleeping son. Grabbed a cup of coffee. "We'll go to the courthouse a little early. Give us plenty of time. Guess our evidence is not as solid against Emma Hawthorne as we thought if a Grand Jury's convened." From the pantry, he snared a couple of granola bars and took a banana from the fruit bowl. "I'll change Ian while you finish your yogurt."

After nursing the baby, dressing in green slacks, a peach pullover, and short, fitted, cotton jacket, Erin slid the walker aside and drew the cane out of the hall closet. The doorbell chimed. Erin let in her mother-in-law, who beelined to Ian in his playpen.

Chipper as a cricket in the thicket, dressed in black capris and white tee, Erica said, "Morning, all. Good-bye. Good luck. See you when you're done. Hey, baby." She rubbed his back and cooed, "Ooo, how's my pretty little grandbaby?"

* * *

In the courthouse, the couple took the elevator and located the room. Judge Shelia Stowe, who golfed with Erica Snow, nodded as the couple entered. She addressed the jury, explaining their duties. "You are impaneled to decide if the Prosecution has the facts and sufficient evidence against the juvenile Emma Hawthorne to proceed to trial." Her instructions continued in her clipped tone. Finally, she turned to the lawyers. "Prosecution, proceed."

Defense Counselor Denise Wilhelm sat with Jack and Emma Hawthorne at their table; she looked comfortably smug, an ease in her posture that Mac never saw at Emma's trial for killing her kidnapper. DA Collins and ADA Lawson sat to the right.

Michael Collins dropped his pen on his legal pad, stood. "We call Detective Erin McCoy." She stood, cane in hand, and shuffled slowly to the chair, perspiring as she eased down on the hard, wood witness chair.

"We're going to review Marjorie Hawthorne's homicide from the top. Please tell the jury the facts that can be verified by CPD evidence. First you discovered her body at the Molly Pitcher gravesite on Friday, March 21, 2009, at 7:00 a.m."

"Yes, sir. She was lashed to the cannon in front of the statue."

"She died from a fork shoved into her chest, which pierced her heart," Collins reiterated.

"Yes, sir."

"Her daughter, Emma Hawthorne, Dr. Donald Davies, and Kevin Lowe were present at the Old Carlisle Cemetery the night before."

"That's correct." Mac shifted slightly to take weight off of her right hip. Her cane stood beside her.

Collins continued marshalling the facts, with Mac verifying, wondering why Wilhelm hadn't sought manslaughter at the first trial. Then, she answered questions about Emma's kidnapping and eventual rescue —skipping the Davies murder, as the teen had been tried and given a suspended sentence for justifiable homicide. Collins took his seat. ADA Lawson addressed the facts about the evidence: hanky and cape, both with mother and daughter's blood, the DNA found on the cigarette butts, an inventory of the Camry's contents, its punctured tire, and a list of the Sixth Regiment reenactors' interviews.

Wilhelm had no questions or statements. The three listened calmly to the proceedings. Finally, Collins dismissed Mac, calling Detective Christopher Snow, who entered the courtroom, holding the swinging gate for Mac as she passed. She took a seat in the first row; perspiration pimpled her forehead.

The DA and ADA asked Snow to verify additional facts relating to Samuel Gray, Jean du Bourbon, the reenactors' camp, the Philly condo, the porn and sex trafficking ring, and more.

"Why did you arrest Emma Hawthorne?" Collins asked.

"She admitted wearing her mother's cape and wresting the murder weapon from Marjorie Hawthorne. Luminol showed Mrs. Hawthorne's blood splatter on the cape. That tells us she stabbed her mother, and then someone lashed the woman to the cannon."

After dismissing Snow, the DA called Dr. Haili Chen to verify the medical findings. The fourth witness—Fire Chief Lane Rusk, related the details of his findings—deliberate arson to cover the crime, but rain had doused the fire.

For the duration, the Hawthornes, faces inscrutable, sat beside Wilhelm, who stood to address the proceedings. "Judge Stowe, jury members, and my esteemed colleagues, I move to dismiss all charges against my client because Detectives Snow and McCoy failed to Mirandize her. They advised her of her rights after browbeating and bullying her for two hours until I refused to allow my client to continue.

"She was traumatized by the kidnapping and torture at the hands of her kidnapper, the trial, the media invading her privacy, and detectives interrogating her. By listing that interview in discovery documents, the CPD denied my client self-incrimination and due process guaranteed by the Fifth and Fourteenth Amendments. They proceeded despite my objections and against the advice of her psychologist, Vicky Alwine." She smiled—a cat in the cream. Alwine, Mary Grace's younger sister, sat behind the defense table, nodding agreement.

Judge Stowe considered the statement. She looked askance at the prosecutors, and then glared darts at the detectives. Back to DA Collins. Glanced at the jury. "Is Defense Counselor's statement accurate?" Collins and Lawson turned to Snow and McCoy, eyebrows raised.

"Well?" the judge stared at the detectives.

"I don't recall. I think we Mirandized her before we brought her into Headquarters." Snow culled back over the night Emma disappeared for several hours, CPD's actions to track her down, and Wilhelm's call to meet in her office the next morning. He shook his head in disbelief.

"But you interrogated my *fifteen-year-old* client in my office for two hours without mentioning that what she said could be held against her in a court of law," Wilhelm repeated.

"A ten-year veteran of the police, and you don't recall?" Stowe's voice climbed an octave. "You should know!" The gavel whacked. "The grand jury will recess for two hours. Find out! Better yet, give me that interview! I'll listen to it myself. Court adjourned until 1:00 p.m. Bailiff, order lunch for the sequestered jury members."

Snow and McCoy glanced at each other, speechless.

When the grand jury reconvened, Judge Stowe declared, "The jury has decided the evidence sufficient to move this case forward.

However, this taped interview," she held it up and waved it back and forth, "and nothing therein are admissible in court. Trial date is set for June 16. As this is Miss Hawthorne's second offense, the defendant will be remanded to a juvenile detention center for the duration."

"What? NO!" Emma wailed.

"Another sound from your client, Counselor, and I'll find her in contempt of court, which carries a $300 fine for starters. Need I say more?" Stowe picked up the gavel, hesitated, but no sound emanated from the defendant. The gavel smacked down so hard it cracked. "The Grand Jury's adjourned."

23

Snow dropped Erin at the bungalow, called HQ, palmed the wheel, and drove to work, cursing. "The chief will tear us a new one! No, we have solid evidence; we'll just have to deliver it by other means," he vowed determinedly.

Erin found a note from Erica on the fridge. "*We took Ian for a stroll around the Children's Lake. Be back for his supper.*" Though weary and her hip burned, she smiled at her good fortune. Shadow whined from the mudroom, so she took the dog out to do her business. Let her run ahead through her obstacle course. "Good girl. No, nothing to find today. Come, let's go in." Shadow stopped to bark at an inquisitive squirrel and sniff the ground. "Leave it! Come!" She rewarded her K-9 officer with a biscuit. "Sorry, I'll do better next time, promise."

Inside, the landline blinked. She punched voice mail. The chief left a brief message. "Assuming you'll be back on duty then, you and Shadow are assigned to assist Mechanicsburg Police on Jubilee Day. Hope you're mending. I'll have a motorized wheelchair available so you won't have to walk all day. We'll reschedule your closing party until you return to work full time."

"Hmm. Guess he hasn't heard about Judge Stowe's decision."

She booted up her MacBook, Googled Rochester, Minnesota, hospitals. Then called Hamilton for a subpoena on medical records from Gavin Mahoney's doctors.

"Snow already took care of that! I'll scan, e-mail those records," Sonja informed her. "How ya doin'? Boss got you working from home?"

"Sorry to bother you. Well, yes. I'm running background checks. Thanks! Have a good day." She phoned Megan Mahoney, requesting any photos and information from their trip to the Mayo Clinic. "May I stop by tomorrow after lunch? Or you could drop by my place if you'll be out and about. How are you feeling? I heard you were hospitalized the other day."

"Well enough. Just got light-headed, hit my head on the corner of the island on the way to the floor." She laughed. "Doctor said low sodium levels. They gave me an IV. I'm supposed to drink more water and Gatorade for electrolytes.

"I can gather what you need by then. We had to keep extensive records for insurance purposes. See you at one?" Mrs. Mahoney sounded accommodating.

"Yes, ma'am. Thank you."

* * *

Next morning, Mac timed herself: an hour to shower and dress, a ten-minute improvement. Today, her dad was watching Ian, spooning cereal mixed with applesauce into his yawning mouth. He whirred the spoon around in the air, making motor sounds: the airplane game. She smiled as she clomped out for a cup of coffee.

"Thought you were on medical leave," her dad said.

She popped another K-cup in the pot for a second cup. "Technically, I am, but I'm just gathering information. Anyway, the exercise will be good for me. I need to get back some strength in my legs. Shadow and I are working Jubilee Day. Chief said he'd have a wheelchair for me. Imagine how that will look!"

"Most people won't even notice. They're too busy spending their money, eating, and gawking at Shadow. Is Chris making any progress on his current case? I notice it's not garnering the press that the Hawthorne case is.

"Around and around—zoom, varoom—into the mouth it goes!" He landed another mouthful into his grandson.

"Emma's facing another trial. Her Defense moved to dismiss all charges because we failed to Mirandize her before we arrested her. The judge threw out our taped interview and everything mentioned on it. Just hope we don't get fired for the oversight."

"That doesn't sound like you to overlook that; I doubt you'd lose your jobs over it. Eat something. I saw yogurt in the fridge, and I brought fresh strawberries. Come on, wee Ian, a few more bites."

"Well, luckily, we have hard evidence." She found strawberry yogurt, sliced a few fat berries over, then sprinkled granola over. Eased down opposite her dad, spooning in her parfait. "Wow, those berries are sweet. From Sandoe's?" He was good about bringing fresh, seasonal produce and usually packed a lunch for all when he babysat. "Thank you for coming. And tonight, we're going out to eat."

He nodded, sipped his coffee, and then set it down out of the baby's reach. "Yes, I heard. Well, little man. Your mother needs you." He unbuckled him from his seat and lifted him up, standing, too. "Let's wash your face first."

Erin grabbed a pillow, unbuttoned her blouse, but waited until the hefty baby dropped to her lap and Dad returned to the kitchen before she opened the nursing bra. Ian's blue eyes studied her; she beamed at him until he bit down. "No teeth, Ian. Hurts mommy." She broke suction, pretended to cry; he stopped, uncertain, his mouth pulling down, chin trembling. "Try again."

Ethan rinsed the dishes, racked them into the dishwasher. "May be time to wean him," he said from the kitchen.

"Heard that, did you?" Erin commented. "We'll see. The pediatrician recommended nursing him for a year. Said he'd have fewer allergies then."

"Is the doctor a woman?" he asked.

"No."

"Case in point. He has no idea what you're going through."

"But I enjoy nursing. It's good for both of us," she countered. "Besides you all give him bottles when I'm not here."

Ethan let it go, humming a Beatles tune. Erin's mind followed,"'Gotta have it your way,' hmm. "Okay, if he keeps biting," she conceded.

"I'm making pastrami Reubens for lunch. Will Chris be home?"

"If I tell him that, he will. What else?" She shouldered the baby, thumped his back; Shadow wandered in, her tug-of-war ring in her teeth, the other attached by a sturdy cord.

Ethan grabbed the dangling ring and tugged; Shadow clamped down, backed away, and shook her head back and forth. "Home-made pasta salad and devil's food, cream-filled cupcakes."

"We'll definitely be here. So would the whole squad if they knew what you made. You're just the most wonderful parent."

Ethan smiled. "Glad you appreciate my efforts. Boosts my self-esteem. I like creating new recipes. Everyone should create something worthwhile while we're on Earth. I mean, children are the first, best choice, but good food's a great second."

"And necessary for survival! What's Liam doing this summer?" Her stepbrother had just finished his sophomore year at Penn State, finally declaring a major in sports medicine.

"Working at college and taking summer courses. Trying to get through in four years. I hear it gets tougher and tougher to do that. He scored a job with the Athletic Department, so he can get valuable on-the-job training under Coach Paterno."

Erin nodded without commenting, switching her son to her left side. She had time to give Shannon Mahoney a call about Jubilee Day; maybe she could hitch a ride with her—if she drove a CPD vehicle, but Mahoney would probably ride her cycle over. "Do you mind if I do some computer research while you're here?"

"Do what you need to do. I'm taking the bairn and the dog outside for a bit. Give any thought about putting up a swing set?"

"It's a bit early for that, don't you think?"

"No, he can sit up; they sell baby seats. He needs to get fresh air and exercise daily. And once he starts toddling around, a wee plastic slide would be fun—or he could just use Shadow's." Ethan let the implication ride.

"I'll talk to Chris about it. Seems like we could hang a swing from a tree. Who knows? He might build a swing set for him."

"That'd work, too. Okay, Grandson, let's get you dressed. We're going out and having fun."

24

When Erin and Chris entered Old Naples, friends and family members jumped up. "SURPRISE! Happy first anniversary!" Balloons and streamers festooned the booths. Their parents, Chris's brothers, Ozzie and Sonja Hamilton, Savage—sitting with Danelle, and the Homicide squad members—all beamed at the couple.

Truly surprised because her joint pain had obliterated all else, Erin glowed despite the cane at her side, her smile wide and eyes glistening. "Thank you all for coming to help us celebrate." She wore her silk spaghetti-strap sheath that shimmered blue and green; Chris's black suit with stark, white shirt delineated his fit physique. One of the wait staff ushered them to the center table by the window amid congratulations on their first year. Caesar salads and hot rolls materialized. Champagne fizzed in the fluted crystal glasses, bubbles bobbing to the surface.

"Tough first year? The rest will get better," Chief March offered. "Or worse, depending on your perspective." More salt than pepper sprinkled his stiff crew, his ebony eyes prominent in a square face. He raised his glass. "But together, you'll weather the storms!"

"Nah, they're still on their honeymoon," Reese stated. He raised his champagne flute. "A toast to the next sixty years! Beyond that, who cares?"

"Here, here! For they're a jolly fine couple," Danelle sang.

"That nobody can deny!" Stuart and Fields chimed in.

"Where's Ian?" Erin whispered to her parents.

"Dreena and the kids are watching him," Chris whispered in her ear, as he hooked her cane on her chair back. "No worries tonight. Happy anniversary, dear."

People pinged their glasses like they had at their wedding. They leaned together for a lingering kiss.

"Save that for later," someone joked good-naturedly.

"Surprised?" Erica asked her daughter-in-law.

"Heavens, yes. Hadn't even realized today was our anniversary. I can't remember the last time we ate out. Seems so long ago," she whispered to her mother-in-law. Truly cheered, Erin raised her glass and toasted the others.

Removing salad bowls, waiters set various entrées before the guests who'd obviously ordered before the anniversary couple arrived. Plates of seafood scampi were set before Chris and Erin. At the next table, the senior McCoys had crab cakes; the elder Snows shared a white seafood pizza. Soon, diners were occupied with consuming the Italian delights, conversing among themselves while instrumental oldies emitted from overhead speakers.

While musicians set up in the far corner, Erica and Christopher Sr. slipped out. "We're sending Dreena in so Jeff has a dancing partner. Stay, have fun. We'll watch the kids."

"Oh, that's kind. Thanks." Erin wilted. She turned to her husband, trying to keep the panic at bay. "I can't dance."

"Of course you can. Trust me." His inscrutable expression gave nothing away as he expertly rolled the pasta on the spoon, then forked the angel hair in his mouth. "Hmm. Perfectly seasoned." He leaned toward her, speared a shrimp and tucked it into Erin's mouth.

Later, two waiters attired in black with black aprons wheeled out a layer cake bearing one large flaming candle on the top tier of Italian butter-cream confection. Chris pulled Erin gently onto his lap. They blew out the candle while camera flashes popped. Kissed again while the wait staff sliced, carted cake and gelato from table to table.

The lead singer for Fifth Gear took up the mic. "Good evening. Congratulations to the Snows; happy anniversary! Thanks for having us back. Shakespeare once said, 'If music be the food of love, play on.' Tonight, we have a skeleton crew, but we'll sing you home. "Chris and Erin, if you'll lead." The introductory bars to "Music of the Night" spilled out.

Chris stood, easing his wife to her feet. He stepped to her right, wrapped his arm around her waist and led her to the dance floor. Without letting her go, he turned to face her, his arm locked around her waist. He glided along, practically carrying her. When he turned, he lifted her good hip with his, smiling at her all the while. "You can stand on my feet if you want," he whispered.

Erin shook her head but flashed him a grateful smile.

"See, you can dance. You are more beautiful now than you were a year ago." Chris claimed. "And just as brave. 'I love you more today . . . ,'" he sang quietly.

Overwhelmed by his support, Erin gazed into his amber eyes. "And you're more loving and gallant, if that's possible. I love you madly, deeply. Thank you." She leaned against his solid strength.

He motioned for others to join them. "Let me know when you need to sit down. I have an oxy." He nodded as Reese and Danelle slid by, she stylish in a black, dropped-waist shift complete with swaying fringe like a 1920s flapper.

"Very retro," Erin commented.

"My best Gatsby interpretation," Reese noted. Hair trimmed, face shaved, and looking rested—a debonair Rufus Sewall doppelganger. His black and grey pinstriped suit with vest complemented Danelle's attire.

"And quite an impression, wouldn't you agree?" Danelle chimed in, her head canting to Savage's attire as her strand of pearls jumped in tune with a jazzy number.

"More like *A River Runs Through It*," Chris added.

"Works for me," Reese said, twirling Danelle slowly.

After dancing stiffly with her dad, the chief, and Lieutenant Stuart, Erin had to take her seat. Her hip pulsed with pain. Chris escorted her back to their table, pushed the white pill surreptitiously across the tablecloth to her.

"How's the pain?" he asked. "You're a bit pale."

"Grinding like a gyro," Erin admitted. "Can we call it an early night? I hate to be a party pooper. You went to all this trouble to surprise me. I'm truly happy but the plain's getting louder." She laid her hand on his. Downed the pill with a sip of champagne and then switched to water.

"Just get well. Hang on for a few more minutes." Chris mingled, thanking their guests for coming. "Enjoy yourselves. Thanks for coming and sharing our anniversary. We're honored. Yes, it flew by. Yes, thanks, Ian's fine—sitting, crawling, and teething."

Ethan and Janelle McCoy stopped by the Snow's table. "No, Erin, don't get up. Happy anniversary! What a night: great food, energetic young people, but it's time for us to go," Janelle said. Both hugged her gingerly.

"You guys fix up nice! Thanks for coming," Erin smiled wanly, waiting for the pill to kick in, her pain etched in the tight lines around her eyes and mouth.

"Get some rest. See you Tuesday." Ethan kissed Erin's cheek.

At home, Chris parked in the garage and carried Erin in, her face tucked in the crook of his neck, her auburn waves tickling his chin and breath soft and warm, smelling faintly of garlic.

Ian lay in his cradle, sleeping on his side, a blanket rolled behind him. He'd kicked off his "boo" blanky.

Undressing his wife, he tucked her in bed on her back, knowing she'd roll to her left side to relieve pressure on her injured hip.

Then Chris accompanied his parents to the door, nodding at their concern for Erin's health. "She's worn out, and I'm bushed. Thanks for watching Ian. Thank Dreena, too," Chris said.

"Poor girl. She seemed drained, though she'd never let on," Erica commented. "Such a trooper, but she'll get better soon."

"We just let Shadow out. She's good for the night," his dad said. "I heard the dog snoring when I passed the gate."

After they left, Chris set the alarm and flicked the light switches off. Went to the bathroom, then sliding his clothes off, eased in beside Erin, slipped soundly to sleep within minutes.

Neither heard the tap-tap-taping in the cornfield.

25

Kelly Sims paced in the parking lot. "Don't think I can do this. Hypnosis—it's a pseudoscience or like what—a séance? I don't need Mary Grace to put me in a trance. I know what's eating me!" She consulted her watch impatiently, scurried back to her car. "I only have an hour; that's not long enough to go into it."

The door shoved open; in an apple-green, knit pantsuit, Mary Grace peeked out. "Come on, chicken. Time's a wasting!" She motioned her inside conspiratorially.

Inside, her friend gestured to a recliner. She'd already drawn the blinds. "Kick your shoes off." Slipping quietly behind Kelly, she applied lavender oil to her temples and wrists. "Relax. Just let your mind go blank, focus on the pendulum."

Kelly reclined, levered up the footrest, her arms floated on the butter-soft leather armrests. "Don't need hypnosis to tell you what irks me: Love is cruel, it enslaves us. Women lose what we value most: our autonomy. American culture thrives on this illusion that love is some ecstatic, vaulted state! Believing the fairy tales, we leap into marriage like blind fools . . ." She counted ten swings of the pendulum, then fifteen. "Denny and I were fine for the first two years, but . . ." Twenty, the pendulum slowed, the arc almost visible. She sighed, closed her eyes.

"Can you hear me?" Mary Grace asked softly.

"Yes, I can hear. You sound far away," Kelly observed.

"What day is it?" Mary Grace asked.

"Wednesday?" Kelly wasn't sure. "Time seems elastic."

"We're going back in time. Comb through your memory for the traumatic event that crippled your marriage. Skip the bickering over the little annoyances, like leaving the lights on or the commode seat up. Those irritate all couples. Focus on that incident that shook you to the core. Tell me about that."

"So many, which to chose?" Kelly breathed a sigh. "So hard to choose just one. Loud, at parties, he sucked all the oxygen out of the room. . . . No, the dinner at Rockwell's with friends. Snowing out. We were ordering. Denny asked the young waitress what time she got off work. Couldn't smile and pretend I hadn't heard, my ears burning, so I excused myself, drove home, leaving him there.

"No." Kelly corrected herself. "It was the time I discovered I was expecting again. Drew was an exceedingly active toddler. Kept us both on the run, from jumping down the slide to crawling through tunnels playing G. I. Joe. So Denny didn't want another child. He'd just started playing with Drew. Said I'd have another kid hanging on my tits for a year. That's when I knew for sure.

"Another time, Denny decided to take down the Smurf collection Drew and I had displayed in an old linotype case hanging in his room. He packed it away and relegated it to our musty basement, a subterranean tomb of forgotten memories because 'the boy was too old for them'—as if imagination had an age. I resented that arrogance—that he dictate our lives like discrete demarcations exist."

Mary Grace said quietly, "That incident affected you deeply."

"Drove me to tears, but Denny said I was too sensitive. Then my parents needed me to drive Dad to the Mayo Clinic. Mom's afraid to fly. Well, Dad doesn't trust his life to the pilots either. "No way but down," he'd say. And they wouldn't leave my fifteen-year-old sister alone in the house or with us. Hell, Mom and Dad were too old to make that trip by themselves.

"Of course, when Camie arrived, Denny adored her. Father and daughter bonded immediately. But . . . there was something wrong with him—or us.

"Denny never showed us any empathy; not once did he extend a hand to comfort the kids and me when we were hurt or sad. Not when I lost a baby, not when Drew was hospitalized for asthma, not when Camie broke her leg playing basketball. But with neighbors, his employees, or even strangers, he would go out of his way to please: run errands, mow lawns, or shovel driveways. Stop and chat. Hand out lottery tickets and bonuses to employees.

"And his sense of timing was skewed, I felt. He told ribald jokes at funerals, made caustic comments about the oddest things. And seemed obsessed with sports trivia. Wouldn't miss a Steelers game, not even on Christmas Eve! Sometimes his conversations seemed scripted—or he depended on platitudes, like 'You can bank on it. Or I'm hungry as the devil.'" Kelly opened her eyes, blinking, canted them to Mary Grace seated beside her. "I'm awake. Am I being hypercritical?"

Her friend smiled. "Some people aren't susceptible to the power of suggestion. Plus, memories aren't veridical. Your dreams and fantasies affect memory, too. And you're also under the stress of uncertainty and the strain on the unknown, plus you're grieving, though Mrs. Independent won't admit to needing any help."

"Oh yes, I do. My family and friends, you mostly, are helping tremendously! I'm only able to function because you all have my back. I can confide in you; you won't gossip about how terrible I am. At work, my assistant Jill handles most issues herself. I know I sound bitchy and ungrateful."

"You're not terrible; you're human! Don't beat yourself up. You did your best as a wife and parent with a full-time job. You'd be surprised how many of my clients feel like their spouses take them for granted in their relationship.

"But sounds like Denny may have had a mild form of Asperger's Syndrome. His manual dexterity was excellent, but the condition manifests in other traits: too loud and dominating conversation, lack of empathy for others, need for attention and inappropriate behavior in social situations. And that type-A personality. That nervous tic in his eye. How about restless leg syndrome?" Kelly nodded. "Don't judge him too harshly. He did his best to provide for you and the kids, too, you know; maybe he felt inadequate." She covered her friend's hand with hers and squeezed.

Sims glanced at the clock, jumped up. "Now you tell me he had a good excuse for his irascible behavior? And I have to get back to work. Why don't you come to the house next week? I'll make lunch. Who knows how long I can keep the house? But that's a topic for another day!"

Mary Grace checked her appointment calendar. "Yes, I can do that. Then Thursday's Jubilee Day. We've lived in Carlisle for thirty years, but we've never attended Jubilee Day. Can you believe that? So I promised to take Alyssa." Made a notation, then stood.

Sims shook her head. "Neither have I! Always working, it seems, but I enjoy work. The camps are in full swing with new ones starting next week, so I need to be on campus to make sure everyone has the supplies they need. Direct the kids to the dorms, cafeteria, pool, or wherever they need to go. Hold their hands until they're comfortable." She hugged her friend. "Thanks a bunch. Couldn't handle the stress without you!" She waved her hand. Stopping in the vestibule to rummage for her keys and sunglasses, she pushed out the door—into the path of Detectives Christopher Snow and Reese Savage. "Grr. Sorry, I have to return to work."

"We'll follow you there. We have a few more questions." They both smiled cordially. "Do you have a private office?"

She nodded and trekked determinedly to her vehicle, frowning and trembling, her good mood evaporated.

26

Jubilee Day dawned overcast, fitful as a tantrum. A fine mist hung in the air, and then a rainy wind slung needles onto sidewalks, vendors' canopies, and unprepared spectators. They scrambled for cover and crowded in recessed doorways as the rain peppered down. Suddenly, the clouds dispersed, and the sun quickly steamed the sidewalks dry.

Workers and volunteers from a hundred businesses, organizations, and eateries had arrived at 6:00 a.m. to set up along Main Street in Mechanicsburg. Vendors handed out coupons and samples. Non-profit volunteers stacked pamphlets to give away. Smoke from grills wafted into the street where people bellied up for London broil hoagies topped with fried onions, mushrooms, and melted cheese. Across the way, a Chinese couple stir-fried lo mein and prepped other traditional dishes. French fries and funnel cakes scented the air. Others hawked fruit smoothies, lemonade, milkshakes, and tropical drinks in coconut shells.

Mechanicsburg police with K-9 officers meandered along the empty street where throngs of people would congregate at 10:00 a.m. for Pennsylvania's largest street fair. More than sixty thousand people would enjoy the festivities. The Carlisle Police Department was sending a contingent as well to assist the Mechanicsburg force.

The Musketeers, Officer Mahoney and partners Chase Rivers and Gabe Summers, traded cycles for horses for the day. Detectives McCoy, Fields, and K-9 officer Shadow arrived early enough to snag a parking spot in the alley. Driving the handicapped van, Fields lowered the motorized chair to the ground while McCoy's fingers fumbled with Shadow's K-9 vest and leash. "Let people watch you," she said. "If you lead, maybe they won't notice me." Mac's first outing in public since her shooting, she felt anxiety creep to the surface, seep through her pores.

By nine thirty, they trolled down Main Street watching the vendors display their wares: NCADV had cards with their hotline number, pamphlets, and placards with warning signs of domestic violence bulleted. Im-Paws-Able Dog Rescue offered adoption information and refrigerator magnets with a cute puppy logo.

Mac made a U-turn at PNC Bank, finally adjusting to her wheels; she had her cane in case she had to assist in an emergency or arrest—just couldn't respond quickly. Her Powershot was stowed in her purse, bottled water and dog treats in an insulated lunch bag.

Few paid any attention to her but eyed Shadow, whose eyes slewed from side to side, nose in the air, mutely assessing passersby. Casually dressed shoppers milled by, stopping to talk to the vendors or ask questions. Teens strolled along in tank tops and shorts, drinking slushies and smoothies. More arrived by the minute, clogging the road. Ahead of her, a lanky clown loped along and whistled a catchy tune. A mass of colorful helium balloons enveloped him, blocking her view. Mac hummed along, "You may be right, I may be crazy . . . ," a Billy Joel song.

Fields jogged toward her from the other end of Main Street. Twelve feet beyond her, a knot of individuals was clustered in the middle of the street. Mac wheeled up. A man lay motionless on the macadam. "Police! Break it up, people. Move along unless you are related to this man or witnessed his fall." Shadow shouldered her way through, throat rumbling; people scattered; Fields scrambled to her side. The man staring at the sky had a letter opener stabbed into his chest with a $20,000 check made out to Salvatore, last name blotted out with blood, signed by

Dennis Sims. The memo noted: 'Paid in Full.' Shadow skirted the body, sniffing.

"Did anyone see anything? Move to the sidewalk, I'll need statements from each of you. I need to check your hands," Fields ordered, palms up. About seven backed up obligingly, palms out.

Mac called it in to MPD. "Homicide at 50 W Main Street, Mechanicsburg, opposite Sunbury Press." Before they arrived, she photographed the body—about her height, dark unkempt hair, eyes glassy, wearing expensive slacks and a dress shirt, sleeves rolled up to the elbows. No tie. She gloved up, snapped a close-up of the body, weapon, and check. Patted the man's pockets, located a wallet. Driver's license read Salvatore Carrelli, DOB 10/31/51. She pocketed the business card.

Mechanicsburg Police surged onto the scene, dropping sawhorse barriers, making a fence with crime-scene tape. Erected a canopy. A burly bulldog of a man stepped up, taking over. "Move away from the body, ma'am. You'll contaminate the crime scene." He called for CSU and a coroner.

Mac flashed her shield. "Erin McCoy, CPD Homicide. My partners and I are guarding him until Homicide gets here." Her head canted to Shadow while Fields took statements. "And you are?"

The uniformed officer scratched his head. "Cole Taylor. How did you arrive on the scene so quickly? Were you tailing or talking to the victim? Did you witness the crime?" He shot questions rapid-fire while adjusting his utility belt, pulling out a spiral notebook. Sweat stained his shirt. His shoulder radio squawked; he ignored it.

"No. We were assigned to assist today—community policing. We came upon a fracas—a knot of spectators surrounding the vic. However, the deceased is connected to a current CPD Homicide investigation, so we'll need to coordinate our investigations." Shadow inserted herself between her handler and the interrogator, sat, looked up at the man, assessing the threat, throat humming in warning. Fields waved curious onlookers along.

"How do you know this?" Taylor asked, pen in hand. He glanced at Shadow warily, stepped back but kept his attention on Mac.

"The check was signed by a dead man—our homicide victim, Dennis Sims," Mac related.

Taylor did a double take, leaned over the corpse to examine the check, and then straightened. "Keep moving, people. Enjoy Jubilee Day. Spend some money." He smiled civilly to ease the demands, which deepened his forehead creases. Turned back to her. "And dead men can't cash checks. It was dated yesterday. When did your vic die?"

"Three weeks ago." She handled over Carrelli's wallet, which she'd dropped in a glassine, dated, and labeled. "I found this. He was a Mechanicsburg businessman who owned a loan company and a pizza place. Our vic owed him $20,000. Looks like he paid up."

"You trying to be funny, Detective?" Taylor looked her over, eyes taking in her wheelchair.

"No, sir." Still, she cracked a smile. "Just saying."

Crime techs swarmed the corpse. A perky little man with a grey crew cut wearing a short-sleeve dress shirt with a blue bowtie marched alongside, sidled up to the body. "Tsk, Tsk. G'day, lady and gents. Gonna be beastly hot; he'll rot fast. Nasty wound. Stabbed in the heart. COD: exsanguination. Well, I can call it a day. Send him to the morgue, Taylor."

"Not quite yet." A white-haired detective in plain clothes—shield winking at his belt, hiked his pants up, raked eyes over Mac and Shadow, and then crouched down to observe the corpse. "Wallet?" Taylor extended the wallet in the evidence bag. "Who bagged this, you?" His sloe eyes assessed Mac, then the wheelchair, and slid to her K-9.

"I was first on the scene." She exposed her shield and sheathed weapon.

Fields flipped his notepad shut, strolled over beside Mac, introducing himself to the detective. "This is my partner, Detective Erin McCoy." He waited a tic, then asked, "And you are—?"

"Loman Richards. Thanks, but we'll take over from here. We'll keep you informed on our progress. If you'll just give us your statements, then you can be on your way. And I'll take those witness notes."

Shadow growled in disagreement. Richards regarded the dog solemnly, stepping away, and clasping his hands behind his back, giving her space. Pursed his lips, waiting.

"Sorry, we need these for our homicide investigation," Fields insisted, and pocketed the notebook. "We'll send you copies, if you have a card with fax and phone—"

Richards frowned, whipped out his wallet impatiently, handed Fields a card. "Now, if you'll excuse us, we'll proceed." Meanwhile, more bystanders stacked up, asking, "What happened? What's the tent for? Did somebody have a heart attack? Shouldn't we call an ambulance? What's that foul odor? Who's in charge here?"

Someone from the booth of a local radio station approached, mic in hand.

Aiming for the sidewalk, Mac said quietly, "Let's go. Shadow, come." The dog was mouthing something. "Drop it!" She held out her hand; a wadded, wet ball of paper landed in her hand. "Good girl! Here's a treat!" Mac dropped it in a paper bag, folded, dated, and labeled it. Pulled the sticky gloves off. Stuffed them in another bag.

Fields noticed the media approaching, "I'm right behind you."

From the alley, Shannon and Gabriel clopped up, the black horses parting, dispersing the crowd. Their massive shoulders and chests were stained with sweat. "You're causing a logjam, folks," Mahoney observed. "Step aside, let the police proceed with their business."

Detective Richards slapped his forehead. "What else? Witnesses, please stay. Everyone else, please move along, enjoy your day!"

Summers guided his horse between the spectators and the tent, forcing them to scatter to avoid being trampled or bumped. Both animals, black with white splashes down their noses, had to be seventeen hands high with hooves like plates.

"Mahoney, got a minute?" Mac asked, guiding the wheelchair up a cut in the sidewalk at the intersection. Mahoney dismounted, exuding lime and coconut scents of her sunscreen. Mac showed the CPD officer Carrelli's photo. A shadow of recognition flicked in her eyes. She whistled. "Damn! Sal! A check from Dennis? How'd he do that?"

"You know him?" Fields stood looking over her shoulder. Summers held Mahoney's mount; his horse tried backing up. He tightened the reins, but the horse shifted his weight nervously, his hooves clacking the macadam.

"Yeah. Denny used him whenever he was maxed out at the local banks." Her sculpted face studied the photo; she returned it to Mac.

"Maxed out?" Mac waited for more information.

"My brother-in-law was a big spender. He had stuff Kelly didn't even know about—a little cabin cruiser docked at the Susquehanna, an RV campsite in Perry County for him and his hunting buddies, an apartment in town. He also kept running bar tabs at local watering holes."

"You seem to know more about him than his wife. You two have something going on the side?" Fields asked.

"Watch your mouth, Zach. You think I'd two-time my sister? You don't know me." She responded heatedly, her low ponytail flipping as her head snapped around to challenge Fields.

"It's a legitimate question, Shannon," Mac said gently, "given what you just said. Okay, so how do you know all this?"

"Most locals know. Kelly's so focused on her career and kids, she doesn't know half of what he did. But it'll come home to roost when she has to liquidate her assets just to break even. I tried to broach the subject, but she says repeatedly, "Let Denny worry about the finances. I'm running the household. Even now she says, 'Don't worry about it.'"

"Did he have a mistress? Someone have a secret habit that needed support? Drugs or baby, perhaps?" Fields asked.

He might as well have slapped Mahoney's face. Her neck and face flushed crimson. "Don't be a dick. How would I know that? Think he'd tell me? I'd tell Kelly about something that serious. Don't jump to conclusions.

"I meant one-nighters, and not necessarily Denny's. His buddies have keys. Often they huddle around a big-screen TV to watch football games and drink beer." She tossed her ponytail, took the reins from her partner, shoved her foot in the stirrup, grasped the saddle horn, and remounted. "Let's go." The cowboys wheeled around, the horses' hooves clattering down the alley.

"Hey, don't know about you, but I'm starved. I could eat—" Fields said.

"Don't say a horse!" Mac retorted.

He laughed, watched her pour some water in a cup for Shadow. "Let's find some shade. I need one of those London broil hoagies. How about you? My treat."

"I'll take chicken lo mein. Ask for a fork and napkins, please. We've got water. When we're done, I want to swing by the Sunbury Press store, pick up a new mystery." But she was talking to herself. As her partner had already galloped off in search of food.

She dug out a chicken jerky for Shadow to munch while they waited. Punched her iPhone button to leave her husband a voice mail. "Chris, we have another homicide: Sal Carrelli stabbed with a letter opener with a $20,000 check attached, signed by Dennis Sims. I'll forward my photos. MPD has taken over the case, dismissing us—even though I mentioned the connection to our vic. But I have an idea."

27

At home that evening, Chris kicked back, cradling Ian on his crossed leg, holding his shoulders, rocking him up and down. Arms hugging his daddy's legs, the baby giggled. "'Gin!" he demanded when Chris stopped to rest.

"Good work. How fortunate to be first on the Carrelli homicide scene. Who wanted to shut him up and why has the check surfaced *after* his death? It doesn't make sense. What's your idea?"

"So he couldn't cash it, of course. I'll bet Sims didn't have the cash on hand. But there's more to the story." She related Mahoney's news. "She nearly took Zach's head off when he asked if she and Sims were hooking up. I'm thinking something happened between them back in the day. Have you ever seen Camie Sims?"

"Yeah, streaky, blonde hair, tall, lean—perfect as a mannequin." Then he caught it. "Like Shannon Mahoney. But Camie has blue eyes; Mahoney's are aqua. The girl's face is fuller, her complexion olive. And my nephew Kyle favors his uncle Jack more than his dad, so that could be genetics. People say I look like my grandfather, so I dunno—it's a long shot."

"Well, aren't you observant! Let me do some research. Which reminds me, I need to check on a wad of paper Shadow took from the crime scene." At her husband's quizzical glance, she explained. "I didn't realize it until the detective dismissed us. We were on our way back to the vehicle." Stopping to concentrate on her movements, she pushed up with her cane, waddled lopsided over to her things dumped on the island. Donned latex. Pulled out the paper bag. Opened it. Laid a paper towel flat. Carefully smoothed out the damp paper over it.

Curious, Chris followed her, jiggling Ian, and peered over her shoulder. "I'll be damned. Where'd Shadow get that?"

"From the crime scene. How prescient: Cameron Annette Sims's birth certificate. Look, parents Dennis and Kelly Sims. Indiana University Hospital. Terre Haute. That's funny. Signed by an ER doctor—not an OBGYN. I wonder what happened." Erin frowned.

Ian lunged forward, grabbing a lock of his mother's curly auburn hair and stuck the strand into his mouth. "No, baby, don't chew momma's hair." Chris disengaged his son's fist, but then the baby started whining, leaning toward Erin, arms extended.

"Here, it's past his feeding time. Come on, Son. You can drink first while daddy fixes supper. What are we having tonight?" Erin asked.

"I'll make pastrami Rueben paninis from what your Dad left. Have to root around the fridge, see what else I can find." He returned to the topic. "Shadow must've taken it from Carrelli's hand or somewhere near the body. Why would he have her birth certificate? Is it real? Is it related to his death?"

"Blackmail?" Erin asked. Shadow whined at the mudroom door.

"How so? Who, why? Look, this belongs to the MPD. I'll have to drop it by sometime tomorrow." He let the dog out, watched her, and then whistled her back in.

Erin located her Canon and photographed it again with her cell. "I'll make some phone calls tomorrow. Should I wad it back up?"

He shook his head. "Let it dry. Transfer it to a glassine. You know what? First, we'll send it to our lab, see whose prints we discover, and then we'll send it on with the results. You'll have to explain how you came to have it."

"I'll tell the truth. Shocking, huh?" She and Ian settled in their rocker as dusk scattered golden ribbons over the

Susquehanna Valley, mellowing the day. Fruit trees swayed gently, cherries ripening outside their French doors. The verdant lawn rolled past their bungalow until it met the eleven acres of walnut, pecan trees, and hardwoods. Perhaps a hundred evergreen trees were dispersed among them. "We live in beauty, Ian. See all the colors. Aren't we lucky?"

* * *

Finally finishing his chores, the stranger swept the mouse droppings into a dustpan and set traps. He'd plaster the holes after catching the dirty little varmints, but they were the least of his worries. His wrist felt better; he removed the brace, flexed it. Changed into woodland-green camo. "Can't imagine why she wants to harass that female cop. How I could have missed that shot? Can't blame the leaves. It's my own fault for rushing, not waiting for a clear shot. And then all those people swarmed the spot.

"And in the hospital, that fag in drag surprised me. Where the hell did he come from? This time, I'll wait until all is ready, until I have the advantage." Double-checked and collected his gear, grabbed some water bottles and granola bars, toting his stuff out to the Jeep. Jogged back in for his watch cap and camo paint. Shut and locked the door. Backed the vehicle down the long drive, onto the macadam, down the steep incline. Palming the wheel, he turned east toward Rt. 34, then north toward Carlisle via Mt. Holly Springs. Destination: 8 Lisburn Road.

"This time, I'm going to study her patterns. Lie in wait. Best place would be in those woods out back, except for that dog.

He glanced at the postcard on his visor, words scrawled hurriedly. "*If you want to get paid, get it done.*"

"Get it done and get out," he repeated. "But I wouldn't mind having a little fun with her first. Comely cop, nice rounded ass and full breasts. In and out, get it?" He snickered at his own joke.

28

Shannon Mahoney revved her cycle, waved good-bye to her sister for the second time in as many weeks. "Thanks for breakfast. See you soon."

"Thanks for dinner last night and your company." Thermos and lunch in hand and her purse looped over her shoulder, Kelly opened her eight-year-old Altima. Her cell chiming, she quickly dropped her load in the passenger's seat. "Hi, Mary Grace. Yes, I remember. I'm fixing lunch." She listened, shoved her key in the ignition. "No trouble—a chef's salad with frozen almond mocha bars for dessert. Okay, see you at noon."

By the time she returned to her house at lunchtime, Mary Grace was parked, car running, thumbing through her e-mails. She cut her engine, climbed out, and pocketed her cell. "Oh, good. I hate wasting gas on the AC but detest hot weather even more."

"Oh, you think this is hot? Wait until August! Come on in. Are you hungry?" Kelly asked her friend.

"YES! I only had a protein fruit smoothie for breakfast. Then ran to my 8:00 a.m. appointment, then met one every hour after that: a troubled teen referred to me by the court. A wayward, bored wife trying to justify an affair. An anorexic inching her way toward eating properly. Anyway, how's your day going?"

"A ballerina had a meltdown because someone else was chosen for the lead in the summer production. I'm wilting! Let's get out of this heat before we melt." She wrangled her house key, let her friend in, and breezed into the seventy-three-degree house. "Oh, that's better! Come on. If you throw the plates on, I'll get the salad and dressings. What'll you have to drink?"

"Oh, water's fine," Mary Grace said.

"Wouldn't you rather have some refreshing iced tea?" Kelly asked as she opened the fridge for the glass bowl of fresh greens dotted with chopped veggies and grape tomatoes, sprinkled liberally with ham and provolone rolls, cubes of chicken, and quartered hard-boiled eggs. She set it on the quartz island.

"Sure, if you have it." Mary Grace laid her purse down, her shades on top. Washed her hands and set the table.

They chatted over salads. Afterwards, they consumed the frozen almond confections coated with dark chocolate. Then the women eased onto comfortable recliners in the great room where blinds were already drawn against the harsh sunlight.

"I'm glad to see you! You seem less burdened, or you're utilizing the coping skills we worked on. I've been thinking. Last week you said your rift with Dennis recurred. Let's go back to the first one, the one that splintered your marriage. If we can get to the bottom of that, discuss that issue, we may make progress."

Kelly leaned her head back, looked up, and kicked off her low-heeled sandals. "I'm not sure I can. It was so gut-wrenching at the time. Even revisiting it gives me goosebumps. I still can't believe that he was unfaithful. Apparently, our wedding vows meant nothing to him." Tears pooled, then spilled onto her cheeks. She whisked them away impatiently. "I'm so tired of it all. Shannon spent the night last night. We cried over it—how he ruined our marriage and her teen years, too."

Mary Grace set her mini CD player, pushed start. Soothing strains of a flute emanated from the machine. "Just shut your eyes and listen to the music for a few minutes. Relax. Remember, this incident happened years in the past. It's over. You survived. Then start when you're ready."

"I was expecting again. Because I was spotting, we rushed to the hospital. Shannon came over to watch

Drew. My OBGYN met me, admitted me overnight. They wanted to run tests, make sure my pregnancy was viable. I returned home the next day with orders to work half days, bed rest in the afternoons. Mom and Dad kept Drew that week. One afternoon a couple of months later, my parents and Shannon came calling. My sister was a mess, sobbing—blubbering about something.

"I was clueless. Slowly, haltingly, the story unfolded." Kelly continued her narrative, relating how her husband had come home that night to find Shannon making out with her boyfriend. They'd been drinking wine. Denny broke it up, sent him home. So he called my parents and told them that she was spending the night here because he didn't want our parents to find their fifteen-year-old wasted.

"Drew was upstairs sound asleep," Kelly said. "Dennis claimed he was trying to help Shannon into the guest bedroom, but he bedded her himself. Tried to convince me that she came on to him. The nerve—he forty something and she fifteen at the time! And in no shape to resist. Those words burned holes in my soul.

"On top of that, Dad was experiencing these debilitating migraines—trekking from doctor to doctor with no results. He'd been to Hershey, Pinnacle Health, Johns Hopkins, and I don't know where else to find the root of the pain." She stopped, swallowed, unable to continue. "Gave mother a scare—she lost weight worrying about all sorts of illnesses he might have."

Mary Grace waited quietly, patiently, while the Native American Spirit CD played, the flute floating, chasing butterflies, followed by the cleansing pitter of rain dripping into running water.

Kelly completed her story. "Now you know. How am I to reconcile that? How does marriage survive such a betrayal? For long stretches, I'd forget, but a glance would send me plummeting into a downward spiral. I put a deadbolt on our bedroom door for a while. He got on his knees and begged my forgiveness but was really riled up that I locked him out of our bedroom."

The images paged across her mental screen.

"I'm sorry, sorry. How many times must I say sorry? The kids had been drinking. Shannon could hardly stand. We did this clumsy waltz into the guest bedroom. She was nearly naked . . ."

I said, *"I don't want to hear a play by play. I'll never get it out of my mind as it is. Go away. Leave! You betrayed our wedding vows! Did they mean so little to you? And you disgraced my family and ruined Shannon's chance of going to college. What's she going to do now?"*

"Let me in. I'll make it up to you, I promise. I love you. I need you. I'm on my knees. I swear it was the first and only time, a weak moment. She threw her arms around me! Please! Let me in."

"When I finally opened the door, he removed the deadbolt."

Kelly tried shaking the images from her mind: "Denny stormed in, ripped off my tee, turning me over, ramming brutally into me, cursing me for holding out. He said, 'I'm not particular. If I can't have your sweet pussy, I'll take your tight ass.'"

Mentally, the scene unspooled.

"OW! OW! STOP! You son of a bitch!" Screaming, she'd fought back, kicking him in the groin. He dropped to his knees. The throbbing pain in her rear radiated out, sending a current of anger surging up her throat, adrenaline fueling her burning rage. Scissoring her legs, she clamped them around his neck. She clung like Death, squeezing until his face purpled. "Why do you hurt me? You think I'll forget? That I'll want to sleep with you? The pain you inflict kills any love I once had." The pain scalded her body and seared her psyche.

"Stop! You're breaking my heart," *he spewed facetiously.* "I'm really sorry, but you retaliated. You hurt me, too, but I still love you. Just don't do that again." *His eyes glittered. Then he grinned manically.* "You're sexy as hell when you're mad!"

"You really don't get it, do you? *Kelly grabbed her lighter from the nightstand. Flicked the wheel; the flame kindled.* "I'm signing up for self-defense lessons tomorrow, but if you ever try that again, then don't go to sleep." *She drew the flame perilously close to the bedspread.*

"You'd do that? Like in that Farah Fawcett movie? You're crazy."

＊ ＊ ＊

But she couldn't tell Mary Grace that.

Kelly concluded. "But in the last five years, he seemed to have forgot . . . acted like his adultery never happened, became increasingly suspicious of me—hovering, nattering on—when he was the one who'd cheated."

Mary Grace waited a moment, and then said, "Transferring his own guilt onto you, a common enough occurrence. And yet you survived. Functioned—one day at a time. Pain and insult—especially from someone who is supposed to love and protect you—is impossible to forget. But can you forgive him? A festering grudge—that angry burden—is destructive to your mental and physical health. It's eating at you still. It's hard, but try to let it go.

"Unclench your hands and your heart. Erase it from your memory now that he's gone." She wiped air with her hand, letting the music play on, quietly waiting. "When you awake, you'll feel refreshed since you unburdened your secret." She snapped her fingers to end the session.

Kelly opened her eyes, flipped the footrest down, and looked around, orienting herself to the present. Shaking herself, she slipped her feet into her sandals. "More tea?" Jumped up to refill their glasses. "Yes, I forgave him, though it took a conscious effort to put that night behind us, but how can I forget? When your spouse betrays you, that trust is nearly impossible to regain. The stain remains."

Alwine smiled. "Thanks for trusting me with that secret." After a beat, she stood and stretched. "Question is what will the police do when they discover this?" asked her counselor in parting.

29

Mac trudged through the side door at HQ, nudging the cane over the threshold, held the glass door open for Shadow, who ambled through. Slid into her office for the dog's dish, clomped down to the break room for fresh water. Peeked into the conference room: empty at 7:00 a.m. "Ah, great! Maybe I can get this done."

Quickly set up to video the conference. The Indiana University Med Center at Terre Haute ER doctor should just be coming off her shift. A plain, pale face devoid of makeup popped up on the screen: blue eyes, drawn features, and ginger hair shot with strands of grey. She wore blue scrubs, the name on the lapel—Irene Sparrow —matched the one on Cameron A. Sims's birth certificate. "You're Detective Erin McCoy? I expected someone . . ."

"Older?" Mac finished the sentence.

"Sorry. I guess you get that a lot," Dr. Sparrow observed.

Mac nodded. "Yes. Thanks for agreeing to this interview." She stated her reasons for requesting her time. "You may not remember twenty-one years ago, but you delivered a Cameron Sims in the ER room, so I was wondering why—" Mac held up the birth certificate.

"I remember vividly. Oh, not the names but the car accident victims. Out-of-towners. We admitted the whole family. Eldest daughter, the driver, was in the worst shape because a trucker ran a red light, T-boned the car at the driver's door. Front airbags deployed, but she lost her fetus. I won't go into details because they were rather gruesome."

"Then Shannon Sims delivered Camie?"

"Like I said, I don't remember names, but the sixteen-year-old was thirty-four weeks pregnant; the baby was crowning when she was wheeled in. We cleaned the infant up, swaddled her, gave her to her mother, but she refused to hold her. She pointed to her sister.

Shocked and shaken by her own loss and injuries, the elder sister took the baby, nursed her while the rest of the family cried. Their grief stemmed—not from the car accident—but some deep trauma that they refused to share. I assumed the younger sibling was single. The parents' injuries weren't life-threatening: the Mrs. had a broken femur and some stitches to her head, her husband a broken wrist when he'd braced his hand on the dash.

Sparrow glanced back at the file. "I called the resident pediatrician and psychiatrist down to the ER. We admitted all four for over-night observation, and we treated the toddler for an asthma attack. A shooting brought three more to the ER that night and an elderly man fell off a ladder, so I lost track of what happened to the family. So they're okay?"

"Well, I'm not certain, but they're part of a homicide investigation, and all withheld the information that you just related. Thanks for your time. Are you off duty now?" Mac asked.

"Yes, sure. Happy to help. Hope everything turns out okay. They seemed like decent but sad people. I'll sign off now." With a flick of her finger, Sparrow disappeared from the screen. Mac left the interview on Chris's desk.

Shadow nosed her way into Conference One, laid her chin on her handler's thigh, brown eyes exuding concern. "Quiet, girl. Let's go. Can't be caught at work; they might want us to stay." As quietly as possible, she reversed her steps, slipping out the side door. Key fob ready, she pressed; the rear door yawned. "Up!" Shadow jumped into her crate; Mac slipped her a dream bone, latched the gate. "Next stop, the courtroom. Need to drop in on Emma

Hawthorne's trial." Parking in the shade, switching off the ignition, she let the vehicle's windows down an inch. "Ten minutes—promise."

Erin watched from the monitor in the antechamber. Dr. Chen was testifying to the particulars of Marjorie Hawthorne's injuries. "The timeline is unequivocal. The fork to the chest was the fatal injury; the restraints, bruising, and temporal bone hairline fracture were post-mortem."

"How can you be sure?" Counselor Wilhelm asked.

"Because the internal jugular vein was intact. No blood pooled in that area, which would normally occur if she'd been alive."

"So the fatal wound pierced the left ventricle?"

"That is correct," Dr. Chen affirmed.

"Would the victim have survived if someone had called 911?"

"No. She expired within three minutes. The arterial spray splattered the cape the daughter was wearing—"

"Just answer the question asked, please." Wilhelm's brows furrowed. Paused, then asked, "How do you know this, Doctor?"

"The defendant admitted wearing the cape at her kidnapper's trial."

Denise held up her hand. "Please strike the reference to the first trial from the record."

"So ordered," the judge assented.

"Thank you, Dr. Chen. You may step down. Defense would like to call Dr. Gerard Drummer to the stand."

Stealing out the back door, Erin hobbled quickly to her K-9 SUV parked behind the courthouse and scooted home. "Looks like they'll wrap it up this week." She checked Shadow in the rearview mirror, her nose tilted up and twitching at the cracked window for fresh air.

Home for lunch, she had time to wash and plucked a bunch of grapes off the stem before her dad brought Ian indoors. He kissed his daughter's cheeks. "He loves the swing! Trade you. He's had strained chicken and applesauce." He passed Ian to her, took Shadow's leash, and eased toward the mudroom door. "I'll let her run through her obstacle course."

Erin sank onto the rocker, nibbling grapes while Ian nursed.

When her dad returned, he laid a piece of brittle, speckled roofing on the island. "What's going on? You guys need a new roof? That's the second piece I found in the backyard." He carried it over for Erin to inspect. "Look, this one's pierced."

"A nail?" she guessed, peering at the hole while Ian nursed quietly. Chills washed over her.

"No, the hole's jagged, shaped like a teardrop. See this little nick? My guess is a grappling hook. Chris needs to climb up there and find out if that sniper who shot you at the reenactment is stalking you. If so, you're in danger. Has Shadow been acting strangely lately?"

Erin shook her head, examining the four-inch square piece of tile. "If she had alerted us, we would've investigated. I'll have Chris check it out when he comes home." She returned it to her dad.

Ethan glanced at her dubiously. "This is serious."

She nodded. "Yes, sir. I'm taking it seriously, but I need to stay calm until Ian's finished."

Her dad nodded, turned his attention to lunch prep in the kitchen. Ducked out to get the fish and corn on the cob from the grill. Set iced tea beside each plate. Back in the great room, he lifted the sleeping baby from his mother's shoulder and carried him into his crib.

Erin joined her father. "Wow—looks great, Dad. What's that?"

"Tilapia with a honey-mustard aioli." He seated himself once he saw that Erin managed hers without difficulty.

"Hmm. See, I'm getting better. Maybe in another week or so, I can ditch the cane." She forked a bite of fish into her mouth. "It's marvelous—sweet and spicy. Thanks again. You're one in a million."

He beamed. "Glad you appreciate your old man. I enjoy cooking. With fresh ingredients right out of your in-laws' garden—"

The landline rang, and her cell chimed simultaneously.

"Hello. Can you hold? I have another call." Without waiting for an answer, she picked up the receiver. "Hello? Chris, I'm handing you to Dad because du Bour—I mean Bowie's on my cell." She listened while her CI updated her on her shooter.

"Think your guy is in the area. Looks like Sheetz in Mt. Holly got him on surveil paying for gas and food. Had a cap on, was wearing woodland green, his face in shadows. We're getting a still printed; Fields will drop it off later. I'm going through the outdoor footage to see if we can get a hit on his vehicle. More later! Over, out." He disconnected.

Her dad related his find to Chris while her husband waited for her. Holding out her hand and looking askance at her dad, she said, "Thanks for holding. I would've told you—"

"I'm coming home now. I asked Ethan to stay until I get there. See you. Bye, love you. If anyone breaks in, you all go to the bonus room. No one will get past that steel door." He broke the connection.

"He hung up! Geesh! You'd think I'm a child, but thanks for your concern. Seriously, I'm not myself, may never regain my agility, but I can manage." Mac punched her fork into the fish, munching in consternation.

Ethan had already lumbered into the garage for the ladder, carrying it around back, extending it to the roof.

Ian on her hip, she followed him out back at a more sedate pace. "Dad, wait. I'm not sure what you expect to find, but please wait for Chris."

The Explorer lumbered up, crunching gravel. Chris switched off the ignition, jogged around the corner. "I've got it. Thanks, Ethan." Scrambled up. Levered himself onto the roof of the bonus room. Climbed up to the skylight, eyes scouring the vicinity. Snapped on latex. Backing down minutes later, he nodded. "Looks like you're right!

"Okay, I need your camera. And see if we have a contact sheet. There's a shoe print up there!" He extended a patch of black cloth. "He snagged something on the corner of the skylight. If we get a print and some information from the cloth, maybe we can track down your shooter before he returns." He smiled. "We'll catch him, babe. Put him behind bars." He rubbed her back, kissed his son and then followed her inside to get what he needed to collect the evidence. "No matter how smart or cunning they are, criminals eventually make mistakes, and this time he left evidence."

Trying to maintain a semblance of normalcy, Erin checked her camera, handed it to Chris, but she was trembling. "Whoever he is, he's brazen enough to watch and stalk us at home. I just wish I knew why this is happening. It's unnerving. My God! Ian's at risk, too. Your parents, Dad, we all are! We need to search the property!"

"He's not here now, lass," her dad said.

"Oh yeah. The black cloth: he stole here in the dark to spy on us." She dropped it into a glassine, labeled, and dated it. Dropped it like a dirty diaper. "Who would be so bold to attack a cop's house?" she wondered aloud.

"We're going to find out. Here, I'll get this to the lab pronto." Chris showed her the zig-zag imprint of the shoe as clear as a photo. "Looks like a size ten." He kissed Erin and Ian and shook his father-in-law's hand. "Thank you, sir. Good work. You're very observant. Now we have more to go on. I'll try to be back by five. Is Ian asleep?" He leaned in to see. "I've got to make some calls."

Erin nodded, leaning into him, needing his warmth and strength, finding that they weren't safe in their own home disconcerting. Despite the eighty-degree heat, chills washed over her again.

Snow kissed his wife quickly. "Thanks again, Ethan." Chris disappeared around the corner of the garage. His engine fired to life; he backed out the driveway and punched in his cell. "Savage, I'll need you and Fields to cover the house for the next three days." He described the scene he'd just left. Next, he called Mac's CI, Bowie. And then made one more call.

Still trying to absorb the shooter's audacity, Erin mused to herself, "And I'm in no shape to fight him off if he accosts or catches Ian and me alone. I've got to find a way to leverage the odds in my favor."

"Which is why you won't be alone," her father vowed. He collapsed the ladder, hoisted it over his shoulder, and stored it back in the garage.

30

The mini-platform in place, he jammed the scarecrow back in the middle. Training taught him to plan. With three secure vantage points near the house, in the woods, and the cornfield beyond, he printed meticulous notes of the cop's comings and goings:

TTh: K-9 training, two men: one like lumberjack; 2nd former military in Redskins' tee/cargo shorts
MWF: M in-law, to and fro w/another young cop/male—partner
S&S: usually home with cop-husband/baby
Trips: Courthouse, Health South PT, Grocery, CPD, K-9 Inst. Site
Visitors: Biker cop, Big man—Dad (?), lawyer, Cop #3
Notes: Cane, agile, neutralize dog; take alone, hand-to-hand
My weapons: Sig, knife, garrote, ketamine.

"Were all amalgams of habits; it's just a matter of observing and waiting until an unguarded moment. Risky. Too many cops around, but if my cousin's paying me $5,000, I can use that to start up someplace new. Still, stakes are high, but I'm an MP, so I can do this, then get the hell out of Dodge."

He lashed the motion-activated camera to a sturdy tree branch. Dug a trench, set a trap, and covered it with dead tree limbs and straw. Lassoed the garrote around the scarecrow's neck. Dripping with sweat in the heat, he paused to guzzle a bottle of water, the crickets' calls ringing in his ears. The sinking sun tinted the horizon salmon. Trees cast stark shadows; long grasses shifted, and cornstalks whispered danger. Time to pack up, hike back to the road where his Jeep was parked, and grab a bite to eat. Then beat a path to his hideout.

Rural neck of the woods, a place called Mt. Holly. Stopped at Hi Hat for a sandwich and onion rings to go. Fountain Coke. Tipped the waitress. Gassed up at Sheetz again, ball cap low over his eyes. Bought juice, an egg burrito, coffee, a bag of bite-sized, powdered-sugar donuts, map, flashlight batteries, and gum.

Gunned the Jeep Renegade down Rt. 34, climbed the road up the mountain while eating. Followed the dark, winding incline—his headlights alone staring for miles. Hauled his groceries and rucksack inside. Cleaned his weapon and sharpened his knife, the snick and snap of metal on metal the only sound inside.

Late. Had to shower, otherwise too sticky to sleep. First, a recon around the perimeter to see if any grass or weeds were beaten down by footsteps or if anyone disturbed the premises. Inspected his traps. Disposed of the dead mice. Cut and hammered boards to fit their holes and caulked them.

"Safe enough to crack the window open?" He breathed deeply; the piney air pierced his lungs. "Fresh and green! Heaven! Yeah, done forever with arid and brown!"

Too adrenalin-fired to sleep, the stranger spread the map open upon the weathered pine kitchen table to trace the best getaway possible. South on Rt. 74 to Dillsburg, then up Rt. 15 north to Harrisburg or south to Gettysburg the most direct. Wouldn't return to the cabin —only one road in and out. Okay, Rt. 174, then 641 east or west also possible options. Or perhaps I-81 would be the quickest route out. Or take all back roads, but he didn't know the geography.

"Soon," he promised himself as he chalked off the days.

31

While ominous clouds curtained the sun, Erin dreamt that their appliances and electronic devices mutinied. The toaster spit out bread, the vacuum cleaner pulled its cord, ran amuck on its own. Her computer whorled the busy color wheel, then regurgitated file after file, words tinkling into her lap—broken black sticks refusing to be reformed. Words destroyed, no more symbols of communication. Meaning denied, or rather jumbled. She brushed them off like strangers who refused to reconstruct meaning.

Suddenly awake, alert—a sound shot to her ears like a sharp retort or shout—a word called out. Stumbling against the end table next to the bed, a hand reached out to steady her, gently pulling her back against his warm body, a hand splayed across her abdomen.

"It's early." His hands caressed her body, resting on her hip.

"I had a bad dream—our electronics mutinied. Toaster spit out bread. Our computer spewed out broken words, nonsensical black sticks. Meanings lost. We couldn't communicate."

"That's okay, babe. Meanings are in people. We'd reconstruct them. Besides, we can communicate without words." Chris kissed her nose and rolled against her.

She stilled. Her mouth tingled. It had been too long without physical contact. Turning to Chris, she whispered, "My mouth is tingling! Rise up, sex me up, and make me bloom."

Bemused, he smiled indulgently. "Your command is my wish." He covered her lips with his, hands tracing the pattern of her curves. Gently, carefully exploring, inching over, fondling satiny soft skin, his hand stopped to heat her ailing hip. Her tongue pushed into his mouth, so he cupped the back of her neck and deepened the kiss, her desire kindling his need to know her again. He entered; she melted into him.

"Help, I'm melting." Finally sated, she smiled against his lips and then propped herself up on an elbow. Her voice roused Ian, who was fussing fretfully but not yet crying, wanting his milk.

Chris changed him and then let Shadow out while Erin nursed her son, who lapsed back into the land of nod. Erin tucked him back in his cradle. Automatically strapping the knife sheath around her calf, she slid her knife into its pouch, slipped into knit lounging pants and a tee, padded to the kitchen. "Where's Shadow?" Grabbed her cell to check for calls and e-mail.

Chris busied himself with scrambling eggs. "I let her out."

"How long ago?" Erin frowned. She never left the dog out unattended, despite the new post and board fence. Slowly, she limped to open the mudroom door and whistled, without results. The minutes stretched out.

She skipped along with her cane, found Shadow lying prone, just under the tree near her obstacle course. A red dart protruded from her shoulder. Punched 911 as she ran her hands over the shepherd's body. "Emergency: K-9 officer down, breathing but unconscious. No blood or broken bones visible. Need vet stat at 8 Lisburn Avenue. Shadow's at the tree line at the back of the property near her obstacle course."

Shirtless, Chris appeared, dashed back into the bungalow for his pistol and cell. Slid a clip home. Called his mother to watch Ian. Dialed CPD. "Requesting backup. K-9 officer wounded. Shooter likely in vicinity."

Outside, Erin warned him. "Shadow's been drugged."

"Okay, go back inside. Wait until Mom comes down." He darted through the trees, weaving and dodging, Glock held down by his side.

"Like hell I will." She checked her dog's pulse—steady, and then hobbled crookedly home for her weapon. Her mother-in-law arrived. "Erica, Ian's asleep. I have to help Chris. My shooter's on the premises; he nailed Shadow! I called 911. She's lying at the start of the obstacle course. Will you direct the vet to her?"

Instantly alert, Erica nodded, motioned Erin out.

A warning shot clipped a branch overhead. Chris was too far ahead for Erin to tell him to look in the trees. Couldn't crouch but used her cane to find cover amid the trees, scanning the low-hanging limbs for boots, a stand, and trace of a stranger. Since Chris had the woods, she skirted the trees, shifted east toward the cornfields. At head height, the dry cornstalks rustled restlessly, swaying, rasping warningly. Her pulse loud in her ears, she smelled the heat of the man. Followed that scent.

She halted, stepping in line with the corn, letting it shield her but avoided grasping husks that would give her position away. The withered leaves wanted rain. Scanning the rows, she notices fresh straw marking the path before her. Her skin crawling, her gut churning, she listens. Peers at the fresh straw—a hole? *What the hell?* Pokes it with her cane; the hidden trap snaps it in two. She stares at the jagged half in her hand, steps past the scarecrow.

Her brain comprehends the new stilt-like platform seconds too late. Her assailant jumps down behind her. She whirls, deflecting his punch, slamming his arm with her cane. Ducks as a knife slashes her forehead at the scalp, blood blooming, running in her eye. She deflects his swing with the back of her hand but drops her Glock. Fumbling for it, a garrote lassoes her neck. Quickly, Mac uses her cane stump to guard her throat. It tightens, cutting off the blood flow, choking. Blood weeps from her wound. Time slows; movement's suspended. Pain and pressure build. Bright dots flash before her eyes. Her pant leg rides up. The garrote tightens. She drops, deadweight, pulling the scarecrow down, forcing him to release her or fall, too. Lightheaded, she reaches blindly for her knife, slices it straight across his groin as she tucks and clumsily rolls under, hip screaming with pain.

The garrote drops. He rears up, raging, knife blade glinting, aiming for a killing blow to her back. A whistling arrow penetrates his bicep. He teeters back, eyes wide: surprised and shocked.

Mac scrambles away from him on hands and knees, gasping for breath, wiping blood from her forehead. Blinded, she hears footfalls approaching.

The scarecrow's left hand, trailing blood, inches toward the arrow; his right still cups his scrotum. He teeters unsteadily.

"You move, you die." Snow chambers a round. Noting that Mac was moving, he steps over her. First, he had to contain the threat. Digs the barrel into the scarecrow's scull.

"So shoot me." The soldier drops to the ground, dripping blood from both wounds.

Jason Lightfoot shifts around the scarecrow. Lifts Mac up. Draws a folded, clean, white handkerchief from his pocket. Presses it tightly against her forehead. Removes his headband from his forehead, winds it around hers. "You'll need stitches—again."

Savage appears, cuffs the prisoner. "Name, rank, and serial number!" he barks.

"Sergeant Daniel Flowers, Army MP . . ." Rattled the numbers. "Help! She gored me!" he exclaimed through clenched teeth.

CI Bowie calls 911. "Officer down with knife wound! Requesting two ambulances at 8 Lisburn in the cornfield east of domicile, approximately a mile from Lisburn. It's accessible from a cart path south of property off of Collier Road. Second one needed for the assailant with arrow and knife wounds to arm and scrotum. Detective McCoy adjusted his anatomy."

"Leave the arrow in until you reach the hospital, son," Lightfoot cautioned. "Less blood loss." The assailant's eyes roll up; he passes out. Her stepfather pressed firmly on her wound. "Can you walk?"

Erin nodded, her lips a thin, blue line, though she wobbled and leaned against Lightfoot.

Lightfoot stayed beside her. "Just like your mother."

Sirens wailed, as ambulances lumbered into the cornfield, brakes squealing, red lights strobing. EMTs jumped out, threw open rear doors, and hauled out gurneys. Pushed them over the dry dirt, kicking up dust. Hemmer loaded McCoy first; others checked Flowers and loaded the unconscious man into the second vehicle.

Back at the obstacle course, the vet Dr. Stacy Wright and Corey Kauffman bundled Shadow onto a stretcher and pealed off to the Boiling Springs Animal Hospital.

32

Hovering between sleep and waking, Kelly Sims stretched, opened one eye—daylight peeped in. She sighed as waking added the weight of her chores on the last day of her leave. Skipping her usual morning shower, she absently tugged on underwear, pulled a tee over her head and stepped into shorts that had been hanging on the doorknob. Then trod down the stairs to the kitchen for coffee. "Do I feel like breakfast?" She rummaged in the pantry, found a granola bar, peeled off the paper, and munched.

Over the weekend, Drew and Camie had come home to help with the eBay sale. The Spode China, a set of pots and pans, ice cream maker, fondue set, Denny's tools, desk, office accessories, and the talking globe had all sold. "All I have to do is address the boxes and ship UPS." They'd also photographed, listed another dozen items, like the bulky BBQ set they'd never used. It'd always been more convenient to drag a utensil from the utility drawer. Drew and Camie also signed over the businesses to her, so she told Abrams to broker the deal.

Her hand rested on the dragonfly Tiffany lamp. She wrote *Keep* on a post-it note and stuck it to the stained glass. Denny had bought the reproduction in New York on their honeymoon. The lamp was dear: all the arduous work and long hours that went into designing, cutting, and fitting bits of colored glass into place and soldering them together. She remembered Nancy Vreeland's labor-intensive description in *Clara and Mr. Tiffany*. The book—written by and about women—reclaimed Clara's story and affirmed for Kelly that hers was as worthy, even if not recorded for posterity. "We were so happy then."

She told the kids to go through the house and stick post-it notes on what they wanted. Drew took his whole bedroom suite. But that was okay. Kelly found a pine four-poster canopy bed at the second-hand furniture shop with a chest to match. Stripped, sanded it, and stained it a honey amber. Slept in it herself rather than in the master bedroom. She'd sell that bedroom furniture, too.

Having strapped and labeled the boxes and stacked them by the front door, she moved on to the next project —defrosting the freezer. It, too, would be sold. "You spend a lifetime accumulating stuff, and then the kids have to get rid of it." She smiled. "I'm helping the kids!" Decluttering made the house feel bigger.

The doorbell chimed. "Mom, Dad, what a pleasant surprise!" Kelly threw wide the door. "Come in! How about some coffee?"

Megan Mahoney threw her daughter a dubious glance. "How about some iced tea? It's nearly ninety out!" She hugged her eldest, shuffled into the kitchen with a tote of produce. "How about I fix a nice salad for lunch? It's too hot for anything else. You have eggs?" She peeked in the fridge, saw the carton. "Six. Good enough."

"How you doing, babe?" Her father bussed both her cheeks. "You're losing weight." He looked around the room at the stacked boxes. "You did all this? We can help you. Did you take off work?"

"Okay! Great! Yes, a week. Everything's running smoothly at work, but I need to go in later to see if my assistant completed the folders. Would you check the garage freezer? Empty the bins if they're full? Thanks. Know anyone who wants a twenty-year-old freezer? I won't use it now."

Her dad said, "Oh, you could put an ad in the papers. I'm sure someone can use it. They don't make appliances like that Frigidaire anymore; I bet it'll last another twenty. Let me ask around. It's a shame you lost the rider and the stuff in the shed. Luckily, I borrowed the push mower the day you and Shannon went to New York. It's on the truck. I'll mow while we're here." He headed for the garage.

Kelly's cell trilled shrilly from the kitchen island. "Hello? Shannon, how are you doing? Mom and Dad are here, helping me clear out the last twenty–five years of clutter!

"What? How do you know?" Paused, listening to Shannon. "I've got to go. I have to get a dozen boxes to UPS. Can you stop by until I get back? You can stall the detectives. Thanks for the warning." Pausing, she listened, then overruled her sister's objections. "So you're on duty? Think of a reason to stop by. By the way, do you need a freezer? You can check it out while you're here. Bye. I'll be back in half an hour." She disconnected.

"Mom, Dad, I've got to drop these boxes at UPS! Be back soon."

Her dad helped her load them in her car and then went out back to mow. Absorbed in boiling eggs and chopping vegetables, her mom apparently hadn't heard her.

On her way, she called Abrams. "I think I'm going to be arrested. Will you come to the house? Shannon called; the Homicide detectives are en route. No, I'm running errands, but I'll be home in a half hour or so. I need to give you the forms the kids signed, too. Thanks." She thumbed end, dropped her cell into her purse. "Damn, damn. I'm a mess. I wanted to get my hair done. Of all the days not to shower!" Then she giggled. "Why today?" What if they drag me to jail? What difference will it all make then?" She felt her heart trip. "Should I call Mary Grace?"

When she returned to the house, Detectives Snow and Savage were waiting. They set their tea glasses on the coffee table, stood.

"Hello, strangers. Are you here to arrest me?" Kelly asked.

"Let's say you're a person of interest in your husband's murder. You've withheld evidence and obstructed an official homicide investigation," Snow admitted. "We'll settle for going over the timeline again."

"Oh, sit down, gentleman, let the girl eat some lunch." Megan Mahoney stood in the arch, salad tongs in hand. "Why don't you join us? Eat a healthy salad, some homemade bread, and explain this to us because Kelly and Shannon were gone that day."

"What evidence do you have?" Shannon leaned against the foyer's doorjamb, arms fisted on her hips.

"The contusion, the broken capillaries in the vic's left eye, the fingerprints inside the kitchen gloves, and Kelly Sims's DNA on the body, for starters," Savage said.

"What about the Carrelli connection?" Shannon suggested.

"That's a dead end," Savage quipped. "MPD's case."

Snow threw Reese a warning glance. "We're looking into it."

Megan Mahoney ushered everyone into the kitchen. On the island sat an inviting tub of salad, a loaf of warm, yeasty bread, butter, plates, and flatware. She handed the tongs to Detective Snow. "Have a seat, sir. Help yourself. Might as well be civil."

He shrugged. His stomach rumbled. "Why not?"

Except for Shannon, the others settled around the table. "Sir?" She was waiting for an answer. "They were married. It's their home. You'd expect her DNA to be present."

"Shannon, please sit down," her mother ordered. "Everyone needs lunch." Handed her youngest a salad plate.

"Several strands of hair pulled out by the roots?" Snow raised his eyebrows. "The salad's cold and fresh. Thanks, Mrs. Mahoney."

"I need to call Gavin. He's mowing. Be back in a jiff." She hurried out the back door waving her arms. The mower droned in the distance, Mahoney's ears plugged against the motor's growl.

"Hair pulling suggests a fight," Savage added, spearing a quarter of hard-boiled egg and dispatching it quickly.

"Or an aggressive kiss," Kelly countered. "But I'll admit we argued that day. But when I left—"

The front doorbell chimed again, Paul Abrams pushed through, stomping his way to the kitchen. "That's enough talking. Kelly claims the Fifth. Did you Mirandize her?" he asked, fumbling for his handkerchief, wiping his brow.

Snow swallowed. "I haven't arrested her. Didn't know you practiced criminal law. Kelly Sims, you have the right to remain silent. If you give up that right, anything you say can be held against you. You have a right to an attorney. If you cannot. . . ," he quoted. "We also found a trace of coffee ice cream on the deceased's left temple. Did you sock him with a brick of ice cream, causing the contusion, which—"

"What? You're kidding? That's ludicrous!" Abrams laughed until his eyes watered, waving away the proffered plate but helping himself to a glass of iced tea. "Do you have the murder weapon?"

Now Shannon was grinning, too. "Begging your pardon, that won't hold up in court, sir."

"Careful, Mahoney," Snow warned. "I may charge you with aiding and abetting a felon, leaving the scene of a crime, and obstructing justice. I can take your badge and weapon, suspend you without pay for the duration." He'd worked his way through the greens, pushed the plate away, but Megan reappeared, offered him a slice of garlic bread. "Thanks. Why don't you join us, Mrs. Mahoney?"

"Oh, I already picked my way through the veggies while I was preparing it. Aren't the tomatoes sweet and juicy this year?" Megan prattled. Her fingers fluttered nervously before alighting onto the back of a chair, griping it firmly for support.

"Absolutely. And thanks for your hospitality," Savage said, a slow smile spreading. "Now, let's look at the facts."

"Please," rejoined Abrams. "They're amusing so far."

Only Kelly wasn't laughing. Her stomach like tilt-a-wheel, she was toying with her salad, hungry and queasy at once.

"Exactly what are we obstructing?" Shannon finished hers, pushed away from the island, and crossed her legs.

"It appears that on your trip to the Mayo Clinic, you omitted telling us about your pregnancy or the fact that Kelly lost her fetus in the car accident. You delivered a healthy, full-term female infant. All of you were hospitalized, but only Drew escaped any injury—though the ER doctor remembers that 'the toddler was shaken and upset.'" He read from Mac's notes. His voice went flat. "You'll admit that information serves as an excellent motive for murder."

Kelly's face flushed crimson; she swallowed and looked away, fighting for composure. "No, not really. It might have made sense twenty-one years ago, but why would I retaliate now?"

"Because he was becoming more controlling, more abrasive and abusive, so you fought back. The court will hear about the mitigating circumstances, the incidents of domestic violence." He, too, pushed back, stood. "Now, if you'll come along with us, Mrs. Sims. We'll do the interview in HQ. If arrested and arraigned, you'll be incarcerated until your trial. With the court's full docket, it looks like August or September at the earliest."

"You can interview her but not arrest her—insufficient, circumstantial evidence based on unsubstantiated hunches!" Abrams bristled as he stood. "Thanks for the tea, ma'am."

Kelly Sims sat frozen, unblinking, throughout Snow's pronouncement. Savage nudged her elbow. "If you'll please come with us."

Slowly, Kelly turned, her eyes stopping at her sister, staring in disbelief, her face draining of color, her mouth working. "Full term? Camie only weighed six pounds. You said eight months."

"Six pounds, eight ounces," Savage noted. "Dr. Sparrow remembered well, then faxed us the records. Your fetus was twenty-six weeks along. We're sorry for your loss. That must have been traumatic and cruel, that your baby died, but Shannon's lived."

"I'm sorry," Shannon mouthed, ascending to her feet and backing away from Kelly's accusations.

"You were already pregnant. You tricked Denny—us—into believing she was his . . ."

"Now, now, Mrs. Sims. Your husband was forty-four, Shannon fifteen. Technically, it was statutory rape," Reese commented.

Kelly still stared at her sister, disbelieving. "How could you? All these years, I've held Denny responsible. Blamed, punished him!" She reared suddenly; her barstool teetered then righted itself. "Leave my house. You're no longer welcome here. Did Mom and Dad know?" Moss-green eyes darted at her parents. Clenching her fists, she dug her fingernails into her palms to keep from crying. "Did you know?" she repeated, her voice rising.

Gavin Mahoney strolled into the great room. "Now, let's settle down. You're not going to arrest either of my girls. They've made mistakes, and, believe me, paid dearly for them. For twenty-five years, Kelly has withstood her husband's ire, his sarcasm whittling away her self-esteem. He bullied her and belittled her considerable talents, despite her best efforts. He treated total strangers better. We all tolerated his passive-aggressive tendencies for your sake," he told Kelly.

"Mom, I have to go," Kelly's eyes filled again. "Don't you see? All these years, I've blamed Denny! Kept him at arm's length. Punished him. The pain nearly crushed me. And it destroyed our marriage. I'll be back in an hour or so, when I've cleared my head." She whirled on her sister.

"Please, Shannon, just leave! It never dawned on me that you could be so duplicitous, so manipulative. Did you get pregnant and then plan to give the baby up all along? Don't you have any shame?" Her voice rose to a pitch. "I don't ever want to see you again!" Tears stung her eyes, her anger electric. Kelly grabbed her purse, thumped through the side door, and dashed to her Altima, leaving the detectives with mouths agape.

33

First, she stopped at the florist's and then drove to Westminster Cemetery, several miles outside of town. Cutting the engine, tugging a stadium throw along, she stalked purposely to the gravesite. The marble marker spelled out his name, birth, and death dates. Underneath, in script was simply written: *son, husband and father.* Just the facts.

Kelly shoved the wreath stand into the earth, and then kneeled on the folded throw to pick the dandelions and pluck the withered flowers away. Now alone, she let the tears flow. "I'm sorry I blamed you when you told the truth about Shannon. I'm sorry I turned my back on our marriage and wallowed in self-pity. I'm sorry I didn't tell you I loved you more, especially if you may've had an undiagnosed condition you couldn't control.

"And while Dad's right—you treated me like a servant, other times you treated me just fine. I love you still and always will. I will never remarry. And I apologize for my part in our failed marriage. But, when you were around, I felt like the sword of Damocles hovered over me. I could never relax—your criticism stung while I stormed around, swallowing the anger burning in my gut.

"But thanks for all your efforts. You did your best, though why you were harder on Drew I'll never know." She gathered the weeds and withered flowers. "I forgive you if you'll forgive me."

She stood, laid the throw next to the marker, sat down, leaning against the cool stone, gazing skyward at cumulus clouds puffing along on the current. Warmth engulfed her, the heat and humidity stifling. Perspiration prickled her scalp.

"Remember our honeymoon at Niagara Falls? Riding the Maid of the Mist, we watched the water plunge into the gorge—thunder in our hearts. Exploding mist glistened like crystal, refracting into rainbows, while the boat inched dangerously close. The mist stung our faces and swallowed our breaths. Finally, the boat keeled hard around to head to port. I nestled against you—rock solid —thinking our love, our lives, would be like that.

"But within the span of five short years, I felt like the Duke in *Twelfth Night*:

The strain again—it had a dying fall.
O, it came o'er my ear like the sweet sound
That breathes upon a bank of violets,
Stealing, and giving odour.

"I'd had enough; obviously, you felt the same. Why didn't we just part company, go our separate ways when the music died? Wouldn't that have been better for us both?"

Jumping up suddenly, she bunched the blanket in one hand, raked the pile of weeds up with the other. "Just listen to me. Now that we can have a meaningful conversation, you're gone, and I'll probably go to jail." Striding to the car, popping the lock, hand on the driver's door, Kelly suddenly realized she wasn't alone. Two men stepped from the trees' lacy shadows, shields displayed.

She giggled at the incongruity, the timing. "Well, if it isn't the cowboys from the Ponderosa."

The first had the wide face and flared nose of Lorne Greene, the Ponderosa patriarch. The second man's round face and bulkier, beefier build resembled Dan Blocker at first. On closer inspection, the first man was not so handsome, the second built solid but not like a linebacker.

"How do you do, ma'am? I'm Detective Loman Richards of Mechanicsburg Police, Homicide." He extended her a paddle-shaped hand.

Kelly wiped her damp ones on her shorts to shake his hand. "Kelly Sims. Are you looking for me?"

"Eric Sanders." The second said, keeping his hands at his side.

"We'd like you to come downtown, answer a few questions about Salvatore Carrelli." Richards motioned toward an unmarked sedan.

"No, thank you. I have an errand to run. As I told the Carlisle detectives, I don't know a Salvatore Carrelli. Apparently, my late husband had business dealings with him. But he's a stranger to me. Sorry." She popped into her Altima and drove off, leaving the officers to follow her.

Speeding until she reached town, she veered into the parking lot in the rear of the Administration Building, still shaking from her brazen departure. A shady space yawned at the end, so she backed the car in until it was shielded from view by a crossover SUV.

She walked into the office building—fifteen degrees cooler than outside. "Thank God for AC." She ploughed through the paperwork; a new batch of campers was due to arrive on campus next week. Her assistant had copied and collated forms with instructions, including a map of the college with dorms, gym, and cafeteria marked. On the reverse, a map of downtown Carlisle with the Back Door Café and other eateries highlighted. A box of Dickinson folders stood beside the stapled papers.

Kelly leafed through them, checking to see that all requisite papers were there. "The health form's missing; we need to know about any dietary restrictions the kids have. Or wait, was that part of the application forms? I've been so preoccupied with everything else . . ." At the file cabinet, she extracted the June camps attendees' forms. Cross-checked the files. "Okay, make a note for Jill to add . . ."

Jill Tanner, her assistant, entered, low heels clicking, carrying a stack of green sheets, placed them on the table with the folders.

"Speaking of the devil. We have another form to add—"

"Kelly, what are you doing here? You're supposed to be on vacation!" She swallowed her surprise. "I mean, how are you doing? I'm so sorry about your husband."

"Thanks." She lobbed the folder to her desk.

Jill patted her boss's shoulder. "I used green for the health forms so they stand out; we can put them first and collect them at the end of orientation, so it won't look like I forgot. Is that okay?"

"Yes, and thanks for the flowers. I saw the card from the department. I'm just distracted. We're still decluttering at the house. There's so much to do like putting things on eBay, bagging stuff for Goodwill, and planning a yard sale. I intend to sell the house, too."

"Yes, ma'am. I can stuff the folders. Two Mechanicsburg Homicide detectives are waiting in the front office to see you. Shall I send them back?" She hefted the box of folders.

But the white-haired Richards and his barrel-chested partner blocked the doorway.

"Sir, will you please bring that stack of stapled forms? I need that box under the table," Jill requested sweetly. Sanders nodded and did as he was bid, stacking the forms into the box and followed the petite blonde—a pencil stuck through the spiky bun on top of her head— back to the front office. She indicated a table beside her desk.

In her office, Kelly motioned to the seat. "Would you like tea or soda? There's a vending machine back down the hallway."

Detective Richards declined, sat down uninvited.

Sims explained her haste. "I've missed nearly a week of work and need to prepare for next week." *Before I'm arrested* she left unspoken.

Richards wiped the sweat from his brow as he waited until Sanders returned, who eased his bulk into the second chair and frowned at her. "Do you want us to arrest you?"

"Whatever for? I told you I didn't know the man, so I'm clueless as to what you want from me." Kelly seated herself behind her desk, back straight, arms crossed—outwardly composed.

"Why did Carrelli have your daughter's birth certificate wadded in his hand?"

"I haven't a clue. You know, the CPD has already covered this territory. Why don't you talk to them?"

"In due time," Richards said. "Where were you on June eleventh?"

"At work. I'm the cooridinator of Summer Programs."

"Surely you must know something." Sanders leaned forward.

"Not relating to your victim. My husband managed his businesses; I had my hands full with work, kids, and running my household. He didn't share his business dealings with me. Before Jubilee Day, I had never heard the name. Detectives Snow and Savage informed me of the man's death when they interrogated me. From what they told me, your victim loaned my husband money."

"You never took a call or had a conversation with him?" Sanders looked dubious.

"Never. I suggest you speak with my late husband's lawyer, Paul Abrams, who was assaulted in his office. Our files were stolen. Or perhaps this Carrelli has employees you can talk to. Now, if you'll excuse me, I have work to do. Then I have to go home and face another mountain of chores before I go to jail." She stood.

Sanders lifted a photo from his pocket, as he lumbered to his feet. "You don't recognize this photo?" He laid it on her desk.

She glanced at it, then picked it up, perused it. "Yes, this man attended Denny's viewing and came to his funeral but left without introducing himself or saying a word to me." Returning the photo, Kelly remained standing. "I still don't know anything about him."

Next, he laid a copy of the paper CPD had sent them. "Is this birth certificate authentic? Why didn't you ask to see it if CPD covered this information?"

Glancing at the paper, Kelly huffed a frustrated sigh. "I have seen it—the day she was born. It's authentic. I don't know why Carrelli had a copy of it. The original, at home in a lock box, has an official state seal stamped on it."

Richards laid his card on her desk. "In case any information comes your way, please let us know. Thanks for your time." He smiled easily, unfazed by her inability to cooperate. "We'll see ourselves out."

"I'm sorry you wasted your time," she said.

"Oh, we always glean something valuable from our interviews. We'll be seeing you." They both shouldered through the door, down the hall, Sanders barely clearing the doorframe. But he didn't duck.

"Is that a threat or a promise?" Sims mumbled to herself.

Jill returned to Kelly's office, concern furrowing her sandy brows. "Sorry, I couldn't help but overhear. Is there anything I can do to help?"

Staring after the Mechanicsburg detectives, Kelly didn't answer, didn't appear to hear her assistant's question. Looking disoriented, she shook her head. "I'm sorry, what did you say?"

Jill shook her head. "It wasn't important. Here, I can put these packets together. Why don't you go home and rest? You're still on vacation. Take a few hours to regroup. These past few weeks have been overwhelming for you, I'm sure. Seriously, boss. I'll call you if anything important crops up."

"Maybe you're right." Sims nodded, collecting her purse, trudging methodically towards the light at the end of the hallway, waiting for the other shoe to drop. Her hands clammy, she felt light-headed when the humid air ploughed into her. Dry leaves edged the sidewalk, withered from the drought and oppressing heat and humidity. Leaning against the building until the vertiginous moment passed, she turned, stepped down, and shuffled listlessly to her car. Popped the lock, collapsed in the driver's seat, keyed the ignition, and blasted the AC.

Her mind like a squirrel ran with images of Shannon's delivery, her refusal to take the baby, giving her to Kelly. "How noble and selfless I thought the gesture, but she intended that all along! Why did she never admit what actually happened? Couldn't she see Denny's betrayal eating at me? Swallowing me whole?"

She pounded the steering wheel with both fists. "Why didn't she tell me the truth?"

34

Mechanicsburg Police Detectives Loman Richards and Eric Sanders entered CPD Headquarters, requesting to speak to Detective Christopher Snow.

"Sorry, sirs, the detectives are attending a briefing. Shall I ring the chief? May I tell him why you want to see him?" Sonja asked, hand resting on the phone receiver.

"It's about our homicide. First, we'd like to lodge a complaint against Detective Erin McCoy for removing evidence from the crime scene. Second, we need to interview her and Detective Fields, the officers who discovered the body in Mechanicsburg on Jubilee Day."

"May I see some ID?" She waited calmly until they produced their creds. "I can handle the first issue, if you're sure." She pulled a form in triplicate from the open file behind the counter and handed it to Richards.

"Do I look unsure, Miss—?" Richards asked, leaning over the counter into her personal space, railroad track creases prominent between his brows. Steely blue eyes pierced hers. Deep slashes bracketed his mouth.

She smiled. "*Mrs.* Sonja Hamilton." She laid the form down. "That would pretty much shut down any cooperation from CPD. Detective Snow is married to Detective McCoy. She's on medical leave after a sharpshooter shattered her hip and continued to stalk her until his arrest."

A full minute passed while Richards considered her words, then he pushed the form back across the counter. "Thanks for the information. We'll return after lunch. Can you recommend a good place to eat close by?"

"Scales on the corner of West High and York Road serves up good homemade soup, sandwiches, and platters. Downtown there's the Gingerbread Man and the Hamilton. The Bruges has excellent steaks. Wendy's on South Hanover is quick. Applebee's is behind the theaters in the MJ Mall."

The second detective opened the door and sauntered out, thumbs hooked into his belt, his holster visible under his khaki sport coat. Surveying the street, he strode toward their Dodge Charger, unlocked the vehicle, turned the ignition, and blasted the AC.

Richards consulted his watch. "We'll be back in an hour and a half. Would you inform Detective Snow that we'd like a few moments of his time? We have questions concerning our homicide. So Detective McCoy is unavailable? What about Zachary Fields?"

Sonja nodded, her lips thinning. "She's on medical leave. The rest are in a briefing or in the field, but I'll give them your message."

"Thanks." Richards nodded, strode out.

Hamilton lifted her receiver, left a voice mail on Snow's office phone. Then sent a TM to Fields's cell. Her heels clicked down the hall, stopping outside the Murder Room where Snow, Savage, Fields, and Stuart huddled in conference. Didn't look like a good time to interrupt, so she returned to her desk.

35

The doorbell pealed. Shannon admitted a bruised and stitched Mac, limping into the kitchen. "Have I interrupted lunch?" Garlic and onion perfumed the air.

"Would you like some lunch, Detective?" Megan Mahoney asked, standing to offer her a seat.

"No, thanks." She addressed Mr. Mahoney. "I just received the lab report from Dennis Sims's toxicology screen. You, sir, are under arrest. You have the right to remain silent—"

"Whatever for?" Mrs. Mahoney's voice climbed an octave.

"Gavin Mahoney's allergic to bee stings," Mac said.

"That's not against the law. What's that got to do with this?" Megan inquired, arms akimbo, her head shaking.

"Let your husband explain," Mac nodded to him.

"As I said earlier, I came over that morning when the girls went to New York to borrow the push mower. I knocked and rang the bell. Couldn't raise anyone, though I knew Dennis was there. His car was in the drive. Anyway, I found him in the kitchen where he must have fallen across the kitchen island, face down, one arm in the sink. Legs and feet tangled in the barstool.

Walking around, I noticed his face was beet red; he was struggling to breathe. Gasping, a nasty bruise on his temple, bloody eye. I said, "Blood pressure up, Son?" Gavin chuckled. "So I helped him along. Put my epi inhaler in his mouth, pinched his nose. Breathe, I told him."

"Epinephrine—adrenaline—would cause his heart to beat faster, Gavin," Megan looked at her husband, surprise rounding her eyes.

"Yes, it does." He agreed. "I said I was helping him along. I told him—"

"Daddy, don't say any more. You need a lawyer. Finish Mirandizing him, McCoy," Shannon said.

"If you give up the right to remain silent, anything you say can be held against you in a court of law. You have the right to an attorney . . ." Mac rattled through the litany. "Dr. Chen said he had too much adrenaline in his system, so in effect, Gavin Mahoney killed him."

Kelly Sims shoved through the front door, stopped, closed it.

McCoy shook her finger at the women. "Officer Mahoney, do not leave town. When we get to the bottom on this, you and your sister may be charged with accessory to murder and withholding evidence in a homicide, obstructing justice, plus other charges unless you decide to cooperate."

"To what end, Detective?" Gavin Mahoney asked. "My daughters have suffered so much damage and acrimony over the years. And consider the community fallout. Both girls could have lost their jobs. Think of the damage this will cause if Drew and Camie find out. Plus, the Sims family could launch a civil or wrongful death lawsuit. We'd be ruined. We were just trying to protect our daughters' reputations."

"We're so sorry, but Camie *is* Kelly's daughter. She's the one who nurtured her, nursed her, rocked her, fed and clothed her, read her stories, helped her grow into a beautiful, accomplished young woman. We're proud of that," Megan added. "And Shannon helped. She never said no to babysitting."

Megan reached out an arm for her youngest, who eased into her embrace, a sob escaping as she laid her head on her mother's shoulder. "No, not once in twenty years. We tried our best. Why, look! To this day, Shannon has remained single. Remember the trips to Disney World, Wildwood, Macy's Thanksgiving Day Parade, and

Hershey Park?" She brushed tears from her own eyes. "Oh, Gavin, why?"

"You know why. You can list a hundred examples. He never gave her a moment's rest, nitpicking about her cooking, her attire, questioning her every move, belittling her job and efforts when I think she's a damned good wife and mother—plus managing a full-time job. Isolating her from friends when he came and went as he pleased. And I finally told him so.

"This is for asking, 'Are you sure that's done? I don't want food poisoning' when Kelly's cooked for thirty years without anyone getting sick, to my knowledge." Red crept up Gavin's neck as he warmed to his subject. "This is for tossing a pack of cigarettes at her, saying you didn't want a fat wife after she had lost her own baby while Camie was still nursing." His fingers pantomimed depressing the inhaler with each example listed.

"*Psst.* This is for leaving her alone with the flu to spend Christmas with your own family."

"This is for sleeping with Shannon. You're an adulterer. *Psst.* Should I go on?" His hands secured behind his back, Gavin Mahoney marched resolutely toward the door, Mac's hand at his back. "I should have done something years ago instead of standing by while Kelly's personality disintegrated. How she's managed to work and raise the kids with any semblance of normalcy, I'll never know. Why, she's been seeing a shrink for years, wearing a haunted, damaged look like Princess Diana," Gavin shook his head sadly.

Shannon's head whipped around. "Mary Grace Alwine? No, Dad, they've been best friends since high school."

"Who happens to be a psychologist? Good-bye, my dears. Don't come for me. I'll handle this." The door whumped shut.

"DAD! NO!" Kelly called after them.

36

At Headquarters, Snow and Savage interrogated Mahoney so Mac could go home. "So you insist on claiming responsibility for your son-in-law's death?" Snow sat across from the man. Mahoney nodded calmly. "You have the right to have a lawyer present during questioning."

"Why pay a suit $300 an hour for him to tell me to be quiet?"

"You realize that you will remain in jail for the rest of your life?"

"Perhaps." Mahoney's guileless face seemed unperturbed.

"All right. Let's go over it again," Savage said. He pushed himself up and paced. "What happened exactly? Walk us through the scene. Why were you at the domicile at 6:30 in the morning?"

"Might've been seven. I wasn't watching the clock. I told you: to borrow the push mover. Mine threw a belt and the landscapers couldn't fix it until the next week. The grass keeps growing, so I went over. Knocked on the door. No answer. I headed around back, got the key, went through the garage's side door, pushed the mower out. Thought I heard a noise—like something dropping, so I went inside.

"Dennis was sprawled across their island, his head hanging over the side, his legs caught in the stool's legs. Looked tangled up, so I walked around to look him in the face."

"Was he alive?" Snow asked.

Mahoney nodded. "He was struggling to breathe. Like I said, I tried to help, giving him bursts of epi—"

"You just happened to have an epinephrine inhaler on your person?" Snow asked, tipping his chair back on two legs.

"I have to carry it with me. Never know when I'll encounter an angry bee. Remember, I'm allergic?" Mahoney said.

"Can't you just stay away from them?" asked Savage curiously.

Mahoney's eyes followed Savage, still pacing in front of the window that mirrored his image. "I try, but when they're pollinating, they tend to get pissed when someone interrupts them. And look at all these yards around the lake, ours included, chocked full with plants and flowers."

"Did you realize Sims had high blood pressure?" Snow asked.

"I did. He took medication for it. Get to a certain age, we're all on meds. Aging's a two-edged sword."

"And what about his temple?" asked Savage.

"Yeah, nasty purple bruise, so he took a blow to the head."

"Did you do that?" Snow asked quietly.

"No, sir. I wouldn't hit a man who's down. That'd be unsportsmanlike." He smiled, his lined face a study in steadfast determination, hands in restraints clasped calmly on the table.

"Would you like coffee or a Coke?" offered Savage, hand on the door.

"That'd be right neighborly of you," Mahoney commented. "A cold Coke would be much appreciated. It's dry in here."

Snow blew out, frustrated. "You're trying to cover for your daughters, aren't you? Kelly brained Sims, and the women ran off to have fun in the Big Apple—alibiing each other. Smart."

"But they *did* go to New York City, would've stayed longer had you not called them back. And they gave you timed parking, play tickets, and receipts, I believe."

"Okay, Okay! Did you see or do anything else? Was he alive when you left the Sims' domicile?" Snow's stomach emitted a long, low, distracting growl. He rubbed his middle to quiet the rumbling.

Mahoney shrugged. "I'm not sure. But I called 911 then. Went back out, put the mower in the truck, went home, and mowed my yard."

"So instead of acting the Good Samaritan, you caused more damage. You're liable for that."

"I called 911," Mahoney repeated.

Savage reentered with Cokes around. They stopped to pop the lids and drink.

"Thank you kindly," Mahoney nodded congenially at Reese, looking from one detective to the other.

"Do you want a trial?" Savage asked.

"I don't know. Would a judge be easier?" Gavin wondered. "I don't want to cause any trouble or cost the taxpayers money."

Snow threw up his hands. "Call the man a lawyer. You need some legal advice, sir. You're giving us no choice. We're arresting you for the murder of Dennis Sims.

37

Robert Orndorf arrived, bustled into the interrogation box, setting his briefcase down, unzipping it, and lugging out a sleek laptop, placing it carefully on the table. Pushed his black-framed glasses up the bridge of his nose, looking studious. Removed his suit jacket, adjusted his tie. Booted up the computer. Extended his hand to Gavin Mahoney. "Pleased to meet you." Nodded at the detectives. "Now if you'll excuse us, I'll confer with my client."

Snow and Savage backed out but watched the men from the mirror in the anteroom. Orndorf asked Mahoney general questions in order to establish rapport. In five minutes, he exited the box. "He just fired me. Acts like he wants to go to prison. Sorry." His wingtips tapped down the hallway to the exit.

"The man's not in the least bit worried," Snow pulled at his chin. "He knows something we don't."

"Oh, I'm sure," agreed Savage, scratching his scruffy chin, which was beginning to itch. "He's taking the fall for Kelly. We can't prove it yet, but she beaned her husband in the head with something."

"A frozen container of ice cream!" Snow leaned against the oblong table. "We found coffee ice cream on his temple."

"Does ice cream get that hard?" Reese looked dubious. "Won't that look silly as a murder weapon? Is that even possible? Not to mention, it'd be difficult to prove; it's long gone by now."

"We'll see. I sent South Street's seven hundred block's trash to the lab. Maybe we'll get lucky. Let's go find out how hard ice cream gets. See what Mrs. Sims's freezer is set at. Wanna bet it contains ice cream?" He stood, unhooked his cell to inform chief where they'd be.

"And if it doesn't?" Savage matched his stride to his partner's.

"Let's go buy several gallons and experiment."

"What if she's not home?" Savage popped the locks, slid into his Bronco, switched the AC on high. Snow climbed into the passenger's seat. "She probably can't lob a gallon container. And what if she buys quarts? And what brand; does that even matter?"

"I'll wager Mrs. Blunt has a key, or better yet, the key's in a vase on the patio behind the house," Snow ventured.

"Okay, I'm game, but what if Mrs. Sims won't cooperate or denies it? We'd have to produce the one she used, if she did."

"Then we'll arrest her for aiding and abetting, leaving the scene of a crime for starters. Let's just rattle her, see what happens."

"She'll lawyer up," Savage claimed as he steered the SUV up the I-81 ramp. Exited at College Street, whipped a left onto Belvedere.

"Abrams is an estate lawyer. Anybody ever tell you that you sound like Eeyore?" Snow asked.

The vehicle stopped at the curb in front of the Sims's domicile.

"Don't we need ice cream?" Snow asked his partner.

"Massey's is right around the corner." Savage switched on the ignition and turned the corner, rocked to a stop within inches of the white brick building with faded awnings over the windows.

Inside, they ordered a quart each of coffee and vanilla.

"I'll have a small chocolate shake," Savage ordered.

"Make that two." Snow pulled a photo out of his pocket. "Do you recognize this person?"

The woman glanced at it and nodded. "Yes, Kelly Sims is a regular. We call her when we make coffee or mud pie."

"How about her husband? He ever stop by?" He showed her a candid of Dennis Sims. She shrugged. "Don't know if I've ever seen him, but we serve hundreds of people every week."

"And how about this person?" He laid a close-up black and white of Mahoney on the counter.

"Yeah, the blonde biker cop. She and the two she rides with come by weekly for shakes."

Snow paid while she bagged up the quarts and set the shakes in front of them. "Thanks."

Bobbing her head, her cropped black hair dusted with silver, she slid to the next window and addressed the next customer.

* * *

The detectives retraced their path, parked in front of the Sims residence as Kelly turned her white Altima into the drive. She climbed out, waited as the men approached. She sighed, unlocked the front door. Pushed it open and stepped aside. "To what do I owe the pleasure of your company?"

"We brought you some ice cream," Savage said, strolling along with her to the kitchen after she unlocked the back door.

She glanced at the bag. "Frozen custard," she corrected.

"Oh, it's not frozen yet. We're here to experiment, with your permission." Snow checked his watch. "You're home early."

"I got light-headed at work when a couple of Mechanicsburg police threatened to arrest me. Technically, I'm still on vacation."

"On what grounds?" Savage stuck the custard in her freezer.

Kelly raised her eyebrows at his audacity. "Make yourself at home. Do they need a reason? Something about Salvatore Carrelli's homicide. They followed me to the cemetery. Didn't know the man. They claim I do—did —because he had a copy of my daughter's birth certificate in his hand."

"Strange, though, wouldn't you agree? Plus, a $20,000 check signed by your dead husband, marked 'Paid in full,'" Snow said, handing her a thermometer. "Would you mind sticking that in your freezer?"

Kelly shrugged, laid it next to the custard containers.

"Set one of you up for blackmail." Savage sat at the island, laid a digital recorder on the marbled quartz. Thumbed it on. "Detectives Reese Savage and Christopher Snow interviewing Mrs. Kelly Sims at 3:00 p.m., June 19, at 769 South Street, Carlisle." He read the case number and other pertinent information.

"When was this?" She pulled her hair back, held it off her neck with one hand, and rummaged in a drawer for a scrunchie. Corralled the chestnut mass into a messy ponytail.

"Jubilee Day." Snow dropped to the barstool beside his partner.

"Denny died weeks before that." She lugged on the fridge handle, withdrew a ginger ale, and popped the tab. "Coke, tea, or water?"

"Coke would be great after that shake," Snow said. "Regular," he directed as her hand hovered between Diet and regular. Savage nodded in agreement, so she withdrew two.

"Did he write that check?" she asked incredulously.

"Yes, our expert says it's your late husband's handwriting. Okay, why would a loan shark be carrying your daughter's birth certificate and a $20,000 check? What's the connection? Did he know that Camie is your niece?"

Sims eyed the recorder. "Correction. Camie is my daughter. I'll repeat that I know nothing about Carrelli other than he attended Denny's viewing and funeral."

Ding-donging flooded the room.

"Excuse me." Sims strode quickly to the door, swung it open.

She blinked, staring at the handsome man before her with wavy sienna hair, wooly brows, and a trimmed mustache—forming a diamond of clear skin over full lips. In a black T-shirt and faded jeans, he wore heavy fireman's boots, which he slipped off and left at the door.

"Hi! I'm Fire Marshall Lane Rusk." He extended a padded manilla envelope toward her.

"Come in." Ushering him into the great room, Kelly said. "I believe you men know each other."

"Is this a bad time?" asked Rusk. Eyes like a winter sky flicked to Snow, who thumbed off his recorder and roved back to Sims. "I wanted to drop the results of our investigation into your shed fire for insurance purposes. Have you filed a claim?"

Rusk reminded Sims of someone—his oval face, squared-off chin, and deep-set, blue eyes. "Not yet. We've been busy with funeral arrangements and . . . ," she waved her hand vaguely at the CPD detectives sitting on her sofa, ". . . a homicide investigation." She looked quizzically at the envelope in her hand, laid it on the coffee table. "Can I get you something to drink or eat?"

Detective Snow stood, pocketed his recorder. "We'll see ourselves out."

"Nice timing," Savage remarked as he brushed by Rusk on the way to the front door. It slammed shut.

"I did interrupt. Sorry. Iced tea would be great if you have it." But the smile belied his words; he made no motion to leave. "And I'd like to offer my condolences regarding your husband. I saw his obit in *The Sentinel,* but—"

"Did you know him?" Kelly's words tripped over his. Releasing her hair, she raked her fingers through the tangles. "No, *thanks* for interrupting. I was about to claim the Fifth and ask for a lawyer. The police suspect me of killing my husband." She extended the frosty glass toward him, took the seat at a right angle to the sofa.

"Don't think we ever met." Rusk studied her: five-nine, one thirty pounds, maybe forty years. Fresh, unlined complexion, a spray of freckles across her nose, lips thinned in resignation. Curvaceous. Chestnut shoulder-length hair fell in loose waves like Katherine Hepburn's or Lauren Bacall's—stylish in the 1940s, but the look suited her.

She blushed. "Thanks. You're not from Carlisle, are you?"

"No. I'm from Camp Hill originally but moved to North Carolina right after college and fire training. Worked my way north over the next decade. Returned home when Dad passed to be closer to my family. Thanks." He took a sip of tea, then a healthy gulp. "It's mighty humid out there. Feels like ninety." He eased himself to the leather sofa. "None of my business, but shouldn't your lawyer sit in on interviews and advise you?" Rusk inquired.

"Well, no, I don't have a criminal lawyer." She shrugged. "Another thing I haven't managed to cross off my to-do list. My husband's lawyer, Paul Abrams, has been advising me on financial matters, but between the Carlisle and Mechanicsburg police, my job, settling Denny's affairs—" She stopped abruptly and crossed her arms. "Sorry. You're a stranger; I didn't mean to dump my problems in your lap."

Rusk smiled. "I asked, remember?" He pulled out his wallet, worked a business card from it, and extended it to her.

She perused the plain, white card embossed with black lettering: "Feldman, Frost and Rusk, attorneys-at-law. Camp Hill, PA." Phone numbers. On the reverse, a D plus a fence. She smiled at the football allusion. "A relative?"

Rusk nodded. "My sister, Swoozie."

"Swoozie? That's unusual." Kelly smiled. "For that matter, so is Lane. Thank you. Do they, would they take . . . I hate to ask; that suggests I'm guilty." She waved the card like a flag of surrender.

"Not at all. It's your right. Don't let CPD or MPD question you further until you've retained council. Imagine they're just doing their jobs, but they want convictions. I've worked with the Carlisle detectives; they're decent but driven—Snow and McCoy especially. And Savage is no slouch either. Watch him, he's sly." Rusk unhooked his cell, pushed contacts, thumbed one, and waited a beat. One, two, three rings.

"Feldman, Frost, and Rusk, attorneys. Hello, Lane. What's up?" Swoozie pushed away from her computer, let her desk chair glide to the window. Looked out at the limp pine needles, the firs demarking a line between properties. Crossed her legs at her ankles and rested them on the low sill.

"I know someone who needs a criminal lawyer. The CPD like her for killing her husband, but she has a solid alibi. They're interviewing her without counsel present. Would you talk to her?"

"Ah, a looker, huh? You always were a soft touch for the pretty ones. What's her name?" Ms. Rusk asked.

"Kelly Sims. I'll hand you over to her." He extended the cell to Sims and gestured her to take it.

Kelly took it, nodded, and cleared her throat. "Hello?" Her voice trembled with trepidation. "I'm Kelly Sims. The Carlisle Police think I killed my husband. I need a criminal lawyer, so Mr. Rusk recommended you."

"I don't accept or advise a client over the phone. Look. I need a break from paperwork. Give me your address. I'll be there in half an hour. How many times have the police questioned you?"

"Three or four," Kelly guessed. "At home twice, once at work and at a restaurant."

"Did they advise you of your rights?" she asked tightly.

"Once, I think. I'm not sure. Time all runs together since Denny died. They've arrested my dad, too, but . . ."

"For the same crime? Be there in half an hour. Block off two hours." The call ended abruptly.

"Thanks. That was really kind of you." Kelly returned the warm phone to its owner. Tears pooled, but she whisked them away quickly with polished fingernails as they spilled over. "She sounded angry."

"She's assertive and specializes in advocating for women—takes justice and the American way seriously. Has a 95 percent acquittal rate. Listen, I need to return to work. If you have any questions about the insurance forms for the shed and its contents"—he indicated the envelope—"give me a buzz. I'll walk you through the process." He set his empty glass in the kitchen sink, laid his card beside it. "Nice meeting you." He extended his hand.

She shook it. Kelly stood, too, accompanied him to the door, her heart beating rapidly. Closed the door behind him, turned, and slid to the floor and cried. "What a mess! Poor Dad, thinking he still has to protect me."

38

"**No driving** while you're on medication, the doctor ordered," Snow repeated to McCoy, who climbed into the Explorer's passenger seat the next morning on the way to HQ for a briefing. "Did you take an oxy last night?"

Mac nodded but stopped moving when her forehead stitches pulled. She snapped the seat belt in place, laid back against the headrest, tolerating the dull ache. Her fingers worried the bandage, rubbing the itch.

"Don't infect your sutures," Chris suggested gently. "Flowers is in lockup, so he's not going anywhere. Savage and Fields escorted him to HQ. Stuart got everybody else's statements. With four eyewitnesses, it's an open and shut case. We have his military file, DNA from the garrote and your knife, his footprint on our roof. CSU is combing the cabin for additional evidence that perhaps transferred from the crime scene."

"Why do I attract the crazies?" Mac adjusted the tape on the bandage covering her stitches. She tied her stepfather's headband around her forehead to hide it. A blue and aubergine scarf hid the bruises tattooing her neck. "And Gavin Mahoney is also behind bars for the Sims homicide. Does that bother you?"

"Yes, not because you got the collar, but because I think the wife did it, but can't prove it. Mahoney's taking the fall."

"How do you know he didn't do it? His reasons sound credible to me. And an inhaler accounts for the increased adrenaline in the body. You know, Occam's Razor," she responded. "Simple—he's taking care of his daughters. Could you stop for a mocha? I just need a shot of caffeine before we get to work."

"Because eighty-five percent of domestic violence victims are women who are abused by their spouse, partner, boyfriend, or someone they know." Turning toward Trindle, Snow braked at Sheetz, jogged in for coffee and a mocha, carried two steaming cups out, handed one to Mac. She blew the froth gently, sipped the scalding drink carefully, grateful for the caffeine in the tasty concoction.

At the station, they ran into a wall of reporters.

"Shit a brick, they're blocking the drive. What the hell?" Snow honked his horn, motioned the cameramen aside, threading his way through the throng. "There's no help for it. See if you can make the side door."

Mac had already stepped onto the macadam, her new cane thumping along. Elena Michaels pushed to the front, but Nelson Daley elbowed her aside. Others crowded in around Mac. The odors of steel, sweat, heat, unwashed hair, and perfume engulfed her. She coughed and swallowed.

"Did you make an arrest in the Sims homicide?" Michaels asked.

"What happened to you, McCoy?" Daley asked.

"You should see the other guy," she quipped, twenty feet to the door, she kept trekking slowly, the cane steadying her gait.

"Did someone assault you?" another asked, indicating her bandage. Flashes strobed the air.

She nodded and touched her forehead. "With a deadly weapon."

"Was that the perp Detectives Savage and Fields escorted to jail this morning? Can you identify him?"

Snow pushed ahead, opening a path for her. "No comment."

"Oh, come on. Give. What's his name?" Lennon queried. "What's his beef with the CPD? Why was he dressed like a scarecrow?"

"Daniel Flowers. He was camouflaged in our cornfield. We're investigating his background now," Mac answered.

"Is the Scarecrow related to last year's needle-pricker case?" Michaels interjected, while her cameraman—a head taller than the others—filmed.

Mac glanced at Savage's ex. "Boy, you're quick." The media just named her assailant; that moniker would stick.

"I'll take that as a yes. What's he charged with? Will he go to trial?" Michaels, wearing a lapel mic with a battery pack, had both arms free. Though the heat was pushing high seventies, the reporter's hair fell to her shoulders like black rain, her makeup perfect, and her navy slacks and sleeveless cream top cracker crisp.

Snow skidded to a dead stop, whipped around to face the crowd while Mac aimed for the glass door ten feet away. "HALT! What part of 'no comment' do you not understand? When our prisoner is fully processed, charged, arraigned, and enters a plea, we'll inform you of the details.

"At the moment, we have an interview, and you are impeding our homicide investigation. When we have pertinent information, we'll hold a press conference and release it. Thank you."

"Can you tell us when? Does this mean the Sims investigation is closed?" another reporter ventured, but the others backed away as the detectives disappeared behind the station's doors.

In the Murder Room, stark photos of the deceased were posted on the whiteboard opposite a timeline of the principals: wife, sister-in-law, in-laws, son, daughter, and employees. Sal Carrelli's photo and info were posted on the second board, an arrow pointing to the first, the words 'Cameron Sims's birth certificate' and 'Sims's check' written beneath.

The chief bustled in, eyebrows in a V. Fields and Savage, already seated, scanned the notes in front of them. Reese was smirking, engulfed in a fume of bad air. Mac dropped to her seat awkwardly as Snow held the chair, then pushed it gently toward the table. "*Phew!*" Her face scrunched. "John's down the hall," her voice rasped.

"Excuse the voluntary emission, Cochise," Savage replied.

She busied herself by getting her laptop out, booted up.

Her eyes looked raw, a curious shade of stippled red—the whites lined with petechiae. Her stepfather's headband nearly hid the bandage covering her stitches. A scarf hid the motley tattoo encircling her throat. Fields pushed a bottle of water and a Coke within her reach.

The lieutenant pushed away from the table to man the white board, as Dr. Chen entered the room wearing a casual, white shirt and flared, gauzy, black slacks, took a seat by the door.

"People, let's report our findings on our current cases. Snow, you've arrested a suspect in the Sims homicide?"

"No, Mac did. Mr. Gavin Mahoney confessed and explained how he came upon our injured vic." He summarized the details, including Mahoney giving Sims whiffs of the epi inhaler. "Would that account for the excess adrenaline in our vic's system?" he asked Dr. Chen.

"It might, but his elevated blood pressure, mood at the time—"

"Let's presume angry, as his wife admits to arguing before she left for New York City that day," Snow interjected.

Chen's almond eyes regarded Snow for a minute, and then glanced at McCoy's injured face. She hated being interrupted, expelled a sigh. "All right. When angry, a person's body pumps adrenaline and cortisol through the system; it's like adding fuel to a fire. Plus, as men age, testosterone decreases, making them angry quicker. And men with a type-A personality have elevated levels of these elements in their blood.

"Epinephrine also increases a person's heart rate, muscle strength, blood pressure, and sugar metabolism, urging the body to fight or flee. Doctors also use epinephrine as a stimulant in cardiac arrest, as a vasoconstrictor in shock, and as a bronchodilator and antispasmodic in asthma cases or those having bee venom allergies."

"In layman's terms, Doc?" Savage asked.

"And when too much floods the system?" added Chief March.

"Epinephrine *is* adrenalin; it speeds up bodily processes, so the heart would be racing, but not in and of itself. As Detective Snow indicated, the man's mood and elevated blood pressure affect the system as well, so no, I could not testify that the epi inhaler *alone* caused Dennis Sims's death."

"And the contusion at his temple?" Stuart scratched his head, nonplussed at the wrinkles in this case.

"Again, whatever weapon used was frozen, so it retarded swelling." She shook her head. "No, that injury alone was not enough to cause death. However, the chain of events together *hastened* the man's demise and caused a massive stroke."

"But we're still declaring his death a homicide?" Savage asked.

"Man didn't kill himself, Reese. And you now have Gavin Mahoney in custody—with a signed confession, so what's the problem?" Chief March asked his lead detective.

"Because I think his wife smacked him in the head with a frozen container of ice cream," Snow answered. "She's as culpable as her father."

"You're joking!" Fields chortled, then laughed. "No jury will buy that!"

"Except she has an iron-clad alibi—she visited the Big Apple with her sister. Officer Mahoney will testify that they were together the entire time in question," Mac whispered. "Plus, they have tickets and parking receipts for the times in question."

"You look rough and sound worse. Do you need additional medical leave?" Chief March turned to the only female detective on the squad.

She shook her head gently. "It looks worse than it feels."

Snow threaded his fingers through his hair and turned to the coroner. "Could the time frame be adjusted two hours either way?"

"To accommodate your theory? What exactly are you asking me to do?" Dr. Chen's back straightened, brow quirked inquisitively.

"Nothing. Is it possible he died before 7:00 a.m.?"

"I feel the window is accurate as stated in my postmortem, from 8:00 a.m. to noon, given full rigor the body had attained. If anything, I'm disinclined to adjust it because other variables, like his clothes and the air conditioning, affect the time as well. It was twenty degrees cooler inside the house when you found him."

"Plus, we have an eyewitness, a neighbor Mrs. Blunt saying the women left at precisely 6:30 a.m. when she let her cat out," Fields read from his notes. "Didn't Mr. Mahoney say Sims was alive at seven?"

"If we can trust his confession. He's covering for Kelly," Savage asserted. "Besides, Fields is right. Do you have any idea what her lawyer would do with the ice cream defense? Laugh us out of the courtroom. The DA won't touch that one." Savage pinched the bridge of his nose. "Is that even possible?"

"We haven't had time to test that theory yet. But I will testify to that effect *if* the frozen container can cause a fatal blow."

"Well, go test it, man. You've got the dad in custody. Want to arrest the widow, too? Why stop there? Why not Officer Mahoney, too?" March looked at Snow like he'd taken leave of his senses. "Try them all together? It'd be a circus!"

"If the evidence points that way." Snow unbuttoned his cuffs and rolled shirtsleeves to his elbows as perspiration trickled down his temples. His brown eyes tracked the others' facial expressions.

"Let's move on. McCoy, can you report anything about your assailant?" March swiveled to Savage and Fields. "Or do you two have the information?"

"Yes, sir," Savage said. "David Flowers, retired Army, is the son of the late Lindy Flowers, the needle-pricker in that inheritance dispute that resulted in the death of Sean Flowers, a.k.a. Richard Benedict, and Luke Flowers, Lindy's husband. Looks like a murder for hire. However, the man refuses to say who hired him. Provided only his name, rank, and serial number.

"He's been arraigned for assault with a deadly weapon, entering a conspiracy to kill a police officer, resisting arrest, and concealing an unregistered firearm in the state of Pennsylvania." Savage nodded for Fields to finish.

"He lawyered up, accused McCoy of police brutality because she sliced his balls. He's threatening a civil suit."

"Let him," Mac said. "Don't forget his assault on my K-9 officer and possessing an illegal substance, ketamine. I was defending my life on our property."

"Do you have photos of your injuries?" Stuart asked.

"Yes sir, both CSU and the ER took photos," Mac said.

"Do we have the clothes you wore—when was it— yesterday?"

"Yes, sir. Bagged, labeled, and entered in Evidence. The ER doc promised to send the lab results over when he receives them.

"Let's send the evidence to our lab as well," Stuart suggested.

"We also have our sworn statements as well as CI John Bowie's and Jason Lightfoot's." Fields pointed to the witnesses present.

"Okay, looks like we can wrap this one up." Chief blew out a breath. "Now let's put the Sims case to bed. Meet with the DA or ADA and the lawyers to lay out your case. See if we have enough evidence to go to trial. If Mr.

Mahoney waives trial, a judge can sentence him. Save the taxpayers some money. Not to mention the havoc and media blitz that the domestic violence issue would cause if Sims's photos leaked or she talks to the press.

"We'll have to let the widow go if your experiment doesn't produce results, Snow. So get to it, people. You all have work to do. I want reports from everyone. "Oh, Mac, how's your K-9 officer?"

"Resting at the animal hospital. They kept her overnight to monitor her injury, but the vet says she'll make a full recovery."

She smiled, relieved that Shadow would not suffer long-term effects of the ketamine used to sedate her. "That's one thing in Flowers's favor; he didn't kill Shadow."

39

ADA Carson Chase Lawson stood as the detectives entered his office with laptops, notes, suspect snapshots, and Dennis Sims's crime scene photos. In the middle of the table, a coffee urn with mugs and bottles of water snuggled next to a plate of cupcakes and packages of snack crackers. His walnut desk backed against the window near the rear of the room. A copy of *The Patriot News* topped the pile of folders, the banner below the masthead proclaiming: TEEN ACQUITTED! A court sketch showed Emma Hawthorne's attorney behind her defendant, grasping the girl's hand, which held an antique fork. Mac's eyes dropped to the lead:

> *"The defendant testified that her kidnapper grabbed her hand (holding the antique fork) and jabbed it into Margie Hawthorne, who subsequently fell across the cannon . . ."*

The young man topped off his mug. "Help yourselves," and sat down, motioning for Mac, Snow, Savage, and Fields to take seats.

"DA Collins has reviewed the case against Gavin Mahoney and is ready to schedule his sentencing once we obtain a judge. What's this new wrinkle?"

Snow summarized their theory re Kelly Sims, the others jumping in with facts, interview information, photos, observations, and the frozen custard experiment conducted at the Harrisburg Lab.

Lawson grinned, then threw back his head and laughed. "You're kidding?" Stopped when he noticed their stern, stoic faces. "And what did the experiment prove?"

"That slammed hard enough into the head, a frozen carton of ice cream can cause blunt-force trauma," Snow answered flatly.

"Did a woman heft that ice cream container in your experiment?" Lawson asked, booting his laptop. His fingers flew over the keys.

"The second time," Savage admitted—a fact they had at first overlooked, and then repeated the experiment with one of the female lab assistants hefting the ice cream carton.

"And?" Lawson stopped keying, eying the youngest detective. "Did she deliver enough force to kill the vic?" He picked up a photo of Kelly Sims.

"Enough to disable the victim with a hairline skull fracture that, along with his other health issues and a high level of epinephrine, led to his death," Fields supplied. "COD was a massive stroke."

Mac slid an envelope across the table. "They include high blood pressure, broken blood vessels in the eye, dislocated pinky and—"

Lawson shook his head. "I'm trying to visualize your scenario, detectives, but I doubt a jury will take this seriously with a defendant already in custody."

"There's the DV issue, too," Mac said. She dumped Kelly Sims's selfies onto the table. "As you know, eighty-five percent of DV victims are women, but most violence against women goes unreported, as in this case. She can claim self-defense."

"That only works in imminent danger situations. No, I didn't know. Jurists in the Commonwealth of Pennsylvania do not keep stats on the DV decisions they hand down. So the motive is revenge?" Lawson winced at the purple bruises on Sims's biceps, along the ribs, across her throat, and purpling her thighs. "Could be rough sex," he added.

"Not sure," Savage admitted. "We think a loan shark was blackmailing Sims, because he thought Dennis fathered Shannon Mahoney's baby, whom he and Kelly raised as their own."

"What's the motive to kill Sims now? Isn't the daughter grown? Why not remove the shark instead of the husband?"

"Someone did. What happened, I think," Mac interjected, "is that an argument turned violent. Sims lunged for his wife, grabbed her. Couldn't get leverage because of his awkward position—stretched across the kitchen island. She was getting an ice pack out of the freezer for her water but grabbed the frozen custard instead and slammed that against his temple."

Snow added. "She swears her husband was alive when she left. Then Sims and her sister tripped to NYC. Gavin Mahoney comes on the scene to borrow a lawnmower, sees the vic injured and claims to *help* by giving him bursts of his epi inhaler. Then he calls 911, goes home, and mows his lawn."

Savage continued, "Kelly and Shannon spend the next fifteen hours in the Big Apple establishing a solid alibi."

"A fire burns down their backyard shed," Fields added.

"And we're called to the crime scene," finished Snow. "Three weeks later, blackmailer Salvatore Carrelli is knifed on Jubilee Day in Mechanicsburg with a $20,000 cancelled check pinned to the letter opener. The man's clutching Cameron Sims's birth certificate. But that homicide's in MPD's jurisdiction. As of now, the case is on-going but they lack the evidence needed for a conviction."

Lawson poured over the items on his desk as the silence lengthened. The detectives helped themselves to coffee and cupcakes while waiting. Savage wolfed down his devil's food with fudge ganache in two bites; the others chewed theirs more slowly. Chased the confections down with coffee.

"Heard the one about the elderly couple in bed? The old man farts, says seven points," Reese quips to fill the time. "The old lady asks him what that means, and he said bed football. So she goes along and—"

"Yes, heard that one—fart football," Snow replied. "Not now."

Lawson coughed. "Detectives, really? My advice? Sounds like Mr. Mahoney's guilty. Otherwise, you'll need a confession from the widow because a quart of frozen ice cream—or custard—won't wash; the jury and press will run rabid with the possibilities. You'll be the butt of a hundred jokes like 'Man Felled by Frozen Custard.'"

"'Or Brain Freeze: Frozen Custard Causes Fatal Fall,'" Fields joined in.

"'Or Marriage Ends with Fire and Ice,'" added Mac.

"Do you know his defense counselor? How will he plead?" Lawson brushed the blond hair off his forehead. The fluorescent light highlighted the sheen of perspiration on his forehead.

"Guilty or No Contest," Snow guessed.

"You'd have to disprove the dad's confession or break the sister's alibi and prosecute one of your own as well. If he goes to trial, it'd be nearly impossible to argue a negative. Plus, the mitigating circumstance of the abuse will play in the widow's favor."

He propped his elbows on the table, cupped his face in his index finger and thumb, considering. Dropped his hand. "On the basis of your *current* findings, I'd have to say *nolle prosequi*. We will not prosecute the widow at this time. You'll have to find her prints on the murder weapon, witnesses to refute her timeline—some hard, physical evidence. Sorry." Lawson pushed their evidence and photos across the table and stood, signaling an end to the meeting.

Disgruntled, the men raked their files and photos back into folders and envelopes. Snow stood first, a frown furrowing his forehead, but he extended his hand to the ADA. "Thanks for your time."

"Don't mention it. What happened, McCoy, you get in a fight?" Lawson indicated her bruising. "Think I'd be at home icing that eye. A bag of frozen peas works wonders. Thought you were on medical leave."

"I was. I will. Thanks." Mac stuffed her evidence into her red canvas tote, tossed her purse over her shoulder, grabbed her soda, and followed her husband out the door. "So this is how it ends—with a whimper instead of a bang."

Behind the couple, Fields turned to Savage. "Now, finish the joke. I haven't heard it."

"So the wife and husband go back and forth, trying to outdo each other, scoring their emissions until the wife leads with a field goal after squeaking one out. Finally, the husband bears down hard, shat the bed, and says, 'Half time, switch sides.'"

Both guffawed, tripping down the hall.

By the time they emerged into the summer's oven, the Snows had disappeared.

"Let's get lunch." Savage motioned Fields into the Bronco.

40

After lunch at home, the Snows hustled to the courthouse for Gavin Mahoney's sentencing. Chris parallel parked on High Street, opened Mac's door, helping her out and holding her cane.

"What time?" Mac clopped along, favoring her right leg, mounting the steps one at a time. Set the cane down, stepped right then left. Repeated the procedure slowly.

"Whenever his case number comes up on the docket."

"Who's in chambers?" Mac paused for a breath at the top. "Does Mahoney have counsel?"

"Judge Acorn. Orndorf should be here to report that the defendant refuses a lawyer and a defense."

People and press were sprinkled sparsely across the courtroom. Officers guarded the doors. Whispers rose, a murmur of insects. The tardy, bespectacled lawyer entered, hurried down the aisle, took a seat. The bailiff entered. "All rise." The diminutive judge entered and took her seat. Court began with several DUIs. Next came two teens who'd vandalized the Ashland Cemetery, toppling some stones and monuments. Down slammed the gavel with each decision.

Finally, Robert Orndorf ascended to his feet, buttoned his jacket, strode determinedly through the swinging gate, and laid a folder on the defendant's table. Gavin Mahoney was escorted in and ushered to his seat.

Orndorf motioned for the guard to remove the handcuffs. He pushed his black-framed glasses against the bridge of his nose, cleared his throat, and summarized the case. "Against advisement, Mr. Mahoney is refusing counsel." But he remained standing.

The judge turned to the defendant. "Is this true, Mr. Mahoney? You are entitled to due process and a trial by jury for the involuntary manslaughter charge."

"Yes, ma'am. Why waste the taxpayers' money?" Mahoney said.

The gallery twittered.

"So you think this is funny?" Judge Acorn sat straighter, her face a stern mask in her small bird-like face, her furrowed frown and dark look roving over the entire room.

"No, ma'am. I'm serious. I admit my role in my son-in-law's demise."

"How does the defendant plead?" the judge asked.

"*Nolo contendre.*" Mahoney's voice stated clearly.

"May I approach the bench?" Orndorf inquired. He carried the folder to the bench and handed it to her. Acorn paged through the summary, evidence and interview transcripts.

Shook her head. "I'm calling for a two-hour recess to review this. Though I have ADA Lawson's notes, I would have appreciated having this file earlier. A man's life is too weighty a matter to pass a hasty judgment. We will reconvene court at 3:00 p.m. to continue the day's business but will postpone Mr. Mahoney's sentencing until tomorrow morning at 9:00 a.m. Mr. Mahoney, I would urge you to reconsider your decision." The gavel whacked again.

The man nodded as he stood, trudged from the courtroom.

Mac sighed, waited for the courtroom to empty before she managed the series of ungainly movements for an action she had performed automatically before her hip replacement. As before, her husband assisted, held the heavy door, then the front doors.

"What more can the judge do?" Mac wondered aloud.

Snow shrugged. "She wants time to consider the case. I don't blame her; he could appeal later on the grounds his lawyer didn't dissuade him from this course of action. Seems silly to send a man to prison who doesn't seem to care—or merit the punishment."

"He's protecting his daughters. He said as much earlier." She climbed into the Explorer, stowed the cane, waiting until Chris was seated. "What's the status on the Carrelli homicide? Has the MDP called?"

"Dead in the water. No. No fibers, hair, prints, or other hard evidence to go on. It's still an open case. No, they haven't called since we sent them the birth certificate. You want to head home?" Chris asked her.

"Yes. Let's pick up Shadow at the animal hospital. If she's able, we'll need to walk the trail at home, loosen her muscles."

At home, Mac eased out of the vehicle, let Shadow out of the backseat, and walked her around to the back of their bungalow.

Chris disappeared inside to check on Ian and say hello to his mother before he returned to HQ.

On the way back to the station, his cell beeped. "Snow." Paused to listen to Stuart's words. "I'm headed in."

* * *

At HQ, a tall, trim brunette with wide, hazel eyes and a practiced smile waited. She'd paired a navy pantsuit with a pale-yellow blouse, the sleeves of both rolled up. She extended her hand and shook his firmly. "I'm Swoozie Rusk, representing Kelly Sims, who stood behind her. Sims had had her hair professionally cut and layered. Reddish brown waves highlighted with copper strands framed her face. Gone were the split ends, and the dried, dusty, drawn look.

"Pleased to meet you. I'm Christopher Snow. Would you step into my office? Can I get you ladies something refreshing to drink?" He followed them in.

"Detective Snow." Sims nodded curtly, sat, hands in her lap.

Rusk got to the point. "No thanks. I'll be brief. I'm requesting all discovery documents pertaining to my client be turned over so we have time to prepare a defense." She tucked her legs beneath the chair, crossing slim ankles.

"That won't be necessary." Still, Snow paged through the stack of folders and bulging envelopes on his desk, pulled one but left it unopened in front of him.

"May I ask why not? I understand you've interrogated my client a number of times without a lawyer present, even when she requested one. That's an appealable offense—"

"Because the prosecution has declined to charge Mrs. Sims for her role in her husband's homicide."

"*Nolle Prosequi*?" She leaned back in the chair. "I'm assuming for lack of evidence, as my client was clearly out of town when that homicide occurred. Well, then, you should have no objection to my having a copy of your folder and ADA Lawson's abandon of charge document should the case ever come before the court."

His brown eyes studied her blue stare, her no-nonsense face—her mouth determined—while he considered her clipped words. Kelly Sims sat statue still, communicating nothing, her moss-green eyes darting between the detective and her counsel. "I'll have our admin copy and mail them to you if you leave your card."

Having one ready, she slapped it on his desk and stood abruptly while simultaneously pulling Sims to her feet. "Thank you for your time, but I'll wait in the lobby for it, if you don't mind. Bird in hand. You understand—in case circumstances change."

"Of course. I'll walk you to the lobby and give Sonja the file." On the way, he punched his cell. "Reese, meet you outside; we need to escort Gavin Mahoney to jail."

41

In her office, Mac's fingers flew over her laptop, writing her report on the Sims case. Her landline jangled. "McCoy," she answered absently, intent on her task.

"Tim Martin from the Harrisburg lab. I'm faxing the results from the trash. We have positive IDs taken from saliva found on a bronchial inhaler."

"Trash?" Mac repeated. She stopped. "From South Street?" Felt an uptick in adrenaline. Her scalp tingled. "Mr. Mahoney?"

"Yeah—the trash. Detective Snow sent the entire block's trash bags over, so it took us awhile to comb through and analyze it all. The inhaler was in the neighbor's trash sandwiched between trash bags. The DNA markers align closely with Dennis Sims's—say a relative—like father, brother or—"

"Son. I'll be damned. How so?"

"The genetic material, part of the cell's DNA, includes codes to construct what the body needs, like proteins. Deoxyribonucleic acid is comprised of four chemicals called bases aligned in specific, repeated patterns. You've seen the double helix—" Martin explained.

Mac interrupted. "No I don't mean a exposition of DNA. I'm asking if you're certain."

"Ninety-nine point nine percent. Wait, I'm not finished," Martin said. "When we tested the saliva on the inhaler and compared the DNA to Gavin Mahoney's as well, the subject's profile shows a correlation to both Dennis Sims and Gavin Mahoney. Plus, this sample matches a specimen taken at the South Street residence May 25. However, his prints are not in CODIS, AFIS, or any database we have, so he has no priors, but it narrows the field considerably. And Dennis Sims's saliva is also on the inhaler. You can see the DNA results for yourself when I fax them over."

"Thanks." Call ended. In Murder One, the fax machine hummed and printer spit out the data. She picked up the receiver to request an arrest warrant. Then rummaged through the interviews, plucked out Andrew Sims's, slid it into her recorder and for the first time, listened to the entire tape.

First, Snow's voice rose from the speaker, listing the pertinent info re the Dennis Sims case. Then came who, where, when, why, and how questions. The son answered, his voice firm, confident.

"And how's your relationship with your dad?" Snow asked.

"Strained. He was a strict parent. I loved him because he was my dad, but he wasn't a very nice person. He treated us kids okay, but Mom bore the brunt of his temper. He was a strange man—very sociable outside but demanding and controlling at home, his mood was either high or low; he could run from normal to raging within seconds."

"So how would you describe him?" Snow's tone remained even.

"He got through life on bullshit and bravado. He dominated conversations. Actually, we didn't converse. He barked commands: Go in the house, eat your supper, get a shower, do your homework, go to bed. It was like living with a dictator."

"Well, he was the parent. So you resented his authority?" Snow said.

"That's not it. He treated Mom the same way. She's a saint for putting up with the shit he shoveled her way all these years. Expecting dinner every night at 6:00 p.m. on the dot. Sending men to tail her. Telling her what to wear!"

"Did your parents always have problems getting along?" Snow asked. Something dropped, pinged onto the table.

"I don't know. Dad never really graduated from the locker-room mentality. Seemed more comfortable with his buddies. Family seemed . . . ," a rubbing sound intervened, ". . . a burden. Oh, he cared for us, but it's hard to describe our family dynamics. He played with us as kids, but often seemed one himself. He had lots of business savvy, but little common sense. Very outgoing and talkative.

"I think Mom would've been happier with someone more like her—serious and cerebral, who liked to read and travel. But she said, 'The heart, not the brain, chooses whom we love.'"

"So your parents loved each other?"

Drew laughed. "I'm sure they had a bond. Honestly? I didn't grasp the depths of their divide until I was a teenager. Self-absorbed as I was, I didn't notice much when I went away to college. Then Camie left for Penn State, leaving Mom alone with him."

"They didn't get along then? Why?"

"He bullied Mom whenever he could."

"Where were you on Thursday, May 21, 2009?"

"At work."

"Which is where?"

"I'm an IT Tech for a waste management company in Lancaster." He reached in his wallet and withdrew a business card with a green garbage truck, the business name in block capital letters superimposed over it.

"Can anyone vouch for that?"

"I need an alibi? Sure, my boss and the drivers. We're working on more efficient runs—more right turns, outfitting trucks with GPS."

"What time do you report to work? What're your hours?"

"Eight o'clock—earlier if I can to check the computers before everyone gets there and we get busy. Hours vary with computer conditions. I'm currently updating the software."

"Can you work from home?" Snow asked.

"During inclement weather."

"So your schedule never varies," Snow stated.

"No, it does, but most days are routine," Drew claimed.

Mac snapped off the recording. Pocketed it. Dialed Chris. No answer, so she left a voice-mail message.

Fields sauntered out of the break room—headed for Murder One. "Did you hear the printer? We must've got a fax." He pulled the papers out, eyes roving over the pages. "What? According to this . . ." He extended the report to her.

"Yes!" She shoved the lab report in the file, the folder in her tote. Tied a green scarf around her forehead to keep her bandage clean. "Come on. We're headed for Lancaster."

"What for?" he followed her down the hall to the office where Sonja handed her the arrest warrant.

"Go get 'im, girl!" the admin encouraged.

"You drive," Mac tossed Zach the keys. "I need to read this report and look up where Drew Sims works."

They arrived at the offices of Penn Waste about quitting time. To the right, garbage trucks were lined up behind a chain-link fence. To the left, a line of parked vehicles marched along the fence. Men poured out of the squat concrete building, most in dress shirts and slacks, making for their cars and trucks. Andrew Sims pushed out the door. Tall and lankly with dark-brown hair and eyes, he loped awkwardly to his car—one leg seemed shorter than the other, whistling, "You may be right . . ."

Mac finally recognized where she'd last heard that Billy Joel refrain—Jubilee Day, the balloon man. Suddenly, the puzzle pieces snapped into place: the clown, the balloons camoflauging his identity and protecting him from blood splatter. His access to the check and the letter opener. Shannon's words: "We all help on Jubilee Day."

But Sims stopped dead when Mac and Fields approached displaying detective shields. His eyes shifted left and right, looking for an escape route, but the high fence encircled the entire building and grounds.

"Your grandfather's in jail, confessing to your father's death," Fields held both arms out, palms out. "You gonna let him take the fall?" Drew stopped, shoulders stooped resignedly. "You have the right to remain silent . . . ," Fields cited the Miranda rule.

"Put him in the vehicle and stay with him while I check the timeline with his boss." Mac strode into the waste management plant, asking for directions to the main office. She displayed her creds along the way until she found the boss, who skirted his desk to shake her hand. Just shy of six feet, he had a broad face, grey eyes. He wore his steel-grey hair in a crewcut; his rumpled, white shirt strained across a middle-age spread. Black slacks were pressed. "Josh Eby. How can I help you, uh . . ."

"Detective Erin McCoy, Carlilse Police. I have taken one of your employees in custody for questioning in a homicide investigation. I have just two questions: "Did Andrew Sims ever ride with the truck drivers? And where was he on the morning of May 21 and June 11?"

"Yes, he's helping drivers with the new GPS system." Eby returned to his desk, picked up his phone, punched a button. "Cheryl, can you please bring me time sheets for May and June for Andrew Sims? Thanks.

"Can I get you a soda or coffee while we wait? It may take a few minutes. Andrew's a fine computer technician; he arrives early, works diligently, and shows patience with the drivers who are unfamiliar with computers. I hope he's not in trouble."

"I can't comment on an on-going investigation. No, thanks, we need to get back to Headquarters."

Heels clicked down the hallway. A woman wearing a navy pantsuit and cream-colored blouse entered and handed Eby the printouts. Nodded at his thanks, acknowledged McCoy with a headshake, and strode out.

"What were those dates again?" Eby asked.

"May 21 and June 11."

He perused the printouts. On May 21, he rode the Carlisle truck. On June 11, he took a personal day."

"Thanks for your time, sir." Mac turned toward the door.

"You said homicide investigation. Surely you don't suspect—"

"Sorry, sir, no comment."

Eby nodded.

As Mac exited the building, she called HQ with a ten-nineteen. "We'll be back in ninety minutes."

42

Snow and Savage escorted their prisoner to Cumberland County Prison until a space became available at Camp Hill for diagnostics. As they entered the grounds, the Explorer idled until the gate yawned. A ten-foot fence topped with coiled concertina wire surrounded the browned field where the concrete block building squatted. The sun had toasted the prison yard. Outside the fence, fronds of grass and Queen Anne's lace hugged the fence; dandelion puffs dotted the landscape. Bumblebees hovered, iridescent wings reflecting light, fat, black bodies buzzing, hovering over the lacy flower heads. Snow swatted at the one that followed them in. Buzzing followed them.

An officer flanking each side, Mahoney took mincing steps, the shackles linking wrists, waist, and ankles severely limiting movement.

A white, paneled medical supply van with a caduceus logo had backed into the loading dock. Snow glanced at the movement—the driver unloading oxygen tanks, presumably for the inmates with emphysema or other respiratory ailments. On the platform, a prison guard, smoking during his break, watched the detectives and prisoner approaching. The beefy guard took one last puff, flicking his butt into the parking lot without looking where it landed.

Snow's eyes caught movement before his brain registered the danger. "Hey, don't flick that cig—" Dropping Mahoney's arm, he ran, but the sudden blast blew him back. Colliding with his prisoner and Savage, the trio tangled and toppled over, butting heads. Squashing the bee, Mahoney hit the concrete walk hard.

Snow's skull cracked a nanosecond later. The truck hiccupped. Another blast followed, engulfing the guard as the driver, sleeves flaming, ran and rolled from the inferno while prison sirens wailed.

Lockdown commenced. Emergency personnel notified.

A fire truck—screaming with urgency—arrived to attack the fire. Black and Whites careened onto the field, surrounding the prison. By the time an ambulance loomed into view, Snow and Savage managed to sit but remained on the ground while EMTs buzzed around them. Snow's ears rang as the explosion echoed. He swallowed the nausea that climbed up his esophagus.

The prisoner hadn't moved. Life had rendered him sere and hollow, a husk with uneven grey hair, his face creased and stippled with stubble. His beer belly a hill, the legs limp.

One man shouted into his attached radio. "I'm not getting a pulse. Remove these chains," he ordered. Savage complied. Leaning over Mahoney, the EMT started chest compressions as the blood trickled from the prisoner's head.

"Stay put, Detective. We have to check you out." Troy Hemmer inspected Mahoney's head wound, staunching the bleeding. Called for a second ambulance on his radio.

Savage noticed the hand swelling. "The man's allergic to bee venom."

"Where's his epinephrine kit?" Hemmer patted the prone man's pockets, waved away the other attendant.

"With his personal effects," Savage said.

Snow tried to remember where he'd left the manila envelope, but his head felt like a split cantaloupe, the ringing thrumming in his eardrums. Dizziness gripped him; the world tilted. He crawled several feet, vomited, then pitched forward.

"Immobilize that detective! Get him to CRMC stat!" Hemmer gently rolled the unconscious Snow over, as his crew hopped to action. Troy jumped into the rear of the ambulance and emerged with a hypo, ripped open Mahoney's shirt, plunged it into his heart. Nothing. He switched to CPR. A breath puffed out. The EMT laid his head against his patient's heart. Faint beating. Hemmer gave a thumbs up. Another started an IV. The second ambulance wheeled into the prison's parking lot headed for the loading dock. On the ground about twelve feet from the charred remains of the guard, the driver sat rocking, both arms burned.

"No, here!" Hemmer waved his arms. "Okay. He waved. We'll take both. Let's get 'em to CRMC stat!" His team loaded the still-unconscious detective on a cot, slid him into the rear, and hooked him up to an oxygen tank. The burned van driver tucked himself in the corner. Hemmer turned to inspect his burns. Doors closed. Lights strobed and sirens screamed as the emergency vehicles aimed for the gates. A guard opened the gates as the ambulances sped through, careened down the two-lane rural road on the way to the hospital.

43

Pouring over her notes and photos, Mac shook her head. She paged through the file again. How had they missed it? They couldn't place Andrew at the crime scene when his dad died. They'd listened to the entire interview again on the trip. Now Drew waited in the box with Fields. Neighbors reported no strange cars in the neighborhood; no one saw anyone enter the Sims domicile either. But a garbage truck? No one would question it. And yes, Officer Mahoney and her sister withheld information about Camie's birth, but did that rise to the level of obstruction?

Shuffling the contents into the file folder, she stood, swiveled, and strode to the interview room, nearly shutting the door on Swoozie Rusk as she entered.

"Not so fast, Detective. I'm here to represent Drew Sims. I need to confer with my client. I'm Swoozie Rusk, by the way." She proffered her hand.

"Of course you are." Mac gave her hand a shake and then stepped aside to allow the lawyer access to her client. She flipped the folder shut. Pushed it over to Fields. "After they confer, you can get his statement. In writing. Then book him for the murder of Dennis Sims. I suspect that he also killed Salvatore Carrelli but can't prove it. The MPD will have to do that."

Savage appeared in her office doorway, canted his head toward the side exit. "Chris is in the hospital. Come on, I'll drive."

"What happened?" Mac asked. "I'm about to question the killer!"

"Zach can do that. I'll explain on the way. Vamos!"

She ducked into her office. Grabbing her purse, holstering her Glock, she paused to inform Fields. "Give me a call if you need me."

Savage tugged her through the door. The Bronco was idling at the curb. He dropped the Explorer's keys into her hand and pointed to it in a nearby parking space.

She followed Savage, twenty questions tripping from her tongue. "What happened? Is Chris all right? Where were you?" she repeated, then noticed a bump on his forehead. "Are you okay? Where's Gavin Mahoney? Did you escort him to the prison?"

"We barely escaped an inferno." Savage folded himself into the driver's seat. Mac took several seconds to carefully step up into the SUV. Briefly, he relayed the incident to Mac as he slotted through traffic.

"They're both unconscious? Are their injuries life-threatening?"

"Erin, I'm not a doctor, but I think Chis has a concussion. Gavin Mahoney's injuries are more serious." Wheeling into CRMC's parking lot, he rocked the car to a stop in front of the ER doors.

Erin clopped down the hall to the ER and stopped in front of the glass cubicles. "Is Chris Snow in the ER? I need to see my husband."

The doors opened; she was directed to room eleven along the hall. Peeked in. The room was dark, quiet; Chris's monitors beeping the only sound. His eyes were closed, his bed elevated, an ice pack beneath his head.

"May I help you?" A woman whose lapel ID read Patel padded into the room, checked Chris's chart, then tried to take Erin's elbow and escort her from the room.

She pulled away and showed her shield. "He's my husband. What can you tell me about his condition?"

"You need to speak with Dr. Cook for that information." Patel stepped back, her hand on the doorknob.

"If you would please locate him, I'll wait." Mac scanned Chris's chart, then sat upon the only chair in the room.

Chris blinked; stared at the ceiling trying to get his bearings. He breathed in Erin's scent—like sunshine and honey. Felt her hand slide into his. Felt fingertips tickling his palm. He groaned. A flash, a fall he remembered.

"You probably have a concussion. We're in the ER at the Carlisle Med Center," Erin explained. "You're scheduled for an MRI and an EEG. How do you feel?"

"Like I lost the fight." He sighed and glanced at Erin without turning his head. "Ringing in my ears, but I'll survive. How's Mahoney?"

Erin shrugged. "I just got here. Fields and I just returned from Lancaster. Reese may be checking on him."

Chris frowned, his eyes tracking her face. "Lancaster?"

"We arrested Drew Sims." She told him the evidence the lab called in. "You know Gavin's story seemed plausible, but stop and think. He doesn't use an inhaler. He delivers his epi with a hypo. But the lab found an inhaler in the neighbor's garbage with Drew's and his father's saliva. Well, with a match to the one you took at the house. He's waiting in the box now. Zach's with him now; I need to question him. And I think he killed Carrelli, too. He was the balloon man at Jubilee Day whistling a Billy Joel tune. A perfect cover—literally and figuratively, but I can't prove it yet.

Chris smiled wanly. "Go, get 'im, tiger."

ACKNOWLEDGEMENTS

Domestic abuse is a chameleon with many colors and manifestations. It runs rampant, crosses all economic boundaries, and leaves an untold number of victims in its wake. The survivors' trauma lasts a lifetime. And that's just the reported violence; most goes unreported for various reasons, but mainly because the victim doesn't want to relive it or be blamed for it. The discourse is detailed and analyzed extensively elsewhere, so I leave that to the experts. But I know that the first step of coming forward is traumatic and dangerous for the ones who do. My character, Kelly Sims, decides to postpone that decision, thus falling deeper into the cycle of spousal abuse that imprisons and paralyzes the victim. For all those intrepid souls who tread that path, I salute you and pray that one day our society will not tolerate such behavior.

As usual, this is a fact-based story, but I've altered the circumstances. I also take liberties with time, geography, places, and events to fit my narrative but try hard to keep the facts and history straight so my fiction is credible. As usual, any errors are mine alone.

Thanks to friends and all family members who encourage, read, and support my efforts, especially my cousins and my late Aunt Lucille. In addition, Sunbury Press provides information and assistance with newsletters, tips, book events, and support. Feedback from consultants, readers, (especially Jim Sclichter's) and editors is always welcome. I owe Joan Sheriff the idea for Kelly Sims's vocation.

Thanks also to Janice's close reading; her corrections, clarifications, and suggestions improved the narrative considerably. Thanks to Crystal for her promptness in getting the book to press. I appreciate Terry Kennedy's updating of my Facebook page (Carlisle Crime Cases by JM West) and my son Jarod for his computer acumen. Finally, thanks, Alida Hodgson, for designing my business cards. Also, the Internet puts encyclopedic knowledge at writers' fingertips. I've also read books, news blogs, social media, and interviewed numerous victims for this novel. Other valuable resources include The Bookery, the Bosler Memorial Library's "gently-used" bookstore. So kudos to Barb, Karen, Bill, and Chuck for a good time, inexpensive sources, and eagerness to share books with volunteers, customers, and friends! And to Kim at History on High in Carlisle; she's such an affable, cheerful hostess at book signings. I'm grateful to Deb Beamer for including me in her author's conference last September: it's fascinating to meet and converse with other PA writers. And thank you, P. J. Heyman, proprietor of The Village Artisans Gallery & Studios for hosting a book signing. Chris Rupp, VP of Online Publishers, Inc. accepted my offer to the Women's Expo as well!

For this novel, I consulted Ramsland's *The Criminal Mind,* Mactire's *Malicious Intent,* McDermid's *Forensics: What Bugs, Burns, Prints, DNA and More Tell,* Kurland's *How to Solve a Murder*, Capuzzo's *The Murder Room,* and Nancy Eschelman's (et al.) *Stabbed in the Heart.* These texts offer anecdotal information, facts, history, and valuable insights. Research is the bedrock upon which I build my texts, so I'm reading and mining data when I'm not writing. Thanks to www.ncadv.org, www.domesticshelters.org, WebMD, and www.verywell.com, among other sites for detailed information and statistics. Again, I thank the police consultants who lent their expertise and answered my questions.

I read books by many talented writers in this genre before attempting the Carlisle Crime Cases series. (David Baldacci, Brunonia Barry, Agatha Christie, Jeffery Deaver, Sir Arthur Conan Doyle, Julia Spencer-Fleming, Ariana Franklin, Tammy Hoag, Ridley Pearson, Louise Penny, E. A. Poe, Deanna Raybourn, Karin Slaughter, Charles Todd, Jacqueline Winspear, et al.) David Baldacci, the main speaker at 2012 Celebrate the Book Symposium in Carlisle, PA, urged writers to follow their dreams. So I queried numerous agents and publishers; Sunbury Press accepted *Dying for Vengeance*, the first in the Carlisle Crime Cases, and published them all. I'm grateful for the opportunity.

Finally, I thank all you readers for following these mysteries to their conclusions. Bless you for constructive feedback and reviews, too!

Continue reading for a sneak peek at adventure number five:

THINGS
STRANGLED

Morning mist climbed off the grass and evaporated as a September sun warmed the earth. Shadow strained forward, sniffing the grass, the fallen logs and leaves. A half-dozen dogs and their handlers had converged at the K-9 Instruction site for training, but Dispatch called Mac with a missing persons—possible kidnapping—case. Relaying the message to K-9 Training Instructor Corey Kauffman, he'd ordered all hands and paws to woods behind the Woolworth "store" where the vic had last been spotted. The men, one woman, and K-9 officers spread out, stalking through the wooded terrain.

"How long has he been missing?" Kauffman asked as his black lab named Inky shouldered ahead, nose roving a six-foot swath to the right. Silence ruled—as a breath held. Acres of fallow land stretched beyond the warehouse where the film crew had reconstructed the site of Frank W. Woolworth's first successful five and dime store. The documentary director decided to film in Carlisle, because he claimed too many tourists mobbed the streets in Lancaster where the store stood originally.

"They're not sure. Maybe twenty-four hours. They'd been drinking after filming, lost track of time." Mac let Shadow draw out the expandable leash. In sweatshirt, jeans, and hiking boots, she tramped behind, trying to avoid the poison ivy and thorny patches of wild raspberry tubers. Eyes scanned the field for broken twigs, bent or flattened grasses—any evidence that people had trudged this way, maybe dragging a body.

"Hell's bells. All of them?" Kauffman jogged to catch up. He wore a Redskins sweatshirt and cargo shorts, its pockets bulging with dog treats and granola bars for himself. "You met the cast and crew?"

"No, just the director—I forget his name, Reynolds. He's youngish. Curly hair like dust bunnies and goatee. I left him ranting about losing his star. A handful of actors were waiting for the star to arrive to film."

"Who's that?" Corey asked. "I see you're not limping anymore. Hip healed?"

"Lance Reading." Mac shrugged, trudged forward, eyes sweeping the brush and hollows. "Yes, sir, I'm fine now." A bird fluttered in the sycamore to her left.

"Never heard of him." Kauffman unhooked his radio, motioning to the vet handling Brutus. "Veer further right. I think we're too tight. I'm swinging out. At this rate, we may walk to Newville!"

"I'm not familiar with him either, but Elizabeth Banks is playing his wife Jennie Creighton. You should see inside. Aisles of sundries, toiletries, hairpins, and hatpins; pin cushions shaped like tomatoes the size of a silver dollar, straight pins, and costume jewelry. Even tiny dolls and toys all displayed on tables with red cambric. The crew added a functioning lunch counter with red leather swivel stools for later. And there's a candy counter. My stepmother manned the candy counter at Woolworth's all through nursing school. She's dying to see the replica, asked if I could get her in."

"Quite the rags-to-riches story, I hear." Kauffman signaled again. Further along, Brutus and his handler moved out of sight.

"His is quite a story. His parents farmed, but physical labor didn't suit Frank. He was determined to make something of himself after an uppity sales clerk in a department store looked down her nose when he and his brother paid for his mother's birthday present with change."

"I remember the store fronts; my mother shopped at Woolworth's," Corey said. "I didn't realize one man was behind the stores. Never really thought about it. And had no idea he lived in Pennsylvania. Thought those department-store tycoons all lived in New York."

Mac continued. "Well, he was from New York and eventually moved to New York City. He revolutionized the way Americans shopped. And he didn't quit when he failed. Just regrouped and tried again elsewhere.

"He owned dime stores, not department stores. Anyway, at sixteen, he left school and took night courses in bookkeeping. Augbury and Moore Dry Goods Store offered him his first job. After several months as an apprentice, he made $3.50 a week! Imagine that! When his store in Utica, New York, floundered, he took the train west, plunking down $30 of borrowed money to rent a 14-foot storefront space for his new store on North Queen Street in Lancaster. He called it Woolworth's 5 & 10c Store."

"Done your homework." Kauffman and Inky pulled away heading further south.

Mac had interviewed the buyer, Larissa Latch. The five-four, persimmon-haired bundle of energy adjusted the placement of displayed merchandise as she described the cast's Friday-night celebration. "We shot the outdoor footage in Lancaster, then drove here and settled into the hotel downtown. The house we're using for the Woolworth's exterior is in the historical district, but the interior's right over there." She'd pointed, led Mac to see the "dwelling," a mock-up of nineteenth-century décor, simply furnished, minus the wall facing the cameras: a kitchen, parlor, living room downstairs, and bedrooms upstairs. A four-poster double bed was centered on the back wall with an antique trundle bed next to it for the Woolworth's young daughter, Helena. A massive wardrobe hung open, revealing several suits and dresses. Stacked trunks and boxes suggested the family was moving in.

Latch explained. "We left the restaurant and moved to the bar around ten: Lance, Liz, Trevor—playing Frank's brother Charles or Sumner, as he was called; the director, JJ, myself, the camera crew, makeup mavens Tammy and Tina Wells, and the stage crew—I don't really know them. They'd wrapped the exterior filming; we just have the store and home scenes left to shoot. Someone said, 'Where's Lance?' He just disappeared. There one minute—gone the next!"

"Is anyone else missing? Perhaps he met someone?" Mac suggested.

"Yes, the costume designer and her assistant left Whiskey Rebellion around nine. Said they had to get the costumes ready for today's shoot."

The director paced the length of the aisle—up one, down the next, checking his watch. "All right, people, looks like we're not filming today, but stay close in the event we can resume later. I expect the detectives to find him soon. I'll be in my office." Reynolds waved his hand vaguely in the direction of the "house."

Ms. Banks, dressed in a long-sleeved blouse with a high, lacy collar and floor-length, grey skirt, pushed off from the counter. Her blond hair had been gathered at her crown and pinned in comma curls. "I better get out of costume if we're not shooting. This outfit takes an hour to press."

At that point, Mac had called her partner Zachery Fields, requesting his assistance. "A dozen people here to interview. Shadow and I are headed to the fields behind the warehouse to start the search with Kauffman and the other K-9 units."

* * *

Shadow bore on, following the scent of the actor's cap. "Let's hope we're on a search and rescue, girl," Mac

remarked more to herself, as her shepherd had stretched
her lead. Slipping a bottle of water from her backpack,
Mac eyed the uneven, rocky, dusty ground. Spindly
deciduous trees with turning leaves gave way to white
pine and fir, the land sprouting mounds, and then hills
as they marched on.

Surging ahead, the shepherd and lab moved as one,
stopping, sitting beneath a dying poplar. Shadow barked
once, her hairs bristling. Mac and Kauffman jogged to the
tree. Looked up. A young man, dressed in baggy trousers
and a tattered shirt from another century had been tied
to the tree. Arms outstretched, head lolling forward, pants
stained down the front, feet lashed around the trunk.
Dark, slightly curly hair. His comely face bore wooly
eyebrows, muttonchop sideburns, an unruly mustache,
and the pallor of death.

Rewarding the dogs, Mac called it in. "Body found. We
need Dr. Chen, CSU in the field behind warehouse on Rt.
641 two buildings down from the Rustic Tavern. Need to
cut him down. Yes, I know she prefers *in situ*, but . . ."

"Someone nailed him to the friggin' tree." Kauffman
whistled. "And it isn't even Easter."

"Not funny, sir," Mac said.

"I'm not joking, McCoy. Why copy the Crucifixion if it's
not significant?"

"Okay. May be a part of the MO. So you think it's a
biblical allusion?" Mac asked.

"I'm not the detective, but it's seems logical given what
we're seeing."

"Someone must've closed his eyes." She waved latex
gloves at Kauffman. While she related info to Dispatch,
Corey and several other guys sawed through the ropes
with Swiss army knives, pried the nail from his side,
lowered the young man to the ground. Kauffman handed
the five-inch bloody nail to Mac, who dropped it into a
glassine, labeled, and dated it. They stuck the damp rope

pieces into a paper bag. She circled the poplar, eyes canvassing the base, trunk, and limbs.

An ambulance roared and whined, bucking over the rocky, rolling terrain, rocking to a stop. Troy Hemmer's lean frame leaped from the driver's door, swung around to the rear, and retrieved a stretcher.

"No need to hurry," Mac started to yell when Shadow suddenly lunged at the inert form, her paws thudding his chest. His eyes flew open, alarmed. He gulped air as Mac pulled her shepherd off, preparing to admonish her.

"Shadow sensed he was still alive!" Corey yelled. "Sharp dog! Okay, men, excitement's over. We're done here. Let's head back to the training site. Heel, Inky." He and the lab turned back. "Oh, say hello to Chris for me. How is he?"

"Good girl!" Mac offered her dog another treat. "Sit. Sure will. He has tinnitus from that explosion last summer, experiences some light-headedness but won't admit it."

"Is he back at work?" Kauffman asked.

"Oh, yes. He missed two weeks, but he's functional!" Mac smiled, remembering her husband's insistence that he return to Homicide despite lingering injuries from the blast that nearly killed poor Mr. Mahoney. "What a chaotic case; all evaded responsibility for Dennis Sims's death except the innocent man."

www.ingramcontent.com/pod-product-compliance
Lightning Source LLC
Chambersburg PA
CBHW022010010726
47494CB00003B/971